Sea Glass Out of Balance

Serenity
Book 3

Stacey Wilk

Sea Glass Out of Balance by Stacey Wilk

Serenity, Book 3

This is a work of fiction. Names, characters, places, and incidents are either the product of the author's imagination or are used fictitiously, and any resemblance to actual persons living or dead, business establishments, events, or locales, is entirely coincidental.

Sea Glass Hidden in Plain Sight

Cover Art by *Diana Carlile*

Published in the United States of America

In loving memory, Dan Ferrigno
Thanks for the dance.

Chapter One

Bailey Russo hid behind the bookshelf in Tea and Tales. Cowardly, really, but she couldn't help herself. The Under the Lilacs book club met every Tuesday night to discuss one thing Louisa May Alcott or another, and if they saw Bailey among the cookbook section, they would invite her to join.

Even though *Little Women* was her favorite book since she was a girl and her sister Maren had read it to her, the last thing Bailey wanted tonight was to sit down with these women as they sipped tea from dainty china cups and giggled over the antics of the March sisters.

These octogenarians were adorable with their gray hair, comfortable clothes, and sensible shoes. Well, except for Cara—who was still adorable—but didn't wear sensible shoes and wouldn't give up her heels. These women were warm and welcoming to all. But Bailey had other plans.

She was leaving New Jersey in a few hours for Colorado, and she hadn't told a soul.

Dust on the shelves tickled her nose. She needed to make her escape before a reverberating sneeze gave her away.

The door to her upstairs apartment was positioned near the book club. She couldn't go that way. She'd have to go out the front of the store onto Main Street and scurry around the back. But those old buzzards—who didn't miss a trick—might notice her running out the door and try to call her back. She racked her brain for an excuse if they caught her and came up empty.

She had joined the ladies in the early months of living above the bookstore as they talked about Louisa May Alcott's books and stories. They often expected her to pull up a chair and join them. And often she did and loved it. But tonight, she needed to get on the road. Her new life awaited her.

Bailey weaved back toward the Mystery section, then tiptoed through Romance, avoiding the spots that creaked underfoot, until she was at the front of the store. The door opened and a blast of sticky, humid air assaulted her. A summer thunderstorm loomed like a stalker.

This time of year was unusually hot. As was the man who had entered the store, but Bailey had never liked spending time with Sterling Billinger III—or was it the fourth or fifth? She didn't know. Sterling, who went by Jack, was Beth's grandson, his only redeeming quality.

"Hello, Bailey." Jack addressed her with a restrained voice. He wore cargo shorts that hung loose on his rower's frame, tall and lean. He oozed of prep school alumnus and blue ribbons, but he was trouble with a capital T.

"Jack, hello. I was just heading out. Your grandmother is in the back with her club."

He rolled his eyes. "How many more times can they talk about the same author?"

"Forever. They're delightful. Leave them alone." She wanted to tell him to pull that giant stick out of his backside, but now wasn't the time to take up another disagreement with him. He was an additional reason she was ready to move on from this place. He was always here, pestering his grandmother about selling her store.

"I'm not bothering them. But if my grandmother put some of that time and attention into fixing this building, it wouldn't be coming down around her." He held up his hands as if he might catch something dropping from the ceiling.

"I don't see you picking up a hammer."

"I prefer to wield my pen. If she'd sell this building, I could have her set for the rest of her years."

"And you'd make a killing too."

"Not me. I'd just borrow some of her earnings and then pay her back with interest."

Problem was, Jack Sterling could not be counted on. At least that was what Beth had told her. Beth loved her grandson, but he had been making one mistake after another in his life. For a man his age, he couldn't get his act together.

"If you'll excuse me. I have to get upstairs." She didn't have time to debate Jack's intentions or Beth's. Bailey had to finish packing and hit the road tonight. Mark expected her in three days.

Bailey brushed past Jack and his aquatic, refreshing smell and without waiting for a reply, she pushed through the glass door.

The July evening's heat turned the air to molasses. Thunder rumbled in the distance. Sweat broke out on her neck as she took her first few steps.

Tea and Tales sat on the corner of Main Street and Spring Street, guarded by a large Japanese cherry tree with low branches that offered shade and a burst of bubblegum-pink flowers in the spring. This tree was Bailey's favorite and was inhabited by a hummingbird with a bright patch of red on its throat. She swore it was always the same one, though there was no sign of him now.

The shops in town headed east on Main Street toward the ocean, leaving Tea and Tales in last place in a row of unique stores to browse. Tourists and residents meandered up and down the street, seemingly unconcerned about the dark clouds hovering. The echoes of their laughter followed her as she ran down Spring Street and around the back of the store, past the patio table, and up the outdoor wooden stairs to her apartment. She had moved in nine months ago as a winter rental, never expecting to stay after Memorial Day, but the Fourth of July was upon them, and she was still in town.

She let herself into her tiny place on a sigh.

She leaned into the space, expecting the cool caress of her air conditioner. Instead, she was assaulted by heat hotter than hellfire and thick enough she could touch it. She checked the thermostat which read eighty-five degrees. The central air didn't seem to be working. Jack was right about this building needing work.

She threw open a couple of windows, but the apartment didn't face the right direction for a cross-breeze from the ocean. She would cook like a chicken roaster up here.

Just another reason to pack her bags and get out. She piled her hair on the top of her head and began gathering the things she couldn't live without.

She would have to tell her sisters of her latest plan to leave town. They would be furious with her for leaving and going to Mark of all people. She hadn't planned on reconnecting with him after all this time, but life often surprised her. They had been talking for months now, and he wanted her to come out to Colorado and work with him in his hiking business. He missed her and wanted to try again.

She wanted a new direction, a new dream, a new vision. Serenity by the Sea had no opportunities for her and she was tired of being part owner of Sea Glass because the ownership was in name only. Her sister Kassidy was the real owner of the restaurant. Maybe Kassidy could buy her out. Bailey would have to find the right time to talk to her about that.

Bailey grabbed her beat-up suitcase covered in stickers and a large duffel out of the closet.

Sweat dripped down her back and pooled under her boobs. By the time she had her things thrown together, she would be drenched. Even if she wasn't planning on being at the Jersey state line in an hour or so, she would have to stay with one of her sisters tonight. Someone could die from all this heat.

Thunder rolled closer as if to prove her point about the apartment being too hot.

She wasn't like her sisters who were rooted in this town or like that hummingbird who had built a nest in the cherry tree. Bailey preferred to have the wind at her back and in her hair. They would have to understand. Bailey would miss them, especially her beautiful niece Emma who was nine months old and always happy to see her.

Once Bailey got far enough into the drive, too far to turn around because of guilt, she'd reach out to Maren and Kassidy and let them know what she was up to.

She should have told them already. Hopefully distance and time didn't keep them apart again. She was behaving like a coward, but she didn't want to see the disappointment on their faces when she told them she was leaving, especially not for Mark.

She placed the bags by the door. She'd leave Beth a note to explain about her skipping out. Bailey hoped Beth would not give in to her grandson and sell, but whatever Beth did was out of Bailey's control. She would also leave a check for August's rent. She wouldn't dream of stiffing Beth.

A knock interrupted her. She couldn't imagine who would be at the door at this hour and with a storm close enough to touch. She opened it to find Beth outside holding a tall iced tea.

"It's dead," Beth said.

"Dead? What is?" She peered past Beth to the ground below, but nothing and no one was there.

"The air conditioner, silly. It's dead. I knew it would die eventually and of course it picked now. I had hoped it would make it through the summer, but this year is just too hot. Anyway, I brought you a cold drink and wanted to tell you to come stay with me tonight." Beth, who barely came to Bailey's chin, handed her a plastic cup complete with straw and lid.

Beth wore her white hair in a curly bob that flattered her round face. Her flowered buttoned-down shirt hung loose around the waist of her tan ankle-length pants. She reminded Bailey of her grandmother on her mother's side.

"Thank you for the drink, but I can't stay with you. That would be too inconvenient." She accepted the drink and took a long cold swig. *Oh, yeah, she needed to get out of this sweatbox.*

"It's not an inconvenience at all. You can't stay here. I won't allow it. You'll stay with me. It's getting late. That storm is almost upon us, and I don't want you to bother your sisters at this hour. I have plenty of room."

"No, thank you. I'll be fine here. It's not so bad." She gulped more of the iced tea to keep the sweat off her forehead.

The plan was to leave tonight so by morning she'd be on

the other side of Pennsylvania. She liked night driving. Fewer cars were on the road. She should say something to Beth, tell her about her plans for moving in with Mark, but part of her worried that things with Mark might not work out again. Once she told Beth or her sisters, this decision to leave would be real. She hoped—not hoped, knew—this time with Mark would be different. It had to be. He had promised.

"Oh, look. You already packed your bags." Beth clapped her hands. "You're a psychic. I always knew that about you."

Beth grabbed the big duffel as if it were empty and disappeared into the dark night. Thunder clapped on her exit, shaking Bailey to her core. Fat rain drops plopped on the small landing outside the door. Lightning broke the sky in half. The lights in her apartment flickered and went out.

She stood there with her mouth grazing the floor. What had just happened? Was the universe giving her a sign?

Beth poked her head back inside. "We'd better hurry. This weather won't wait for us. I'll meet you at the car."

Bailey took a quick look around. In all the months of living here, she had barely put out any personal items. The apartment had come furnished. Everything she owned was in her two bags and one had gone off with Beth.

She didn't see that she had much choice, at least for tonight. She'd sleep at Beth's in the comfort of some air-conditioning and in the morning, she'd hit the road. One more night wouldn't hurt anything. Mark would wait.

Chapter Two

J ack hurried into the office building of Billinger and Associates. He was running late again. He wanted to avoid his father's disappointed glare, because to Sterling Billinger III, tardiness was an act of defiance, but Jack was due to be in his father's office five minutes ago and wouldn't be able to avoid the family patriarch and managing partner if he were a runaway locomotive and Jack was tied to the tracks.

He stopped out of sight a few feet from the glass office to suck down a deep breath and right his tie. He hated ties.

His father probably wanted to talk to him about Jack's latest screwup. He would rather have a root canal than talk about the worst thing he'd ever been involved with. He wished he could rewind the days like an old cassette tape and return to the hour before he lost everything.

On false bravado, he entered his father's office. Sterling turned away from the window with the view of the Hudson River. His father was the picture of financial freedom in his expensive, designer navy-blue suit and silk tie that could pay Jack's mortgage for one month. The overhead lighting sparkled in Sterling's cuff links. He wore his expertly maintained salt-and-pepper hair cut close and never arrived anywhere without a clean shave. Sometimes Sterling stopped at the barber shop in The Lombardy Hotel to sit under the sharp blade of the skilled Jerome.

"You're late." Sterling glanced at his Tag Heuer and tsked.

"The train was running late." Using the train as an excuse for his tardiness was a feeble attempt to keep his father's scorn at bay, but he was too tired to come up with something more creative.

His father's pristine office displayed only one personal item. Sitting on the credenza behind Father's desk was a picture of Jack, smiling at the camera with a fish in his hands. He was nine and had caught that fish in a competition. Winning was important to Sterling. It was the reason Jack stopped trying to win at everything when he was in high school and started hanging with the kids who were the best at finding trouble.

"You should've bought a townhouse in Jersey City instead of near the beach," Sterling said.

"The Statue of Liberty scares me."

"Stop being so obtuse."

Jack shifted in the chair. He had purchased a home in Rumson, not Jersey City, because it would aggravate his father and was the town where the most successful people in Jersey lived. He had also wanted a yard for the family he never had.

But what Jack wanted or needed didn't often factor in to Sterling's ideas. Jersey City was a more practical commute to Lower Manhattan where the office was located. Sterling didn't do sentimentality or emotions.

Now the house was for sale and about to go under contract. He was sorry to see that house go, but he couldn't make the mortgage payment any longer. Once the house sold, he still wouldn't be ahead.

"What did you want to see me about?" His father had sent him a text late last night, asking for this meeting first thing. Jack didn't know what his father wanted, but he did know whatever it was couldn't be good.

"I've heard from one of your ex-girlfriends." His father tapped his pristine desk.

"Really? Who and why?" He wasn't expecting Sterling to say that. Jack had braced himself for his father putting a spotlight on how Jack had been scammed.

"Sloane Van Salis."

Jack groaned. He and Sloane had dated off and on for a couple of years, but that was ten or more years ago. He couldn't think of one reason why Sloane would reach out to his father. If she wanted to find Jack, all she had to do was search for him on social media.

"What could she want after all these years?" He could hardly remember their time together.

"Well, my son, apparently you made a child with her."

11

He choked on his own spit. "What? No way. Not possible. She's nuts. She must want money or something." He had done some dumb things in his life, but sex without a condom wasn't one of them.

"I thought the same thing. In fact, I said as much. But she was insistent. Claims she came to me instead of you to prove how truthful she was being."

"So, you just believe her?"

"I didn't at first. I assumed she was after our money or something else. Connections maybe. Her family had suffered that scandal a few years back."

"But you believe her now?"

"I have proof." Sterling pulled out an envelope from the top desk drawer, then handed it over.

Jack's hand shook as he reached for it. Inside would be the proof his father would have demanded. Sterling wasn't a man who could be fooled—unlike Jack and the recent real estate scam he was suckered by—and would have gone to great lengths to get the facts. Sterling wasn't going to allow anyone access to his money without a fight.

"What's inside?" He didn't have the stomach to look.

"I offered my own DNA sample. I didn't want you involved if she was lying. My DNA would be close enough to prove I was a grandfather. It appears I have a ten-year-old grandson named Luther."

Jack dumped his head between his knees before he threw up all over his dress shoes. A kid?

"Sterling, please look at the DNA results." His father tapped his shoulder with the envelope.

"Jack, Dad." He opened the envelope, then unfolded

the piece of paper. Proof in black and white. His father was matched to a child by twenty-five percent. A grandchild.

"What does Sloane want?" He tossed the paper on the desk as if it were hot.

His father returned to his chair and dropped down. "Sloane is very sick. She's going to Europe for the remainder of the summer and most of the fall for treatment. If she doesn't make it, she wants Luther to know his father."

Sloane sick. He couldn't imagine it. She had been the picture of perfect health when they were together. She ran seven miles a day and could outswim him. She ate clean and never drank alcohol which was sometimes a problem in their relationship. She had wanted him to stay away from it. He didn't understand how someone as young as she was could be so sick she might not be here in a few months.

"Isn't she married or with a partner? Isn't there anyone else who can take care of him? He doesn't even know me. Why would he want to live with me?" He didn't have the kind of life that a child fit into. He didn't even own a car. He drove a motorcycle. Didn't kids have to sit in a car seat or something?

"She's divorced. The ex-husband doesn't want Luther. Her parents are deceased now. She has two siblings, which you may or may not remember, who might take him, but Sloane's wishes are for her son to know his father. I don't think that's a lot to ask from a woman whose life is limited."

Jack pushed out of the chair and stood at the window. "What if I refuse?"

"Then you will actually be the lummox you have pretended to be your entire life. You're over forty, Sterling. It's time to grow up. Luther will be brought to your house."

"I sold the house."

"I'm aware. You'll have to figure something out forthwith. And by the way, you're fired."

He spun around. "Excuse me?"

Even though he expected this very thing at the start of the meeting, the words sucker punched him in the gut. He forced his body to remain upright and his face neutral. He had practiced his stoic reaction the entire forty-five years of life. Sterling Billinger III did not appreciate emotional outbursts.

"Will you cite a reason? I have never failed in my duties here once." He knew the reason. He wanted his father to say the words.

"My financial risk manager, my son, got hoodwinked in a real estate scam any teenager would've recognized. How can I tell my clients that we are taking care of their multimillion-dollar businesses when the financial risk manager can't identify a fraud when he sees one?"

His father's logic was spot-on. Jack hated to admit that he would probably fire him too if the tables were reversed.

But he had checked all the risks. He had done all his due diligences, and the seller had checked out. All that planning and prepping had been for nothing. The con artist had run off with all of Jack's savings, enough money to choke a horse. He had nothing to say for himself. He should've known better.

"If that's it, then I'd like to pack up my office and be on my way." He could apply for unemployment. The money wouldn't be enough, but it was something and he had earned it.

"I had Margorie do it. The boxes are on her desk. If you can't carry them back to the train, I can have them delivered to you at home. You aren't closing for a few days." His father kept his gaze on his desk and pulled at a string on the leather blotter.

"I would appreciate it if you could have Margorie ship them this afternoon." He wanted to be done with this place as soon as possible. He had never wanted to work for his father, but like most things, his father got his way with Jack's employment at Billinger and Associates.

"Luther will arrive tonight at six. Make sure you're home."

"Who's bringing him?"

"Sloane."

"Why didn't you tell me about this sooner?" He deserved a little time to get used to the idea he was a father. He had a son who walked the earth and Jack didn't even know. He had questions for Sloane he wanted answers to. He needed time to adjust. He wasn't ready to be a father.

"I didn't want to give you time to find a way out of it."

"You think I wouldn't stand up and be a father?" He had toyed with the idea of being a father one day, but he'd never found the right woman. He also worried about passing on the Billinger genetics for overworking.

"Would you have?"

Jack turned to go.

"Sterling, one more thing."

Jack stopped. He hated the name Sterling, but his father refused to call him by his middle name, the way his mother had. What would she say about her son losing his shirt in the most humiliating way possible and fathering a child he didn't know about with a woman he hadn't loved? He'd like to think she would put her arms around him and tell him he'd be okay.

Jack faced his father.

"You're going to need a new career. No one will hire you now. You must know you've been blacklisted. There's nothing I can do to help you."

"I don't need your help." He never did.

Chapter Three

J ack paced the foyer of his house in Rumson. The
six-thousand-square-foot home would only be his
for a few more days before he sold it for what he
owed on it. This was supposed to be the house
where he grew old. Maybe with a wife or at least a long-
term partner—someday. Now it would belong to a power
couple with four girls in various ages of elementary
school and he would still not have any money.

After the real estate scam, he couldn't afford to make
the mortgage payment on this house. He had no choice
but to sell. He also had nowhere to live.

He was about to meet his elementary school-aged
son. Jack's hands trembled. He shoved them in his
pockets while he continued putting miles across the plat-
inum vinyl barnboard. Meeting his son—Luther—among
a few moving boxes and the echo of an empty house was
not how Jack imagined becoming a father, if he ever
became one at all.

A father. Him. He had barely committed to anything in his life. He hadn't seen the point in getting too attached to anything or anyone. Everyone left eventually. He wanted to be the one to go first. Which was how he had left Sloane. Not one of his better exits. If he had known she was pregnant... maybe he would have stuck around. Maybe not. He wasn't proud of that thought, but he was being honest with himself for a change.

The doorbell rang. He jumped, then reprimanded himself for being such a coward. This was a kid. Jack had been a kid once. How hard could parenting be? His father had managed well enough.

He opened the door to Sloane Van Salis. Ten years may have passed, but he would recognize her anywhere. Her blond hair was cut short with slanted bangs across her forehead. Her once bright eyes had dulled some, but considering what she was going through, she still shone.

"Hello, Sloane."

"Hello, Jack. You're looking well." She tugged on her oversized t-shirt.

He took a beat to realize she was thin enough to swim in anything she wore. He wasn't sure if he should pay her the same compliment. They would both know he wasn't telling the truth.

"It's nice to see you again." His words were hollow. This was not some random meeting in a coffee shop. "Where's... Luther?"

"In the car." She glanced over her shoulder to the Toyota in the driveway. "I wanted to speak with you first."

"Do you want to come inside?"

"No, thank you. I told Luther he would be able to see me the whole time."

"Okay." He closed the door, then stepped onto the porch. Sloane backed up a few feet.

No hugs. No tearful reunion. The tension between them could light up the sky. He blew out a long breath.

"First, I should apologize for never telling you about Luther. By the time I was certain, we had broken up. You were on to another woman. I believe her name was Michelle."

He had no idea Sloane had known about the bed he had jumped into after hers.

"Anyway, you had been clear about us from the start. No strings. No permanent attachments. That was fine by me. I didn't need you to raise a child. And I didn't want my son to have a father who couldn't commit to him. But keeping his existence from you was wrong. I should have given you the choice. I'm sorry." Her eyes filled with tears.

"I would have stayed around." He wanted to believe he would have done the right thing, but ten years ago... He couldn't be sure, and he didn't like that about himself.

"The past is the past. I made mistakes. You made mistakes. I'm worried about the future. I may not be here to see my son grow up." She gnawed on her lip. The tears returned, but she blinked them away. "He should know his father. We had some good times, you and me. You're older. I hope wiser. With the last name Billinger, Luther will have doors opened for him. I want him to have all the best possible chances in this life. Right now, you're it. Will you take our son and raise him to be the kind of man I know you are deep down?" One tear slipped free and ran down her cheek. She didn't move to wipe it.

"My father said you're going to be back in the fall." He ignored the dig about the man he might be. He wasn't perfect, but who was?

"I hope so. Life doesn't give us guarantees. I think we both know that. I am asking for this one, though. If you take Luther, then I need you to promise to be the best possible father you can be, and if I don't make it back, then you have to keep him. He's not a pair of shoes you can return, and you can't dump him for something better."

"If you think I'd do something like ditch him, why are you taking a chance with me?"

"Because he's your son and your son deserves to have a father who loves him. He deserves the best version of you. And I happen to remember that you wanted to be a different man than your father is. Here's your chance."

Jack never got along with his father. Sterling was an uptight control monger. He had expected Jack to toe the line, to follow in his footsteps, to live his life by Sterling's choices. His father cared more about money than he did people. The only person Sterling had ever loved was Jack's mother. She had died when Jack was five, and Sterling had buried his heart with his wife.

"Does he want to meet me?"

"He does. If you don't want to take him, my sister is waiting for my call."

"We won't be living in this house. I've sold it. I don't have another place lined up. I don't even own a car. I can't drive him around on a motorcycle." He had sold his car to make a couple of mortgage payments a few months ago.

"Your father filled me in. The timing isn't ideal. I realize that. But I'm leaving in two days. I can't wait for you to get back on your feet. I know I'm asking a lot of you, but Luther is a good kid who deserves this."

If he turned his child down, he would be the bone-head his father thought he was. Jack never pretended to get into jams. Sterling could claim that all he wanted. Jack had found plenty of problems to twist around his neck like a noose. Problems weren't hard to find if he looked in the right places.

"I'll do it."

"Thank you." A small smile tilted Sloane's thin lips. "I'll get him."

Jack waited on the porch while Sloane returned to the car. He would have to find a way to get his hands on one. He had a few credit cards. Maybe that would work until he could convince his grandmother to sell her store.

He would manage the money for her, set her up so she didn't have to worry about anything for the rest of her years. He would borrow a lump sum from her, pay her back with interest, and get back on his feet, with a house and a career. His father was right about being blacklisted. Sterling had seen to Jack's placement on the list.

A skinny boy, tall for his age, with light-brown hair

that flowed around his face and a little over the top of his ears, followed Sloane.

"Jack, this is Luther."

Luther stared at him with stern green eyes. If Luther wanted to meet him, Jack couldn't tell from that look or the set of this kid's jaw.

"Hey, Luther. Looks like I'm your dad." He held out his fist for a bump. Luther hesitated but gave in and bumped back. That was a start.

"I have Luther's bags in the car. I'll get them."

"No, let me. Pop the trunk." He pushed past Sloane. The color had drained from her face during this exchange. She looked as if she might fall over. Getting the bags also gave him a minute to catch his breath.

He didn't know how to feel about being a father. Was he cut out for it? What if Luther didn't like him? What if he didn't like Luther? Sterling didn't like him very much. Was it genetic?

He was afraid he wouldn't know how to do the right thing now. The timing couldn't be worse. What did he have to offer this kid? Shouldn't a parent at least be stable? He also didn't think it was right to tell Sloane no in her condition. She had to make it back. She just had to.

He carried the four bags to the porch, then placed them by the door.

Sloane had cupped her hands around Luther's cheeks that still had the plumpness of a little kid.

"I need to leave now. I have a long drive back," Sloane said to Luther. "You can call me anytime, okay?

And I'll call you and check in. Jack will introduce you to your great-grandmother, Beth. You'll love her. I did."

Luther nodded. "I'm going to miss you."

"I'll miss you more. You and your dad will have a good summer together. He's a lot of fun. You'll see."

Jack watched the conversation like a voyeur. He wanted to run inside and give them privacy, but he stayed, unsure how to handle the situation.

Sloane pulled Luther into a hug. They held each other for a minute, then she eased away first. She brushed Luther's hair away from his face. "You're so brave. I love you, little man." She kissed Luther's head, then turned to Jack.

"Thank you, Jack. I put a folder in one of the bags with all my information in it. Call me if you have any questions. I'll get back to you as soon as I can." She hurried to the car without looking back.

He and Luther stood on the porch until Sloane pulled away and her car was out of sight.

Luther turned to him. "Now what?"

"Good question. Have you eaten? Because I'm starving."

"We already had dinner." Luther stared off in the direction his mother went as if he might want to run that way too.

Jack still couldn't believe he was the best option. He had no idea what he was doing—about any part of his life.

"Listen, I'm going to be honest with you."

Luther's serious gaze held his. "Okay."

"I don't know a whole lot about kids. We're going to

be figuring this out as we go along." He grabbed two of the bags, then pointed to the others for Luther to grab.

"I always wanted to know who my dad was." Luther held the suitcase handle with two hands and leaned it against his thin frame as he followed Jack.

"Your mom never told you about me?"

"Nope. She said you were some old boyfriend she lost track of. You weren't worth the time and we were better off just the two of us."

"Ouch."

Luther shrugged and dragged the suitcase into the foyer. "I told her I still wanted to meet you. Wow. Are you moving? Those are a lot of boxes."

"We're moving. We can only stay here a few more days."

"Then where are we going?"

"Your guess is as good as mine."

Luther's brows furrowed. "You don't plan very well, do you?"

"I've never been a planner."

"That explains how you got my mom pregnant."

"How do you know about getting pregnant? You're barely old enough to read."

"The internet."

"Hard to argue with that."

Chapter Four

I f she left now, she wouldn't have to explain to Beth where she was going. Bailey straightened the bed and debated her options—wait for Beth to wake to say goodbye or sneak out like she had something to hide. Which she did.

After they returned to Beth's house two nights ago—somehow one night had turned into two and Bailey was still in Jersey—they sat up talking about *Little Women*. Bailey had pulled up scenes from the recent movie on her phone for Beth. Watching Beth's face light up as her favorite characters came to life, poured some pride into Bailey's heart. Beth had seen the version with Katherine Hepburn, but Beth's love for that story ran deeper than the ocean. She enjoyed every adaptation and Bailey appreciated exposing her to another.

Her relationship with Beth filled something inside her. From the minute she moved into the apartment above the store nine months ago, Beth had checked in with her to see how she was doing. Bailey could go days without talking to her sisters, chalking it up to busy lives, but the constant presence Beth offered was new to Bailey. Her own mother didn't check in with her all that often.

Bailey didn't want to see the disappointment on Beth's face when she realized Bailey was leaving for good. She'd wait until Beth was awake, then she'd say goodbye and promise to keep in touch. She would too. Maybe Beth could come out to Colorado and meet Mark.

Bailey opened the curtains and let the sun stream through the dust-coated window. The unblemished sky shone against the treetops. Of all the places she'd been, nothing compared to the sky in Serenity by the Sea—not the mountains nor the desert's red rock. She would miss the ocean in her backyard.

But she had to give this thing with Mark another try. They always had the right love at the wrong time. Now was their time.

She'd put her bags in the car for now. With her hands full, she fumbled with the bedroom door. The knob banged against the wall, and she cringed. She hesitated, listening for sounds of Beth, but the house remained quiet.

Bailey's phone trumpeted in her purse. She dropped everything on the floor with a thud and searched her handbag to silence her phone. If Beth was still sleeping, she didn't want to wake her. Though it may be too late.

A text from Kassidy pulsed on the screen. Bailey could ignore it, but it wasn't like Kassidy to text early. She only hoped this didn't have to do with Sea Glass. Bailey was not going to cover the breakfast shift today. Kassidy would have to figure out something else.

Guilt had her swiping to the messages app.

GM! Emma and I are up. Want to go looking for sea glass with us? You can see her cute new beach hat.

Bailey read the text three times to make sure she got the words right. Her dyslexia was always worse when she was tired.

She had hidden her disability from everyone, including her sisters, for years. She had been out of high school before she realized what was wrong with her and could explain it to others.

Teachers always thought she was dumb because her tongue tripped over every other word when she read aloud. Her test scores had never reflected her actual level of intelligence. Back then, no one paid much attention, leaving her flapping in the wind like a beach warning flag. She had worked hard to overcome her condition. Some days she could almost forget she had it.

Hiding her problem hadn't been hard. Growing up, Bailey didn't live full-time with Maren and Kassidy. They had a different mother than she did. But she never wanted to give herself away to them. They were both smart and earned good grades. Their father always praised their school performance while he would tell Bailey she needed to study harder and stop trying to be the class clown.

Kassidy had put herself through college at night and worked all day. That kind of focus might've sunk Bailey.

She had learned to compensate from a young age.

The reason her own father had never known was because Bailey had sworn her mother to secrecy. Her mother had agreed without much effort because she suffered too, and Mom put her attention elsewhere.

At least Kassidy wasn't asking her to go into the restaurant this morning. Seeing Emma in any outfit was tempting. She loved her little niece and wanted to devour every second with her.

Bailey used the voice recorder to reply. *Hi. Can't. Crazy day. Call you later.*

The lie hurt her heart, but she had to get out of town while the getting was good. Mark was waiting for her, and she wanted to put some miles on her car before any more time went by.

Maybe she could come back in the fall when she was settled in with Mark. By then, her sisters would see this time was different for them, that Mark meant what he said, that he and Bailey had a real chance at happiness. She would take Kassidy and Maren on a hiking tour too.

Walking up toward the bookstore now. Meet us outside for five minutes. We could grab a coffee from Mr. D. Kassidy's text jolted her back to the present moment.

Not there. Too hot. No A/C.

Kassidy would only take half a second to ask where she had slept because her sister would wonder why Bailey hadn't walked the few blocks to her house or had at least called. Kassidy was the one who always wanted the three sisters close. If it wasn't for Kassidy, Bailey would never have returned to Serenity by the Sea. She was glad she had. For the past several years, she had lived near her sisters. They had grown closer after time apart and Bailey was glad for that.

But now it was her moment. Maren and Kassidy were both successful businesswomen with men in their lives who loved and respected them. They both had children, something Bailey had always wanted. When she had been with Mark the first time, he hadn't wanted a family. They had talked about kids recently. He was more ready than before. She took that as a good sign.

Did you go to Maren's? Just as Bailey had suspected, Kassidy's curiosity got the better of her.

As if Bailey would want to spend the night with Maren and Shane and watch them make googly eyes at each other, all in love. Maren's daughter Peyton was spending a few weeks at her father's house and couldn't provide a much-needed buffer. When she did venture over, she and Peyton would sit cross-legged on the floor and dish about all the latest gossip while Maren and Shane did whatever it was they did, which Bailey didn't want to know about.

Bailey had loved Mark from afar for years. After they broke up, she couldn't get over him. That had to mean something. Every other man who had shared her life was nothing more than a vague memory.

I stayed with Beth.

You could have stayed here.

I know. Got to run. Love you. She shoved her phone in her pocket to avoid another text. She didn't want Beth to hear her speaking into the phone.

"Oh my." Beth's loud voice bounced off the walls somewhere else in the house, startling her.

A bang, crash, and thump followed.

Bailey ran through the house into the kitchen. The room was empty, but the basement door gaped open.

"Bethy?" She stood at the top of the steps and stared into the dark, damp room below.

"Hello, Bailey, dear. It seems I lost my balance."

Bailey hurtled down the old, wooden steps, hoping they didn't give out beneath her, into the dark and dank basement. Beth struggled to sit up, pushing her back against the cinderblock wall. Her legs sprawled out before her. Her pedal pushers were up around her knees.

"Are you okay?" She squatted down by Beth and looked for signs of scraped skin or blood.

"I think so. Well, except for my arm." Beth held up her right arm. The forearm dangled out of line from the elbow.

Bailey sucked in a deep breath to keep from passing out. "You might have broken your arm."

"Do you think? That would be inconvenient."

"I'd say. Here. Let me help you up. I'll drive you to the hospital." She put a hand under Beth's good arm and pulled her to stand. The woman weighed as much as a sack of flour and Bailey wondered if Beth had been losing weight.

"I can do that myself." Beth attempted to push her away.

"Absolutely not." She wrapped an arm around Beth's middle. Bailey's fingers could outline Beth's ribs. "Can you handle the steps, or do you need to sit a minute? Where's the light down here?"

"It's over there by the washer and dryer."

"You come down here to do laundry?"

"I've been down here doing laundry since long before you were born." Beth laughed. "I'm not that old."

"Beth, going up and down those rickety steps has nothing to do with old. I wouldn't want to carry my laundry down here. Why hasn't Jack moved those machines for you?"

"Jack? My grandson? Oh, pooh. Jack doesn't know the difference between a flathead screwdriver and a Phillips." Beth took the first step up and Bailey kept a hand on her back as they navigated the stairs.

"If he's going to come into the store and try to convince you to sell, he could at least make sure you're safe at home." They took another step.

"Oh, don't worry about Jack. He has a big heart. He just doesn't know it. And he couldn't convince me to sell. I just let him prattle on about it."

She wasn't sure if Beth encouraging Jack to keep talking about the sale of the store was a good idea. Jack seemed determined to see his grandmother hand it off and wouldn't give up on his notion. He was a pompous fool. She wanted to shake him for not appreciating his grandmother more.

"How did you fall?" Time to steer away from thoughts of Jack Billinger. He might be easy on the eyes, but that's where the easy stopped. Beth had told her many stories of Jack as a teenager, a young man, and a full-grown adult who stirred up trouble wherever he went.

"It was silly, really. The room spun out from under me. I reached out to steady myself and lost my balance."

"Does getting dizzy happen a lot?" Dizziness could be a sign of many things. Some that didn't relate to anything dangerous, but at Beth's age, she couldn't be too careful.

"From time to time. Usually when I skip breakfast." They made it to the kitchen.

The sun streamed in through the window above the sink filled with dirty dishes that Bailey hadn't noticed the night before. The smell of bacon lingered in the air but just out of reach. The rest of the room was in order. Besides a toaster, nothing else was on the counter. The kitchen table had been wiped clean. The floor was polished.

She made sure the door to the basement was closed tightly and pulled out a chair. "Sit down. Keep your arm still. I'm going to drive my car around and take you to the hospital."

Beth plopped into the chair. Her face had paled, and dark circles outlined her eyes. She had to be in pain and didn't want to say. Bailey would have been complaining and crying up a storm if she had broken her elbow.

"I hate hospitals. Can't you just put my arm in a sling? You have that wellness business."

"Not nearly the same thing as practicing medicine. Do you have any ibuprofen?"

"I never need anything like that."

Bailey had some in her purse. "Since I don't know how to set a broken bone, you need to see a doctor. And I want you to mention the dizziness."

"Oh, pooh. There's nothing to tell, dear. A little drop in blood sugar is all. I'll be fine as soon as I have some orange juice."

Bailey opened her mouth to protest, but she didn't want to waste any more time. "I'll be right back."

"I'll be right here. Oh, and my purse is by the door. You'll need my Medicare card."

She would have to be the one to fill out the forms for Beth while the doctors and nurses set that arm. Bailey disliked filling out forms more than eating anchovies. But for Beth, she would force her traitor eyes to work.

Bailey ran to her car. She debated on telling Jack where they were headed. He was Beth's next of kin and should be at the hospital, but Bailey didn't have his number. She'd get it later from Beth when they knew more. Or Beth could call him herself.

Looked as if her plans to leave town would have to wait.

Chapter Five

"It's just a silly broken elbow." Beth waved Jack away—again.

His stubborn grandmother would not allow him to help her into the house. She insisted on climbing the front steps herself and using the key with her nondominant hand to unlock the door.

The hospital had kept her overnight because she had bumped her head and had mentioned some dizziness.

Bailey hadn't called him until this morning to tell him what had happened, saying she didn't want to disturb his sleep. He had expressed she should always get a hold of him when it came to his grandmother.

When she had called, he left Luther at the house and raced down Route 35 to the hospital in Neptune where Bailey had taken his grandmother. She was his only living relative on his mother's side. He wasn't ready to lose her.

Bailey waited on the front walk with a look in her hazel eyes that said something like he was wasting his time arguing with his grandmother. He hadn't expected Bailey to be the one to be there for his grandmother. He hadn't known Bailey spent the night at Grammie's either until she had called, and he would find out what that was all about as soon as possible.

Bailey didn't like him. Most times she glared at him since she found out he wanted his grandmother to sell the store, but he was grateful to her for having taken care of everything at the hospital.

Before today, he hadn't noticed how her spiral curls bounced against her shoulders when she walked. Even her step held a bit of a bounce as if helium filled her shoes.

Bailey saw the best in everything—except him. Not that he wanted her to look at him in any particular way. Besides, she wasn't his type, and he wasn't looking for any kind of relationship. Not even friendship. He could barely hold up the broken pieces of his life. He was like the damn sea glass Bailey had named her restaurant after. Well, it was really owned by her sister. He had checked.

Jack helped his grandmother to the sofa in her small house that needed some love and attention. The rooms could do with a coat of paint, maybe a new roof. She had some dead bushes that needed yanking as well. Now that he was unemployed, maybe he could come over and take care of some of the things that needed attention. He could teach Luther how to use a hammer. Luther. Jack wasn't sure if he should have left Luther alone, but he couldn't take him on the bike.

"Will you be okay here? You can come back to my

place, or I can stay a few days here." He would have to explain about Luther too.

"Don't be ridiculous. I have one good arm and two good legs. I can take care of myself. Besides, Bailey is staying with me."

Bailey poked her head around the doorway from the kitchen. "Beth, I can go back to the store apartment if you want some privacy."

"You can't stay there until I get the air conditioner fixed."

"I can stay there." He needed a new place to live now that his house was almost ready to close, and that apartment was better than nothing.

"Anyone would stifle to death up there. It's why Bailey is staying with me. You have that beautiful home. Why would you want to stay in that apartment?" Grammie regarded him with suspicion.

He wasn't ready to divulge the whole story. Especially not with Bailey in shouting distance. "If I stay over, I can fix the air conditioner."

"You can?" Beth and Bailey said at the same time.

He glanced between the two women and their surprised expressions. "I don't just crunch numbers, you know." He liked working with his hands, but his father never encouraged him to pursue those interests. He was a Billinger and Billingers worked in finance, according to what his father always said. They hired other people to work with their hands.

Sometimes, late at night, Jack tinkered in his garage, and whenever something needed fixing in his own home, he did it himself. He hadn't ever told anyone.

"You could've fooled me. This might be one of the first time I've seen you in anything other than a suit." Bailey carried a tray with iced tea, a tuna sandwich, and the prescription painkillers for his grandmother.

He glanced down at his t-shirt and shorts. He wouldn't be needing his suits for a while. Maybe he could sell off a few for the extra cash.

"I took the day off."

Grammie Beth eyed him again. "You want to leave your spacious home to stay in that cramped apartment." She turned to Bailey. "No offense, deary. The apartment is special. Louisa May Alcott stayed there, but it is small."

"None taken." Bailey sat on the floor cross-legged. "But isn't it rumored that she stayed there?"

"Rumor. Truth. Who knows." Grammie turned to him. "Jack, I don't understand. How can living in that apartment be better than your home?" She took the pill and washed it down with the drink.

"I want to make sure you're okay."

"I can do that, Billinger. You worry about your fancy New York career, and I'll take care of Beth."

"What about the store?" he said.

Grammie Beth and Bailey exchanged glances.

"Bailey can handle that." Grammie's smile brightened her eyes and put a little color back in her cheeks.

Bailey dropped her gaze and picked a fuzz off her pants. "Oh, Beth, that might not be a good idea. I've never run a physical store before."

"You work the restaurant with Kassidy."

"I just take orders and help out in the kitchen. I'm only a partner in name. Kassidy does all the hard stuff." A red blush ran up her neck and blossomed on her face.

Jack wondered what that was all about. He hadn't known Bailey to seem embarrassed by... well, by anything. Her confidence rivaled that of the sun's.

"You'll be fine." Beth slapped the couch cushion. "It's settled. Bailey will run the store."

"I can't. I have a trip planned. In fact, I'm supposed to leave today."

Relief washed over him. He couldn't afford for Bailey to get in the way of him convincing his grandmother to sell her store. Managing the sale of the bookstore was his last and only chance to salvage what was left of his existence. Now he had his son to think about too.

Bailey could just bounce her way right out of town for all he cared.

"Trip? You never mentioned a trip. How long will you be gone?" Grammie straightened herself on the sofa. Her feet dangled above the floor.

"A while."

"A long time? Are you leaving Serenity?" Grammie's eyes narrowed.

"Why don't we talk about my trip later. I can postpone leaving for a couple more days to help you around here."

"But what about my store?"

Heat burned his cheeks. His grandmother wasn't even considering him as a possibility to take care of the store. He had to admit, she didn't yet know that he lost his job, and he *was* trying to convince her to sell it. But Bailey was a better choice? He didn't see it.

"I'll run the store, live above it. We don't need Bailey."

Bailey glared at him. "I didn't say I wouldn't do it."

He had one last card to play. He needed a place to live that wouldn't cost him money he didn't have. "There's another reason for me to take the apartment and Bailey live here with you until your arm is better."

Confusion ran across both women's faces.

"I have a surprise. I just found out myself." He had to take a deep breath to continue because up until now, Luther still didn't seem real even though he was a living person in Jack's house.

"Go on," Bailey said.

"I have a son."

Grammie gasped.

"You? A son? How? Well, I know how, but are you even in a relationship?" Bailey sat beside Grammie.

"No relationship. Luther is ten. His mother is Sloane Van Salis. Grammie, do you remember her?"

"The gold digger?"

"I thought you liked her."

"Well, I did, dear. But it was obvious the way she spoke about expensive things all the time and how she wanted you to take her on trips. She had even asked me once why you hadn't bought me a nicer house. Now she must want access to your inheritance."

"I did not know about the house thing. Sorry."

"What made her change her mind and tell you now?" Bailey handed Grammie half a sandwich. Grammie shook her head.

"She's very sick and spending the next several months abroad for treatment. Luther wanted to know his father. Me. In case, she doesn't make it." The heat returned to his face again. He had no idea how to be a father, he wasn't the best boyfriend, and Sloane still wanted Luther and him to have a chance. She may have dated him for his money all those years ago, but that seemed to be the least of her concerns now.

"Do you know if he's really yours?" Bailey said.

"I do. He is. He's at the house. I should get back soon." He checked his phone. No texts or calls from Luther.

"I can't believe I have a great-grandson. Jack, you go get him right now and bring him here. I want to meet him and not waste another second of not knowing him. Do you hear me?"

"Yeah, Grammie. I hear you, but I have a problem."

"What kind of problem this time?" Grammie scrunched up her nose.

"I don't have a car. I sold it. I can't bring him here on the bike. It's probably not safe."

"You have that much right," Bailey said.

"I'll get a car somehow, and then I'll bring him over. Okay?" He would have to call his friend Aaron for a ride. He and Aaron had worked together, and he would have heard by now that Jack had been fired.

"Wonderful." Grammie tried to clap, but grimaced when her hands met.

Bailey stood and turned to Grammie. "Since you have a lot on your plate and it's what you want, I'll work in the store and help out here for at least another week."

Bailey glared at him as if to dare him to contradict her.

"Excellent. The store has some summer events planned for all my Louisa May fans and the Under the Lilacs book club."

"Just a week or so. I don't know if I can stay for the events. I have to take my trip. I have a friend waiting."

"I can handle any events and your lady friends too." He must be half out of his mind, wanting to take on those women. He has never even read *Little Women*. He wouldn't have the first thing to contribute to their conversation and he wasn't about to wear one of those silly hats they wore.

Grammie arched a brow. "Oh, no, dear. You wouldn't last five minutes with the Lilacs. Bailey has more in common with the ladies. She's sat in with us many times."

Bailey crossed her arms over her chest and nodded.

He could accept defeat for now because he would have his way in the end. Bailey was only promising a week or two. After that he could convince his grandmother that it was time for her to sell the store. She was getting older. The building was in desperate need of renovations she couldn't afford. He didn't want the bookstore even though it had been in the family for generations. He needed a loan, and she couldn't borrow against the building or her house to give it to him. He wouldn't allow her to do that, but sell the store? It was time.

Because if he didn't find a way to get money and quickly, he and now Luther would be homeless. Luther didn't deserve to suffer because of him. He'd suffered enough. Jack would have to find a new career and he didn't have the faintest idea how to do that at his age. He should be planning for retirement, not starting over. He had no one except his grandmother.

And nothing except that store.

Chapter Six

Bailey walked up to the boardwalk. Beth had decided to take a nap and Jack returned to Rumson. He claimed he had some loose ends to tie up, but he would be back as soon as he could to help out. She wondered about the validity of that statement.

Bailey needed some air and the ocean breeze against her heated skin cooled the burn in her veins. She was supposed to be on her way to Colorado, but she couldn't leave Beth right now.

She also needed to call Mark—a phone call she did not want to make—but pulled up his number in her favorites list and hit the call button.

"Hey, babe. What state are you in?" His familiar voice spanned the distance but did nothing to settle her.

She plopped down on the hot sand. The beach was full of sun worshippers and those on vacation unprepared for the UV rays. Someone's music blared over to her on the wind.

She had promised to check in with Mark this morning, but she hadn't, and half the day had gone by already. Fatigue burdened her mind. Sleeping on the chair next to Beth in the hospital hadn't added up to a good night's rest.

"Is that the ocean I hear? Did you drive past Colorado?" He laughed at his own joke.

"Mark, I need to talk to you."

"Oh no. What happened?"

"I'm going to be here for another week." She braced herself for his response. They had been planning this next stage of their lives for months. They had wanted to close the distance on their relationship. This time things between them would be for real.

"Your sisters are guilting you into staying. They hate me and don't want us together."

Bailey might not use the word hate, but Kassidy and Maren were not exactly fans of Mark. They had good reason to dislike him, but he was different now. So was she. She wouldn't be fooled again.

"I haven't told my sisters about us yet."

"Where do they think you're going?"

"I haven't told them that either." Her choice to keep a secret from them was like the time when she was fifteen and borrowed Kassidy's top without telling her, then ruined it at a beach party she wasn't supposed to be at in the first place. She had known back then how mad Kassidy would be when she found out—just like she would be now.

"Bailey, if you aren't willing to tell your sisters about us, are you sure you want to be with me?"

"Of course I'm sure." She had waited years for him to return. She had always loved Mark. She hadn't planned on moving to Colorado when they first reconnected. She had built a life in Serenity by the Sea, but she also hadn't thought she and Mark would end up planning a future together.

"I hope so. If your sisters aren't the reason, why are you staying longer?"

"Beth Parnell had an accident. I want to be here to help her."

His audible sigh shook the phone line. "When will you be leaving New Jersey?"

"A week from now. Once Beth is comfortable and moving around a little better." She hated the idea of leaving Jack alone with Beth. He would push harder for her to sell the store. She was older and now injured. That building was in bad shape which gave Jack a good argument.

"Okay. I get it. Beth's important to you. I'm just disappointed."

"I understand." But she wasn't sorry. She would not leave Beth without help, even though Beth had plenty of people who loved her. Beth had been like a grandmother to Bailey.

"Let me tell you the latest with the business. Naomi came up with this great idea..." He went on about his marketing manager, but Bailey wasn't paying attention.

The heat beat down on her. She decided to walk back

up to the boardwalk. She wondered how Jack felt finding out he had a son after all these years. The mother of the child must have had reasons to keep the boy from his father until now.

She didn't know Jack very well. He was aloof a lot of the times their paths crossed. Beth had told her about some of his antics as a teenager and a young man. Trouble seemed to find him. He had a wild streak, still rebelling against his father. If she didn't stick around, who would make sure he helped out his grandmother?

"Bailey, are you listening?"

"Sorry. I missed that last thing. A car went by."

She stood on the road and waited to cross as a pack of bicycle riders pedaled with fury down the street.

"I've got to run. I have a meeting. Call me later, okay?"

"I will. Thanks for understanding, Jack."

"Jack?"

"Did I call you Jack?" Where was her head? "I'm so sorry. I guess I'm just tired from being at the hospital all night."

"Is Jack an old boyfriend I should worry about?" Mark's words held a hint of teasing mixed with what she wanted to believe was worry.

"Hardly. He's Beth's grandson." And not her type. He was too stuck on himself, too into money.

"No problem, then. Talk to you later."

"Okay. See you." She ended the call before she stuck her foot in her mouth again.

She hurried across the street and waved to Mr. D

who owned Bella Notte bakery and stood on the sidewalk with his broom. He was a cute older man who made the best pastries. Mr. D waved back with his big smile. His wife Sophia was one of Beth's book club lady friends.

Bailey also couldn't allow Jack to take control of the bookstore. He'd probably wait until Beth was half out of it with her painkillers and get her to sign ownership of her store over to him without her knowing. He didn't seem like the type to do that, but she really didn't know him that well.

Bailey didn't understand why Jack wanted the store so badly except to make the profit that would surely come with selling. She also wondered if Jack wanted his grandmother in a home so he wouldn't find himself in the position to care for her if she ever became unable. He was her only living adult relative. He must have the power to displace her.

She had allowed her mind to run rampant. Jack was not an evil dweller. He was just Jack and not her problem. Maybe some retail therapy would get her to stop thinking about him.

She stopped outside Intentions Clothing. Even the sidewalk baked under her feet. This July must be a record heatwave.

The door handle burned under her touch, but when she stepped inside the store, the cool, crisp air met her like an old friend. The scent of oats and lavender drifted over to greet her.

Maria Lopez owned the store and stocked the shelves and rounders with organic clothing and bohemian beachwear. Bailey loved coming in here for the flowing pants and skirts and the textured tops with flowers and patterns.

Three women huddled around the display of long gold necklaces, expressing sighs of glee. Bailey fingered the long gold necklace she wore regularly and had purchased from here. Maria stood behind the counter folding cotton tissue tees.

"Hello, Bailey. How can I help you today?" Maria's black hair was streaked with white. Her smile was a mile wide and available for anyone who walked into her store. The skin around her eyes crinkled as a sign of years living in a beach town.

"I need a mood booster, Maria. And I think a hat for my head. This heat is killer."

"I just got in those distressed caps. They should fit over your curls. Boy, I would kill for your hair." Maria pointed to a shelf of adorable baseball caps that appeared soft, worn, and well loved in a fashionable way.

Bailey grabbed the sky-blue one. "Thank you, but the curls can be a lot sometimes. I'll take this too." She waved a beige hair tie made from rope.

"Why do you need a mood booster?" Maria put the folded shirts on a nearby table.

She couldn't tell Maria about her call with Mark and how something seemed off-center for her. The feeling could just be nerves about the trip. She missed him and was disappointed she hadn't left on time, but this pause in her plan and Beth's accident gave her some time to think about what she might be leaving behind.

"Beth Parnell broke her elbow. I'm helping her out for the next few weeks."

"I heard about the fall. I hope she's okay." Maria rearranged a display of cotton tote bags.

"She's doing well, a real spitfire. I'll give her that."

"It's nice of you to help her. Let me know if you need anything. I can always pop over."

Bailey could not deny Serenity's community and the way the year-rounders stepped up to help out their own. She would have to ask Mark if his town had that kind of connection.

"I'll let you know. Thanks."

"Kassidy was in here the other day. She ordered a few things, and they came in this morning. I was going to drop them off on my way home. Is there any chance you're headed that way? You'd save me a stop. I have to pick up Miguel at work. He's taking beach badges down at Spring Lake."

Miguel was Maria's youngest teenage son. She had four children spaced apart. Bailey didn't know how Maria took care of her family and ran a successful store that was only open April through October.

If Bailey was going to appreciate the community, it would serve her right to be a part of it while she was in town. Beth would help Maria and drop off that package with no questions asked. Bailey could do the same.

"Sure. I'll walk over there now." Then she could have Kassidy drive her back to Beth's.

"Thank you. You're a lifesaver." Maria rang up the

items and she bade Maria goodbye as the threesome of women brought their choices to the counter.

Bailey pulled out her phone and brought up Beth's contact information. She spoke into the phone and composed an audio message.

"Are you okay if I visit with my sister for a little while?"

A text came back. *Take your time. I'm fine. Waiting for Jack to return with his son. I can't believe he has a son!*

She couldn't believe it either. Bailey sent a heart emoji and opened the group text with her sisters. She started the voice message.

"Hey. I'm walking down to Kassidy's. Anyone up for s'mores?"

The cap might not have been the therapy she had needed, but chocolate and marshmallows with her sisters always was.

Even if she had to keep her trip to Colorado to herself.

Chapter Seven

"I wish I could hang out tonight, but Grant and I are taking Emma down to the boardwalk to watch a movie on the beach."

"Does she watch movies?"

Kassidy laughed. "Grant and I will try and watch it. She's too little. Did Maren get back to you? Maybe she's around. Cute hat by the way." Kassidy took the package from Intentions Clothing out of Bailey's hand.

Bailey patted her new find. She and Kassidy stood inside the front door of Kassidy's house. She had two front rooms on either side of a small foyer. The room to the left had been turned into a playroom for Emma. Toys scattered across the floor in a jubilee of color and creative expression. A child's table for four sat under a window, waiting for a little person to come along and make use of it. The bottom half of one wall was now a chalkboard for little Emma to draw on to her heart's content. The space was filled with love.

"No reply from Maren. It was last minute." She tucked away the unexpected envy. Bailey was used to flying solo and happy to be that way most of the time, but lately she longed for a committed relationship and a family of her own. Everything she had wanted was in reach. She should be on her way to it.

Kassidy had a full and complete life that didn't include her sisters. She had earned that life. All of their childhoods had been pocked with uncertainties and abandonment. Kassidy had fought hard for the blessings in her life, and Bailey was happy for her. But her happiness for her sister didn't fill the emptiness inside of her—an emptiness she didn't know was there until recently.

She missed spending time with her sisters, sitting in Kassidy's backyard roasting marshmallows, and would miss it more when she moved. But that habit was before Emma arrived and before Maren and Shane became a couple. Her sisters had slipped away like fog against a sun-filled morning. She hadn't even noticed at first.

Bailey had nothing in this town to ground her to it. She was like a kite caught in a gust of wind. Sure, her sisters loved her, but they were caught up in the folds of their own worlds now. They didn't have time for Bailey.

"We can do it another night. Thanks for bringing the clothes by. I had ordered a few things for Emma." Kassidy's smile spread wide and lit up her dark eyes. Motherhood looked good on her.

"Where is she? Could I give her a little squeeze?" Maybe if she snuggled with her niece for a minute, her heart would fill some. She wondered what kind of a father Jack would be and then immediately shoved that thought aside. The less she knew about him the better.

"I'm sorry. Grant already took her down to the boardwalk. He wanted a little time with her since he'd been away for a few weeks." Kassidy checked her phone.

"I'm holding you up. I should let you go." She had overstayed her welcome. Kassidy would never say so, but she didn't have to say anything at all. The worry in her eyes gave her away.

Kassidy pressed her lips together in a thin line. "I hate to run. Grant just sent a text wondering where I was."

"You'd better get to it, then." She turned to go.

Kassidy put a hand on her arm. "Is everything all right? You don't seem like yourself lately."

She hesitated. She hadn't been hiding her plans as well as she thought. Now wasn't the time to tell Kassidy about moving while she had one foot out the door. She didn't want to rush through her explanation, and she'd like Maren to be present when she did spill the tea. Bailey only wanted to tell the story once.

"I'm fine. Everything's fine." She would be fine too, just as soon as Beth was on her feet and she was on her way to Mark. Until then, Bailey could fake it till she made it. This wouldn't be the first time.

"Do you want to come to the beach with us?" Kassidy glanced away, then glanced back.

"Kass, you don't have to take pity on me. Go spend time with your family. I'll head back to Beth's."

"How long are you staying with her?"

"A week I think." Or longer if Beth needed her.

"What about your clients?"

"You know what? Grant is going to get mad at me for keeping you from him." She gripped Kassidy in a big hug to keep her sister from reading her expression because Kassidy paid attention to the details.

As soon as Bailey settled in with Mark, she would merge her health and wellness clients with his hiking business. She had told each client that she was going on vacation for two weeks and then relocating. She'd have to send an email updating them that her vacation would be a little longer.

She hurried from Kassidy's and walked back toward Main Street. Kassidy lived on the edge of the Topside Community. Bailey didn't understand the draw to these foldable houses that stretched out during the summer and cost more than a four-year college education.

She waved to Kate and Howie sitting in rockers on their front porch. Someone's grandfather, Bailey couldn't remember whose, had won the tent in a poker game in the 1920s.

Every house had a history and a section that remained standing all year long and a section that came down.

Serenity's residents found the community charming with their small lots and striped awnings. The space inside was cramped with little to nowhere to move. A resident could stand on their front lawn and see into the house next door.

She wanted space to roam, rooms that echoed with

her steps. If she couldn't have that, then she wanted to at least see the vast sky or mountains in the distance. Not Howie in his underwear.

She crossed Main Street. Tea and Tales was open, and Bailey went inside. She paused to take in the smell of old paper and wooden shelves. The light flickered above her. The lightbulb would need to be replaced soon. The store was too dark and could use a facelift, but Beth loved the store the way it was. Nothing had changed much since Beth's grandfather bought the store. Bailey understood Beth's need to keep the past, but if the store had a bit of a facelift, would it attract more customers, especially young tourists?

Even with the old carpet and poor lighting, entering the store was like receiving a hug from an old friend. For all the painful effort it took Bailey to read, she loved books and the worlds they held.

Growing up with divorced parents and a mother who always searched for the next exciting thing, Bailey's favorite stories were the constant in her life. She loved *Little Women* because of the four sisters who watched out for each other. Even though she only had two sisters whom she saw infrequently as a child, she imagined that she, Kassidy, and Maren were exactly the same as the March sisters. They weren't. They had grown closer in the past few years, but she still held back from telling them about Mark and her big move.

Eventually she would tell them, but she didn't want them to say she was the ditzy one, the one with wings and no roots.

Women's chatter drifted toward her from the sitting nook by the window and distracted her from her errant thoughts.

The Under the Lilacs ladies were huddled together in their usual meeting spot, except it wasn't Tuesday. They would have word of Beth's accident and were probably planning a meal train with Sophia DeFazio in the lead.

Beth's only employee, Amy, sat behind the counter, hunched over the latest bestseller. She worked at the store every day for a few hours to help out Beth. Bailey would need to talk to her about the daily duties.

"Bailey, dear, could you come over here?" Cara Raines waved her over from her perch by the window.

"We were just talking about you," Natalie Lowe said. Natalie chewed on gossip like a starving man knee-deep in a feast. Nothing happened in Serenity by the Sea without Natalie's knowledge. She could recite names, dates, and details better than a census report. In fact, Natalie kept Serenity's census report.

"You were? How incredibly sweet of you. What were you saying today?" Bailey tilted her head and flashed her brightest smile. She tried to keep the sarcasm out of her voice, but she may not have done a good enough job. Sophia pursed her lips and looked away.

"We know Bethy put you in charge while she heals. We think you should cancel the Afternoon Tea and History event," Natalie said.

"Not all of us." Sophia folded her hands in her lap. "Some of us think the event should continue as is because we've sold out tickets and a lot of people look forward to spending a day learning about Louisa May Alcott."

"She's just annoyed because Giovanni is slotted to make the desserts and now he won't be able to dazzle the guests with those cookies the size of a garbage can lid." Cara waved her fingers. The gemstones on her hands caught the overhead light.

"Ridiculous." Sophia swatted the air with her hand. "Gio doesn't need to spend all day making pastries for this event. He doesn't even get paid."

Cara stuck her tongue out at Sophia. Sophia said something under her breath in Italian and stabbed her pointer and pinky fingers at Cara. Bailey didn't know what the gesture meant, but knowing Sophia, she probably just cast a spell on Cara.

"Ladies, I thought you were all good friends. Don't fight."

"We aren't fighting. We are the best of friends." Cara grabbed Sophia and Natalie's hands. The three women exchanged warm glances. "That's why we want you to cancel the event. It's too much for Beth to worry about."

Bailey understood their dynamic of arguing one second and reaching for each other the next. She and her sisters behaved a lot like these three. As soon as Beth was better, Bailey would tell her sisters in person about Mark and her plans. She could trust them.

"I'll have to ask Beth what she wants to do." She took out her phone and left herself a voice memo to check with Beth.

Natalie stood. "Are you recording our conversation?"

"I'm taking notes." She held out her phone to show Natalie the screen.

"I like pen and paper better. Keeps the memory sharp." Natalie tapped the side of her head.

Bailey preferred her fingers circled around a sleek pen and the scratch of the point against lined paper too. She always wanted to keep a diary as a little girl, but writing for long periods of time gave her a headache and her handwriting was terrible even when she wasn't confusing letters. She used to carry a small tape recorder around with her before smartphones became a thing. She'd be lost without her phone.

"I'll talk to Beth."

"Don't do that. She'll tell you not to cancel. She's too stubborn," Cara said.

"She's a pretty tough lady. I'm sure she'll be able to direct the event even with a broken elbow." Bailey would help with whatever Beth needed even if she had to phone in from Colorado.

The bell above the door announced a patron. Bailey turned to find Jack walking toward the back. *What was he doing here?* He was supposed to stay with his grandmother until Bailey returned.

"Excuse me, ladies. I need to check on something."

Natalie grabbed her arm. "You're going to cancel, right?"

"Leave her be," Sophia said. "She's a smart girl. She'll do the right thing."

"I'm not canceling that event if Beth wants it to happen. Please excuse me." She peeled away from Natalie's grasp and hurried after Jack who had disappeared into the back room.

The back room doubled as storage and an office area. Beth kept extra copies of some of the bestsellers back here along with rolls of receipt paper, order forms, and who knew what else. Bailey would have to find out what was here.

Jack stood on a ladder and reached for a box on the top shelf. He hadn't heard her come in because he didn't acknowledge her presence. Or he was ignoring her. Either was likely.

She took a deep breath and said, "What are you doing here?"

Jack jumped. The box he had grabbed tumbled to the ground as he lunged for the ladder, pulling himself against it. He squeezed his eyes shut.

"Are you crazy coming in here and shouting like that?" He couldn't look at her. If he did, he would fall. Instead, he gripped the ladder with both hands and kept his gaze on the books inches away.

"I didn't shout."

"Yeah, okay." He hadn't seen her when he came into the store. If he had, he might not have picked now to search for the rare books his grandmother kept.

"Are you all right? You look like you might puke."

"I'm fine. I need a second." He needed more than a second. He hated heights, always had. He avoided rooftop restaurants and bars. He'd never been to the top of the Statue of Liberty or climbed The Empire State Building. He hadn't lied to his father when he said The Statute of Liberty scared him.

"You're afraid of heights." She stated the obvious, but he didn't bother to point that out.

"No, I am not. My heart almost burst through my ribs from your yelling, that's all. What is it you want, Bailey?" He still didn't look at her. Sweat rolled down his neck. He needed to pull himself together.

"Fine. Play it all macho and don't admit to the problem you're having. I thought you were going over to your grandmother's this afternoon with your new son."

"I am. I wanted to stop here first." He had sat with Grammie until she fell asleep. Then he called his friend Aaron for some help. Jack needed a car and fast. Aaron could help with that. Jack had also called Luther to see how he was doing all alone. Luther didn't seem to mind. Jack had an Xbox. He set up Luther to play while he was gone.

He descended one rung but kept his gaze in front of him. He could have called his father to come over, but Jack didn't want to ask for help from Sterling in the first twenty-four hours of becoming a dad. His father would only say Jack was already screwing things up.

"You look like you need some help." She took a step forward.

"No, thank you." He came down one step at a snail's pace. He would be stuck on this ladder all day at this rate.

"What happens if your grandmother wakes up and

needs something and you're not there? I should've known better than to believe you would be helpful."

He put his foot out to reach for the rung below, but he only circled the air. He couldn't look down to find the rung. He hadn't been this affected by heights before. Sure, bridges weren't his favorite thing, but a ten-foot ladder? Since when?

All the recent stress must have brought the panic about. If his father saw him, he would call Jack weak. Sterling would be right too.

"I don't need a lecture right now. My grandmother is okay for an hour or two if she wakes up and I'm not there. She has a broken elbow. She's not an invalid. If you're done, please go back out into the store. I'll be there soon."

"I can't believe what I'm witnessing. You walk around with a swagger to your step, with more money than the universe and an answer for everything. How are you afraid of a ten-foot ladder?"

He wanted to focus on the part where she said he had a swagger. It gave him the courage to take another step down. Bailey had paid attention to him. He had no idea she even noticed him except to snarl when he came by to visit Grammie.

Bailey moved closer to the ladder.

Heat burned his cheeks. He didn't want her help. Not like this. He needed to save some of his pride. "Please back away, Bailey."

She backed up with hands in the air. "Go ahead. Fall on your backside. See if I care."

Chapter Eight

Jack stood before Bailey. A splash of red spread across his neck and cheeks.

She took him in for what seemed like the first time. She had never noticed the way his light-brown hair stood up in the front like he'd just run his hands through it but was really an expert cut. His blue eyes were close together and accented his thin nose. He had the classic square jaw that gave every man a rugged look even in a suit.

She liked him in the blue t-shirt he had on today instead of the suit he usually wore. His legs went on forever in those jeans. She shook the thoughts away. What was happening in this moment?

He opened the box and rummaged through.

"That box can't wait? Don't you need to get back to Luther? You said this morning you left him alone."

"He's fine. I checked and told him to text me if he

needed something. I just wanted what was inside the box before returning to get him."

She had no right to tell him what to do with his child even if she wouldn't leave a ten-year-old home alone. She had been left home alone a lot when she was that age. Her mother always had a date she was running off to.

"What are you looking for?" Her curiosity had the best of her.

He pulled out a thick book with green binding, held it up, and gave it a small shake. His smile spread wide. The edges of the spine were worn and tearing in places. The title was etched in gold, but she couldn't read it because some of his hand covered it.

"What book is that?"

He glanced at it, then back at her. "It's a *Little Women* first addition." He opened it to the title page and held it open for her.

She ran her finger over the publication date. "Eighteen ninety-six."

He frowned and turned the book toward him. "Eighteen sixty-nine."

"That's what I meant." The numbers had jumbled because her pulse quickened, standing close to him. She had caught a whiff of his aquatic scent. She backed up. "I didn't know Beth had one of those."

Bailey longed to flip through the pages and look at the illustrations, but she wouldn't ask for that favor.

"I don't think she realizes she does either." Jack flipped a couple of pages.

"Are you going to bring it to her? That would be a nice treat right now."

"I'm going to have it assessed." His eyes narrowed.

"You're going to sell it? You can't do that." She should have known this wasn't about a kind gesture on his part.

"I don't believe what I do with this book is any of your business. My grandmother may want you working in the store, but the inventory isn't any of your concern."

"You're going to sell it. You're going to sell off all the inventory while she isn't looking, and then she'll be forced to sell her bookstore. Well, I won't let you do it." She lunged for the book.

He jumped back but tripped over the box still on the floor. He fell on his butt and the book skidded across the cement floor. She dove for it, but he was quick and grabbed the book at the same time she did. They tugged. The cover gave under the strength of their hands. The rip of the binding echoed around them.

"You broke it." She scrambled to his feet.

"You're the one who tore it." He pushed to his hands and knees. "Now it will have to be repaired."

"At least you can't sell it." She had accomplished one goal.

"Do you know how much this book is worth? She has both volumes."

"I don't care how much it's worth. Those books are part of her legacy. She would want Luther to have them, then his children. Shame on you for wanting to sell them for a buck."

He opened his mouth but shut it. The red splotches

invaded his cheeks again. He put the book under his arm and brushed past her without another word.

She needed to catch her breath and bent in half, her hair falling over her head in a waterfall of curls. She took two deep breaths, then rose to stand. The man pushed her every nerve. The book tearing was unfortunate. Even fixed, the damage could affect its value, but she believed Beth would never want to sell those books.

Jack was up to something. Bailey didn't like it, but she would find out what his motives were. He seemed to love his grandmother. She hated to think he might love money more.

Bailey returned to the store. The Lilacs were gone. Jack was gone. Only Amy remained, still glued to her book.

"Hey, Amy, can I ask you a question?"

She looked up from her book and rolled her eyes. She placed a bookmark between the pages and closed the book with exaggeration. "I guess so."

Bailey fought the urge to point out that Amy was an employee, getting paid to pay attention and help customers and that this wasn't her lunch break or the public library. She'd deal with Amy's attitude later but made a mental note to add a conversation to her to-do list.

"How well do you know Jack?"

"Beth's grandson?"

"Are there any other Jacks around here?"

"Sorry. I wanted to be sure. He doesn't talk much. Kind of a stick in the mud. He's never rude or anything but only talks to Beth when he's here which isn't often.

At least he's cute to look at." Amy grabbed her book and smiled for the first time.

Bailey could agree. But wouldn't. She wanted to keep an eye on Jack Billinger. He was up to something with that rare book, and she would find out what.

Somehow.

"Luther, I'm back." Jack's voice echoed in the empty foyer. He placed the *Little Women* book on top of some boxes. The binding hadn't ripped as badly as he had thought. Aaron would be here soon. He had a used car for Jack. The book was the down payment.

He made his way to the back of the house and the oversized family room. Luther sat on the leather sofa, his gaze glued to the big-screen television. His small fingers moved over that video game controller with a speed Jack had never mastered. When he was Luther's age, video game controllers consisted of a joystick and one button. Unless a kid was born into the world of face buttons and directional pads, he was at a serious speed disadvantage with today's technology.

"Hey, man, how's it going?" Jack moved into Luther's peripheral.

"This game is awesome. Thanks for letting me play it."

"Sure thing. Stop before you think you'll throw up, okay?"

"Okay." Luther kept his gaze on the TV.

"My friend is going to stop by for a minute. Then I want to take you to meet my grandmother. We're going to be staying in her apartment."

Game Over flashed on the screen. Luther dropped his shoulders. "Why can't we live here? This place is cool."

Jack didn't know how cool this house was. The whole place was packed up except for this couch, television, and video console. He'd been sleeping on the sofa for over a week. He had sold his bedroom furniture along with a few other items in the house for the cash.

"Because someone else will own it in a few days. We'd be trespassing and probably get arrested."

"Arrested? We're going to get arrested?" Luther's eyes widened to his hairline. He was a good-looking kid with his wavy hair and bright eyes. Jack didn't have to look hard to see the resemblance.

"No, no. Calm down. We're going to move out. Those boxes in the foyer are going into storage. We'll live over my grandmother's bookstore for a little while." Until he could get back on his feet.

"My mom didn't tell me that."

"She didn't know." Sloane hadn't bothered to mention the kid either. He was in no position to raise a child. Sloane should have contacted him, asked if now was a good time to take on Luther. Jack would have said no.

"Can I call her later? She said I could."

"On your phone?" Because he couldn't afford an international charge at the moment.

"Yeah. Can we get something to eat? I never had lunch." Luther pushed off the couch.

"After my friend comes. Grammie will have something for us at her house." He hoped.

"What am I supposed to do until then?"

"Play more video games?"

"Nah. I'm bored. Do you have board games or cards? We could play that."

"Nothing like that here." He had some non-fiction books, but he doubted Luther would be interested in the world of finance. "Can you play on your phone for a little while?"

"I want to go outside. Do you have swings?"

"Luther, man, I'm a grown-up. Grown-ups don't have swings. I owned a set of dumbbells and weights. That's how I played. But I sold those. You'll just have to hang out. My friend will be here soon. I'm going to wait for him outside."

He wasn't ready to introduce Aaron to Luther, even though Jack had told Aaron about Sloane's surprise. Jack continued to try and get his head around his new circumstance. He didn't know what was up and what was down.

Aaron pulled into the driveway behind the wheel of an old Honda Civic. Jack hustled down the steps to meet him. The car was silver with some rust over the front wheel. It had to be from the early 2000s. Jack had never owned a car like that. His last car was a Beemer. He'd spent a small fortune for it. He missed it.

Another car, a brand-new German number, pulled in behind Aaron. Aaron hopped out, but the other driver stayed put. Jack couldn't make out who was driving the new car. The sun's ray bounced off the darkened window, blinding him.

"Hey, I came as soon as I could. She ain't much, but she's reliable." Aaron patted the roof of the Civic.

"Thanks, man. I just need something with four wheels right now." He handed Aaron the book. "This is worth a lot. You'll be able to sell it online or to a collector. I also have some cash."

Aaron took the book but shoved his hand away. "I know someone who will take the book, but I don't want the cash. The car is yours free and clear. What your old man did to you is disgusting. Who blacklists their own son?"

"Sterling."

"He kicked you when you were down. Any one of us could have fallen victim to that scam artist. Whoever they were, they were the best to get one over on you."

"Thanks for saying that, but I made the mistake. I should've known."

"No way to have known. Don't beat yourself up about it. You'll get back up in no time. How's it going with Luther?"

Jack and Aaron had been friends for over a decade when Aaron first showed up at Billinger and Associates. They connected over sports, money, and beer. They played hoops on the weekends until Aaron got serious with Stefania, a New York City Broadway dancer. Aaron spent more time with the woman he loved and less time with Jack, but they remained good friends. Aaron might be the only friend he had.

"It's weird. It's like he's not really my son and I'm just waiting for the actual father to show up and take him. I don't know what to say to him. I half expect him to throw himself on the ground, crying and kicking his legs."

Aaron laughed. "This isn't the movies. He's probably a good kid. He might be scared and missing him mom. Just keep talking to him."

"I think that's about all we can do for a while. I have to save my extra cash. I can't take him to a game or something. I don't even know what he likes to do." Besides video games.

"So, shoot some hoops with him instead. Be the father yours isn't." Aaron handed him the keys.

"Thanks. And thank you for helping me out of a bind."

"I'm here for you. Good luck with Luther. Call or text if you need anything else. I can help you move some of those boxes if you want."

"I'll let you know."

Jack stood in the driveway until the fancy new car drove out of sight with his friend in it. He should've asked who was driving. Probably Stefania. She wasn't his biggest fan. Always complained he was a bad influence on Aaron. He could tell her a thing or two about her husband, but Jack would not betray a confidence.

He dumped a couple of small boxes in the trunk and his and Luther's bags into the back seat. It was time to get to Grammie's before Bailey found out he was still gone and she handed him his head.

Her feistiness was a turn-on. Too bad because she hated him and had seen him at his worst moment on that ladder, behaving like a fool.

Anyway, he had no business coming on to a woman at this moment with nothing to offer.

In another world, another time, he would ask her out, romance her until her head spun, then he would take her to bed and make her forget about him sweating it at ten feet off the ground. He would show her the man he usually was.

She also scared the hell out of him.

Chapter Nine

Jack ignored his ringing phone. He had no interest in talking with his father. Instead, he led Luther up his grandmother's front walk. The cement had some cracks in it that would need to be addressed eventually. The bushes in front of the house needed some trimming too. He could handle that much, but he couldn't lay cement. Something else that could be paid for once the store was sold. Grammie's house was old. He could probably find other projects demanding attention.

"Are you ready?" He turned to Luther.

"I haven't had a grandmother in a long time. My grandparents died when I was six."

"I'm sorry to hear that." Sloane's parents thought she was making a mistake by getting involved with him.

He might be a Billinger, but he never cared for the life that name brought. Maybe that financial mistake he had made wasn't a complete mistake.

He didn't want to think about the possibility he was looking for a way out of his life and deliberately allowed himself to mess up.

"Can I knock?" Luther looked up at him.

"We don't have to knock. Grammie wants us to walk in. If she's sleeping, we don't want to wake her." Jack opened the door to let Luther pass, but the boy didn't move. "I'll go first. You can follow me."

The living room was empty and cast in shadows. The sun was in the back of the house this time of day and streaming through the kitchen windows.

Grammie sat at the table reading. A cup of tea waited beside her. She looked up when they entered. Bags puffed up under her eyes like blowfishes. She smiled, but it did not lift the fatigue in her eyes. Her elbow must be bothering her.

"Oh my, this must be my Luther." She threw her good arm in the air. "Is it cool to hug your great-grandmother?"

Luther nodded and went in for the hug. Grammie rocked him back and forth, then kissed his head.

"It's so very nice to meet you. I hope we can be fast friends," she said.

"I don't have a grandmother," Luther repeated his earlier declaration.

"Well, now you do. Your dad can tell you what a good job I do as a grandma. Would you like a snack?"

"Yes, please." Luther nodded with vigor.

"Polite too." Grammie pushed out of the chair.

Jack tried to stop her, but she waved him away. "I can do it. Go sit down."

He was too wired to sit. "I can get the snack."

"Nonsense. This is my home and I'm the grandmother around here. Luther, sweetie, are you comfortable calling me Grammie or would you like to try on something else?"

Luther looked between him and Grammie. Jack shrugged. "Up to you, pal."

"I guess Grammie is okay for now."

"Perfect. Your father started calling me Grammie when he was just about one. His father, your grandfather Sterling—have you met him?"

"Not yet." Luther turned to him. "Will I?"

"Do you want to?" He hadn't thought about bringing his father into the picture. He could deny Sterling the right, considering he had thrown Jack to the wolves.

"Is he nice?"

Grammie shot him a look over Luther's head as if she expected Jack to answer. He wasn't going to lie.

"My father is very strict about how things are done. Maybe you can meet him in a few weeks after we figure ourselves out? Good?"

"Okay. Good."

"Like I was saying," Grammie continued as if the conversation hadn't gone off course, "your father started calling me Grammie. Sterling wanted me to be Grandmother. That's a lot for a little mouth to spit out. So, your dad could only say Grammie and it stuck. But you are old enough to come up with your own name for me."

Grammie glided around the room as if her left arm wasn't in a sling. She sliced pound cake and poured iced tea.

"Jack, why don't you run over to Vic's and get some pizza for dinner for us? My purse is by the front door. I have money in my wallet."

"I can pay for pizza." He'd prefer not to, but he couldn't let his grandmother pay for his food.

"I'm sure you can. But I want to, and Luther and I would like some time to get to know each other. Why don't you stop by the apartment first and make sure it's to your liking." She shooed him out of the kitchen and followed him to the door.

"Here." She shoved cash at him.

"I don't want your money." He handed it back.

"Then why do you want me to sell the store so badly?"

"Because it's becoming a hazard and needs too many repairs you can't afford. The land will always be valuable and get you the most money. If you sell it, I can make sure you're comfortable for the rest of your life. Why is that so bad?"

"I'm not ready to retire and I want that store to stay in our family. It's our legacy."

"I don't want the store. I've told you that a thousand times. I don't want to own a bookstore or any retail store in Serenity by the Sea."

"You might not, dear, but Luther may. He's going to have a chance to decide."

"He's ten."

"I guess I'd better live another eight years. Now go."

She closed the door on him, leaving him no choice but to go and get the pizza.

Bailey walked the surf with Kassidy, looking for sea glass. The wind came in off the ocean, grabbing hold of Kassidy's new baseball cap. She shoved it back on her head for the millionth time.

The early morning tide was out, a great time of day to find treasures, but they weren't having any luck today. Bailey didn't want to see the lack of sea glass as a sign of things to come.

She had spoken to Mark last night after she left the bookstore, but she had been distracted by her encounter with Jack and his taking that rare book. Mark had noticed she wasn't present when he shared his good news about more hiking tours booked for the end of the week. She wanted to be there and promised when she was, she would be fully involved.

She had told him she loved him.

"Hurry home," he had said instead of I love you too.

That meant I love you, didn't it? She wanted to ask Kassidy, but now wasn't the time. Bailey hadn't even told her about the move.

Months ago, returning to Mark had seemed like coming home, but since Beth's accident, she wasn't in the same hurry to get to him. Must be the stress of it all.

She had debated on telling Beth about Jack taking the

book but decided against it this morning when Beth told her all about meeting Luther last night. Jack and Luther were gone by the time Bailey had returned. Jack a father. Wonders never cease.

"Bailey, are you listening to a word I'm saying?" Kassidy stopped in her tracks and held up three pieces of green sea glass. "You didn't even budge when I yelled."

"Sorry. My head is somewhere else."

"Like where? The bookstore?" Kassidy shoved the sea glass in her pocket.

Bailey had watched her many times clean the sea glass off and add it to her growing collection. Later, she would wash it off and add the find to her growing collection. Kassidy was a lot like their dad in that way. She had displays of sea glass all over her house.

"Yesterday Jack took a rare book from the store. He wouldn't say what he was doing with it." She was surprised how afraid of heights he was, but once he got back on the ground, the fear was replaced with determination to leave with that book.

She would have to find out which dealers bought old books to sell. If she had the money and wasn't too late, she could try and buy it back.

"Did Beth ask him to have it appraised?"

"I don't think Beth knows. I debated on telling her, but I couldn't do it." She told Kassidy about Luther and how happy Beth was to have someone else in the family. "She didn't even seem to care that this child has been hidden for ten years."

"Maybe the mother had good reasons to keep her son

from Jack." Kassidy brushed aside wet sand but came up with nothing.

"Maybe. But Beth too?" The wind grabbed at her hat. She slammed it back on her head.

"Telling Beth would mean telling Jack." Kassidy kept her gaze on the surf and sand.

"I guess that's true."

"Would you have told him, if you were the mother?"

Kassidy's question caught her off guard. Jack was too focused on money for her. He had a reputation as a giant goof off since he was a teenager, according to Beth. Ten years ago, he could have been messing up in a big way.

"I don't know what I would've done, and I can't imagine what that mother was battling back then, but I would want to know if I had a child somewhere."

"The good news is, if you have a child in the world, you will always know about it." Kassidy chuckled.

"Truth."

"Why don't you wait and see if Jack tells Beth about the book. That's his place anyway."

"I just hope he's not up to something that will hurt his grandmother."

"You'll find out."

She didn't want to find out Jack was the worst possible person, trying to pull something over on his sweet grandmother.

"Do you want to keep walking toward the pier? We might find some sea glass down there." Kassidy pointed north.

"Might as well keep looking." She'd keep watching

for what Jack was up to also. If he took another book and didn't tell Beth, she would.

Jack swept the hardwood floor of the tiny apartment above the bookstore—his and Luther's new home for the next several months.

He tried not to think about the fact he could walk from one end of the living space to the other in less than thirty paces. The kitchen and living room were really one room. At least the windows let in some good light.

He had given Luther the one bedroom that was tucked in the corner of the apartment. Jack would sleep on the sofa much like he'd been sleeping on the sofa in his house which would not be his in the next two days.

He would need to get rid of some of these boxes, so they had a little more room to move around. The cabinets and closets wouldn't hold all their stuff. Unpacking had little appeal to him. Finding a spot for everything would mean they were staying, and somewhere in the back of his mind he hoped this reality belonged to someone else.

He tried to think about Aaron, telling him he'd get back on his feet, but he was having a hard time believing it. He'd lost his home. He drove around in a junk car and lived above his grandmother's store. He didn't care that this building had been in his family for generations or that Louise May Alcott might have stayed here to finish a book. He didn't even like her stories. He would never tell

Grammie or her flower friends that. They might stone him.

The kitchen in this tiny apartment faced Main Street, and the top branches of the cherry tree swept the window on a breezy day. A hummingbird had taken up residence in the tree and might drive Jack batty with all its singing.

He caught a whiff of nectarine and honey every time he went in the bedroom but couldn't figure out where it was coming from. Hopefully, Louisa May Alcott wasn't haunting the place.

He swept the same spot three times. He and his father hadn't spoken since Jack left the office a few days ago. He couldn't imagine what Sterling Billinger had to say to him now. His father hadn't left a voicemail the other day. Whatever he wanted couldn't be that important.

"Jack, do we have to stay here all day?" Luther stared up at him with wide eyes.

Jack. He tried not to allow the disappointment to choke him and didn't understand why he was disappointed Luther wouldn't call him dad at the same time. He hadn't wanted to be a father, hadn't asked to be, but now that he was, the idea had begun to take root somewhere inside him.

"Do you want to go to the beach for a few hours?"

"I guess. I... I... never mind." Luther flopped onto the couch.

"Never mind what? You can tell me." He propped the broom against the table, then joined Luther on the sofa.

"I've never swam in the ocean before."

"Really?"

Luther gave him a sideways glance. "My mom doesn't want me to, and I never had a dad to ask."

"If I had known about you, I would have been around." He had to believe that.

"My mom said you never wanted a family."

Sloane had been right all those years ago. Back then, he had been doing the New York party scene every weekend. He went out with his buddies from college and work. She had wanted their relationship to be serious. He had only wanted his next good time.

"Like I said, if I had known, things would've been different."

"Is there a boardwalk here?"

"Not one with rides and games if that's what you mean." He had no problem changing the subject. Staring his mistakes in the face took courage he didn't have today.

"Do you know how to swim?"

"Yup." When he was younger than Luther, his father had paid for swimming lessons at the best swim school in the county. Sterling had dreams of him being on the swim team. Jack had other ideas.

"Can you show me how to swim in the ocean?"

"Can you swim at all?"

Luther stared at his hands. "No."

"We'll have to change that. You can't live at the beach and not know how to swim. But the good news is, you can jump waves even if you can't swim."

"What's jump waves?"

"I'll show you. Do you have a bathing suit?"

"No."

He had a lot to learn about Luther and had questions for Sloane. How could she allow their son to be unable to swim? "Okay, we'll stop at the clothing store on the way."

"What if I can't do it? You know, jump the waves."

"Everyone can do it. You'll like it. I promise."

He hoped.

Chapter Ten

Bailey's phone vibrated in her skirt pocket with a call. She tugged it free. The screen read Beth.

"Hey, Kass, I need to take this. It's Beth." Bailey waved her phone in the air.

"Sure thing. I'll walk ahead a little."

"Hi, Beth. Are you okay?" She pressed her phone to her ear and her other hand against her other ear to block out the wind and crashing waves.

"It's not Beth, deary. It's Cara. Beth is napping. I took her phone to call you. The Lilacs and I have been talking. We're concerned about the Afternoon Tea event Beth has planned. If someone can't handle it, you really should think about canceling it."

Bailey was still getting her bearings at the store. Beth's event hadn't been a top priority. The notes on the event were disorganized, some written on scrap paper. Bailey had struggled to make heads or tails of it. Her dyslexia hadn't helped either when reading someone's scratchy handwriting. She wanted to wait to discuss the event with Beth when she was feeling a little better, but the right time hadn't appeared.

"The event is important to Beth. She's been talking about it for months."

Beth had planned a day filled with Louisa May Alcott history. Attendees were encouraged to dress up from the time period. Beth had partnered with a local tea shop as well. The event was scheduled for the end of the summer. She wouldn't be here to see the day unfold, but Beth's arm should be much better by then. Bailey couldn't see a good reason to cancel.

"Are you at the beach? I can hear the ocean."

If Cara could hear the ocean, why had she asked? Bailey clamped her mouth over that question. "I tell all my clients that fresh air is good for them."

"It's a thousand degrees out. You'll get heatstroke."

"It's only nine hundred by the water."

Cara humphed. Bailey tried not to laugh.

"I'm glad you're concerned for Beth. I am too, but we should ask her what she wants. Can you and the Lilacs meet tomorrow morning? I can bring Beth to the store, and we can discuss the event together."

Bailey appreciated Cara and the other ladies' concern for their friend. She glanced at Kassidy, still searching for sea glass. Her sisters were always worried about her too even when they didn't have to be. The Lilacs were no different.

"You will not bring in Beth. She needs to rest. I've never seen her so tired. I think something else is going on besides that arm." Cara lowered her voice. "She's not saying, but I didn't like her coloring today and she didn't eat a thing."

Cara was probably overreacting. Beth seemed fine this morning. She had eaten the eggs Bailey had made.

"She can decide for herself if she would prefer to rest. Can you get the ladies there by nine?"

"Fine, nine o'clock, but you're wrong. Something is going on with her. She told us about Jack's son. That's caused her undue stress. She's too old to have so many major changes in her life."

"Cara, you underestimate Beth. She's very excited about Luther, not stressed. The elbow is unfortunate, but she's handling the whole thing like a champ. Stop putting her in the grave too soon."

Cara was the Lilac who saw every glass half-empty. She worried over every cold and flu season or if the heat index was too high. Storms had her scurrying like a squirrel. She didn't drive at night because people pretended to be police officers who attacked old women, and she didn't want to get pulled over alone on a dark street by an impersonator.

"You're too young to understand. But you'll see when you're my age." Cara ended the call.

Bailey would never be Cara's age. The number didn't matter. Cara was an old lady in her twenties. Bailey would bet on it.

Jack handed Luther a towel. "What did you think?"

They had come down to the beach about an hour ago. Jack had shown Luther how to jump the waves before they crashed on him. Luther had protested at first, but after watching him do it a few times and body surfing one into the sand, Luther had tried.

The kid was a natural. He had taken to the water much the way Jack had as a kid. Athletics had always come easy for him. He suspected Luther might be like him in that way. He would shoot some hoops with Luther like Aaron had suggested. Jack still had his gym membership for a few more weeks. They could go there.

Beachgoers filled Serenity's beach with their bright towels and chairs sunk into the sand. Everyone seemed to be out today. A group of boys about Luther's age played volleyball at a nearby net.

"That was cool." Luther wiped his face with the towel.

Jack didn't have any suntan lotion. A pink tint covered Luther's fair skin. He should've thought about that when they bought a bathing suit from Intentions Clothing. If he was going to be a dad, he needed to do better.

"You're good at it."

"Thanks. I'm going to tell Mom when she calls." Luther wiped the droplets of salt water from his legs.

"Maybe we should wait on that one. I don't want her to worry." If Sloane decided she didn't like Luther's newfound interest, she might send her sister to come get him. Jack didn't want that.

Luther's face fell. "Mom and I don't have secrets. That's our promise."

Jack kept a lot of secrets from his father. If his mother had lived, maybe he would have told her everything.

"Okay. No secrets. Sorry."

"Can we go back out?"

The lifeguard blew his whistle and waved in some people who were too far out in the ocean.

"Looks like the water is getting too rough. We'll have to come back another day." The last hour had worn him out. He was ready to grab a beer, something to eat, and chill.

Or he could spend more time trying to convince Grammie to sell the store. She hadn't been convinced by dropping revenue and now with Luther in the picture she was more determined than ever to keep it. He needed another angle.

"Tomorrow?"

Luther's question forced Jack's thoughts back to the beach. His gaze landed on two women walking his way. One wore a light-blue baseball cap and spoke on the phone. The other made stops to squat near the sand, looking for something.

His body recognized Bailey before his mind did. He had admired her for months even when she scowled at him. He liked the scowl too. Her beauty rivaled any sandy beach or cresting ocean wave. He could look at her longer than the constant pull of white foamy water against the surf.

"Jack, can we come back tomorrow?" Luther tugged on the waistband of his board shorts.

"Hey, dude. Careful. I don't want to flash the ladies." He moved Luther's hand away.

"Sorry," Luther said with a pout.

"I don't know about tomorrow. We'll see." He glanced over at Bailey again.

"What about Grammie? Can she take me?"

"Grammie hasn't gone in the ocean in thirty years. It's me or no one for now. Got it?"

"I could come down by myself. You said I was good at it." Luther's face filled with hope.

"I did and you are. But you can't go in the ocean unless I'm with you. That has to be our promise."

"Okay. Promise." Luther's gaze dropped to the ground.

"Luther, man, let's high-five on it to make the promise official." Jack held up his hand and hoped this was the right thing to do.

Luther hesitated. Jack held his breath.

Luther caved and high-fived back. "It's official."

"Good. The ocean has to be respected. Don't forget."

"I won't."

"Hello, Jack," Bailey said, startling him.

His throat dried up. He hadn't expected her to come over to him, appearing like an apparition even though he had spotted her only moments before.

He soaked her in. She wore a long print skirt with a slit up the side, revealing a toned and tan leg. Her tank top stopped short as if the maker had run out of material.

A speck of silver winked at him from the intimate spot of her belly button.

He had to swallow to be able to speak. "Bailey." He did a lousy job of it because his mouth closed over any other words he tried to utter.

"Hi, I'm Kassidy." The other woman stuck out her hand.

Jack shook but kept his gaze on Bailey.

"Kassidy is my sister."

"Nice to meet you." He remembered his manners and looked Kassidy in the eye. She resembled Bailey with the same nose and eye shape, but that was where the similarities ended.

"This is... Luther." His tongue had tripped over the word *son*. He would have to try that out a few times in front of a mirror before he delivered the revelation to the world.

"Hi, Luther. Your Grammie told me all about you. Welcome to Serenity by the Sea. I hope you have an amazing time this summer." Bailey held up her hand for a high-five much like he had done moments before.

Luther swung with some force, missing Bailey's hand and getting her arm. Bailey lit up with delight. Joy danced across her eyes. Luther bellowed with laughter. Jack didn't understand the instant connection between the two of them and wanted to be a part of it.

"We jumped waves today. It was awesome. Can I show them, Jack?" Luther stared at him with anticipation.

"We have to get back. Sorry."

"I hate that apartment."

He did too, but he would keep that to himself in present company. "It's getting late. I've got some stuff to do."

"Have you had a chance to fix that air conditioner?" Bailey said.

"Not yet. I'll get to it tonight or tomorrow." He had kept some of his tools. They had been shipped to the storage unit by mistake. He would either have to drive over there or borrow some from his grandmother if he was going to make any headway tonight so he and Luther didn't cook in their sleep.

"It's really hot up there. Last night Jack and I had to sleep in our underwear," Luther said.

"Luther, you don't have to tell the women that."

"It's okay. I slept in my underwear too." Bailey ruffled Luther's wavy hair.

Jack tried not to picture Bailey in lacy underwear, preferably a black thong. But he had the image in his head, and it wasn't going anywhere anytime soon.

"If it's okay with you, Luther is welcome to look for sea glass with us. We're headed down to the pier. Then you can do your stuff." Bailey gave his shoulder a small shove. Her touch set his skin on fire.

"Yeah. That would be fun," Kassidy said.

"What's sea glass?" Luther looked between the adults.

"Kass, you do the honors of explaining." Bailey put an arm around her sister's shoulders.

"Unless Jack wants to," Kassidy said.

"Go ahead. I'm no expert."

"Well, sea glass starts out as garbage thrown into the ocean. Something like a piece of glass from a bottle or a vase or anything. I don't recommend polluting the water, but people still do. After years of tumbling in the salt water, the piece of glass will wash up to shore, but this time the edges are dulled, and the glass has become textured and clouded. The glass is transformed and now it's beautiful."

Kassidy pulled a few pieces out of her pocket. "Here you go." She handed the green and brown pieces to Luther.

"They're pretty," Luther said.

"They are. And they mean that even when something is broken, it can be beautiful again as something new," Kassidy said.

"Like my mom." Luther's gaze remained on the sea glass.

Bailey narrowed her eyes.

"Sloane isn't feeling well at the moment," he said.

"She's going to come back from Europe in the fall better. Like this sea glass." Luther's face lit up again.

Bailey ran a hand over Luther's head. "That sounds great, buddy. You can keep those pieces for good luck. Right, Kass?"

"Absolutely."

"So, what do you say, Luther? If Jack agrees, do you want to go looking for more?" Bailey said.

"Can I?" Luther looked at him with innocent wonder. "I don't want to go back to the apartment yet."

He didn't have the heart to tell this kid no, and he didn't want Bailey to think he was the callous guy who refused a kid with a sick mother a small consideration.

"I'll wait for you here. Thirty minutes. Then you have to be back. Can you tell time?"

Luther rolled his eyes. "It's on my phone. I'll grab it from our stuff. I'll be right back." He ran off.

"He's cute," Kassidy said.

"Thanks. We're figuring things out."

"I wonder if you ever get the hang of being a parent. Emma is only nine months old. There's so much to learn and I'm overwhelmed most of the time," Kassidy said.

Luther ran back, kicking up sand in his wake. "I've got my phone, and I set an alarm."

"Okay. I'll be up at our chairs." He turned to Bailey. "Thank you."

"No problem."

Luther threw his arms around Jack's waist and squeezed. He pulled Luther closer. His kid smelled like the ocean and possibilities. Jack couldn't remember a time in his own life when everything was possible.

"Thank you, Jack," Luther said.

"No problem." He struggled to clear his throat.

Bailey took Luther's hand and the three of them sauntered off, talking and laughing.

Jack watched for a bit. He was glad for the short break if only to catch his breath. He wasn't used to having to entertain someone all the time and he sure wasn't used to the surge of emotions that clobbered him out of nowhere.

He spent his adult life never answering to anyone about what he was doing or where he was going. The second he could be out of Sterling's house, he had made up as many of his own rules as he could. Now that he no longer worked for his father, he wouldn't do any of Sterling's bidding.

Sloane had probably kept Luther to herself because she believed Jack was a selfish prick, but Jack deserved the chance to know his child from the start. He had missed too many years. If Bailey's sister felt overwhelmed, he was that times a thousand. He was thrown into the big leagues without ever having played the sport.

He walked back to his beach chair. His cell phone rang from the pocket of his backpack. He tugged out the phone to see that his father was calling again.

He couldn't imagine what the urgency was unless Sterling had found himself in the hospital, but Jack suspected his father would have his assistant reach out to tell Jack about an episode in the emergency room.

He debated on answering. If he didn't, he would have to call back. Or he could answer and get the pain over with.

"Hello, Father."

"Hello, Sterling. I'm glad I finally reached you."

"Is there something I can help you with?" He dropped into the chair and stretched out his legs.

"I called to check on Luther. How is he adjusting to Serenity by the Sea?"

Not *how are you?* His father didn't care how Jack was doing. Jack had to figure out his problems on his own.

Sterling had told him many times in his life that he had to deal with whatever was bothering him and move on. Billingers didn't have time for unnecessary emotional baggage. That was for people with fewer opportunities.

"Luther's fine." Most likely having a better time than Jack was.

"Has he met Beth?"

"He has."

"Did that old woman scare him away from me yet?" Something that resembled sarcasm—Sterling was too well bred for that—came across the line.

"Father, Beth isn't like that," he said. Not that he should have to point out that fact.

"She poisoned your mother against me."

"I have a feeling you did that all by yourself."

"I won't tolerate the disrespect. I only called to inquire after my grandson."

And there was the indignation his father was so well known for.

"Now you have." His patience for his father wore like a sun-damaged beach umbrella filled with holes.

"I'd like to spend some time with him."

"I'm busy right now. I need to find a job. Someone saw to it I'd never work in finance again. Do you have any idea who would have done that?"

"You did that one by yourself." Sterling ended the call with the echo of Jack's words in his ears.

For a long time, Jack had believed Grammie had turned his mother against Jack's father. When his parents had married, the stories were all about them being in love.

Old photos showed two people who stared at each other with nothing but adoration.

But over the years, Priscilla fell out of love with her handsome and successful husband. According to Sterling, the only thing that had changed was Beth's constant badgering of her daughter.

Once Jack was old enough to understand the kind of man his father was, those stories about Grammie didn't hold water. Grammie was like a second mother to him. He only spent a few weeks a year with her, but she had showered him with love and affection. She never once called him Sterling. She encouraged him and supported him when he had messed up over and over.

Sterling only wanted to be rid of him.

Chapter Eleven

Bailey lagged behind Kassidy and Luther as they searched for sea glass. She replayed the moment when Jack held his son until it wore a groove in her mind.

She wasn't expecting to see such emotion on Jack's face when Luther threw himself into his father. The stoic veneer cracked, and a warmth spread into Jack's eyes. A warmth that was rarely there when she was around.

The ocean crashed into the sand and foamed around their feet. The water dampened the hem of her skirt. She didn't want to think that Jack had a heart. Knowing he had more than one dimension might change her opinion of him, and as long as he wanted his grandmother to give up her store, Bailey needed to keep her opinions of him the same.

She was still curious about the Louisa May Alcott book and what he had done with it. She suspected he would return to the store for other rare finds.

He must want the money. He had sold his home in Rumson and moved above the bookstore. He wouldn't do that if he had a decent cash flow. She assumed he still worked for his father or did he no longer have a paycheck?

She never cared that much about making the big bucks. She wanted to be comfortable, to be able to travel as she wished. Her happiness was more important than the dollar. That was why she had agreed to move to Colorado and be with Mark. He had made her happy once.

"We got some." Kassidy pumped her fist in the air and interrupted Bailey from her thoughts.

Luther squatted down beside her sister as they pushed sand away and gathered the stones. Luther was a sweet boy and a mini version of his father. She had liked him instantly with his stylish wavy hair and Jack's eyes.

"Bailey, come look," Luther said.

He dumped a few pieces into her palm.

"Great find. I love the green and white ones."

"You can keep them," he said.

"No way. Finders keepers. Put them in your pocket to keep them safe."

"Can I share them with Jack or maybe Grammie Beth?" Luther ran his fingers over the pieces.

"You can share them with whoever you want."

"All the pieces are textured like Kassidy said." He stared at her and Kassidy in wonder.

Every summer when she came to stay with her dad and sisters, all they did was search for sea glass. Their father would drive up and down the shore from Sandy Hook to Cape May, looking for the stuff. She used to hate the long car rides when they had a beach in their back-yard. What she hadn't known way back then was her father was saving all the sea glass for something only he understood.

"My mom and I don't come to the beach much. She doesn't like the sand." Luther shoved the sea glass in his pocket.

That explained why he probably wasn't familiar with sea glass.

"Here's another." Kassidy handed a brown piece to Luther.

"For me?" Luther's eyes grew wide.

"Of course. I have tons all around my house. I just like looking for it. Being out here reminds me of our dad."

"Where's your dad?"

"He passed away a few years ago," Kassidy said.

"I hope my mom doesn't die." Tears filled Luther's eyes.

"She's going to be fine." Bailey gripped Luther's shoulder and hoped she hadn't told a lie.

"I hope so. I don't want to live with Jack forever." Luther wiped away a tear.

A truth that shined brighter than the afternoon sun.

"He's not so bad. Give yourself time to get to know him."

Kassidy shot her a questioning look.

With Luther present, she had no way to say that she was just defending Jack. Kassidy had to know what she was thinking. Jack had his issues—plenty of them—but for that short moment when he held on to Luther, she witnessed another side to him, a side she might want to explore.

Kassidy's phone sounded off. "I'm sorry." She fished it out of her pocket. "It's a text from Grant. He has to leave for a gig. I forgot."

"You forgot? That's not like you," Bailey said.

"Sometimes I struggle with this mother, wife, career schedule. I didn't realize how hard it would be or how much energy it took." Kassidy brushed her hair out of her face.

"You're doing great, Kass. Being a mom is hard work." Not that she had any idea what it was like to be a mom, but she had coached several clients who struggled with their new existence as mother and career person. Women were told they needed to keep their balls in the air no matter how many they had to juggle. Women had been lied to.

"I have to run." Kassidy offered a quick hug, then turned to Luther. "It was nice to meet you, Luther. I hope I get to see you again." Kassidy scurried away.

"She's nice," Luther said, looking after her.

"Yeah, she is. Okay, shall we look for some more sea glass or how about some ice cream?" She was ready to get off the beach and into some shade. The heat bored right through her hat. Maybe she should've worn the straw one that provided more shade.

Her phone vibrated in her skirt pocket again. Because it could actually be Beth this time, she pulled it out. Not

Beth. Mark. She debated on taking it. He would ask when she was leaving, and she didn't have a new answer for him. He was running his hiking business just fine without her. An extra week or two in Serenity shouldn't matter.

"Hey, Luther, I have to grab this call, but I'll be quick."

"I think I want to show Jack the sea glass."

"Okay, hang on. I'll just say hello and then walk you back." She hit the accept button. "Hi, Mark."

"I didn't think you were going to pick up again. I wanted to talk to you about a few things."

"Can you hang on a second?"

He huffed in reply, but she ignored him and moved the phone away from her mouth. "Luther, where are you going? I was going to walk you."

Luther had already begun the trek back to Jack.

"You don't have to. I know where Jack is sitting. See you later, Bailey." Luther waved.

She watched until he blended into the crowd, then second-guessed her decision to allow him to return alone. The beach wasn't that big, and this was Serenity by the Sea where people didn't even lock their doors. The only time they had trouble in town was when someone decided swimming too close to the jetties at night was a good idea.

"Bailey. Bailey. Are you there?" Mark's voice sprang up from the phone.

"I'm here. Sorry."

"Who was that you were talking to?"

She hesitated, avoiding any mention of Jack. Mark didn't have to know about the two of them taking care of the store. Her life here was separate from the life she would begin with Mark.

"Kassidy's employee's son. He was looking for sea glass with us." The words tasted bitter. She should not have lied.

"That's nice. When do you want to announce that you'll be coaching my clients on nutrition? I'm making graphics and want to post them."

His clients. "I don't know. I'm still not sure when I'm leaving, and I'll want a few days to settle in before I take on new clients. I also have to check in with my clients once I'm there."

"In other words, you want to fly by the seat of your pants."

Mark was her opposite in many ways. She didn't feel the need to plan out every step, but he did. "An extra week or two isn't going to matter. Tell them the end of August."

"The end of August? I've already started talking about new services."

Not her problem.

The heat gave her a headache, or maybe it was this conversation. She was ready to get back to Beth's and sit in the cool air-conditioning with an iced tea.

"I have to run. Maren is calling." Another lie, but she was not in the mood to keep talking about his promises to *his* clients.

"Fine. Call me later, but please find a date sooner.

Bye." He ended the call without any terms of endearment.

She could count on one hand how many times he had said, "I love you." He wasn't big on romance, with sappy words or sending flowers that would die anyway, but she wanted to hear it once in a while. That wasn't too much to ask for. s

She pushed thoughts of Mark away and scanned the beach crowd again. The sun worshippers were staying late today. She couldn't see Jack or Luther. They had probably headed back to the apartment.

They would suffocate up there if the air conditioner hadn't been fixed. She should move out of Beth's so they could move in. But she would no longer have an excuse to stay in town and she wanted one. She wasn't ready to leave the way she had been only a few days ago.

In a week or two, she would set sail and take the long trip across the country. Mark may have not said he loved her, but he did. He would wait.

For now, she'd grab a salad for her and Beth on the way back. She would ask Beth to watch one of Bailey's favorite shows. She'd like to read a book tonight, but her head hurt too much from the heat to concentrate on letters that jumped and skipped across the page.

With a final look for Jack and Luther, she bade goodbye to the beach for the day.

Chapter Twelve

Jack fought the anger weighing on his chest but was losing at record speed. Bailey had said she'd return with Luther in a half hour. Ninety minutes had passed, and they weren't back. He wasn't prone to overreacting, but he had no plan if his son went missing. No one had coached him that could happen on day three of being a parent.

Grammie had taken him to Disney World when he was about eight. She had placed a business card in the pocket of his shorts and told him if he got lost, he should find a mom and have her help him call. At the time, the idea of losing his grandmother in that crowd of people had frozen him in place. In the end, Jack had never strayed far from his grandmother, worried he might lose her. He had already lost his mother. He didn't want to lose Grammie too.

Now he shoved the scream back down his throat.

He didn't have Bailey's number. Rookie mistake on

that one. He tried his grandmother an hour ago to obtain it, but the calls went straight to voicemail. She had also not responded to any of his texts. She must be asleep or forgot to charge her cell.

Luther and Bailey could still be down by the pier. He would try that location first and when he found them digging in the sand, he would tell Bailey to stay the hell away from his son.

As he walked closer, the only thing before him was the ocean waves wrapping around the wood piles that held up the pier. No one was looking for sea glass or playing in the sand. The closest person to the pier was a scrawny guy in orange board shorts with a beard down to his collarbone.

"Excuse me," he said to the man. "Did you happen to see a woman with a blue baseball cap and a little boy with wavy hair over here?"

The man's eyes were vacant. His mouth hung open. "Not me, man. I didn't see a thing. Nobody here but us surfers."

Jack doubted the man could swim let alone surf. The lack of a surfboard was a big giveaway. "Thank you."

He decided to zigzag his way back to his chair. Maybe they had run into someone Bailey knew and were saying hello. But every step brought him nothing. Luther was not among the bodies lying on their towels or slumped in their chairs, all hiding behind sunglasses as if they all had secrets. He had secrets. His biggest secret was his failure as a man and now as a father.

Luther had taken his phone. Jack lunged for his. The

screen was black. The battery had died. He smacked his forehead. "How stupid are you?" he said under his breath.

Jack searched the horizon. Had Luther gone into the ocean again? He hoped Luther had listened to what Jack had said earlier. Luther had a lot to learn about swimming in the ocean.

He stood by the lifeguard stand. Luther and Bailey were not in or near the water. He ran up to the boardwalk. Maybe they had decided to get a drink or Luther needed the bathroom.

Panic burst through the anger like a flamethrower. Where was his son? He turned in circles. People walked the boards, some in bright colors, others eating ice cream.

He cupped his hands around his mouth. "Luther."

A few teenagers walking ahead of him turned at his outburst. One gave him a dirty look; another gave him the finger.

He yelled again. Not a single person stopped to ask him if he was okay, had he lost someone. This was a small town. Where was the community they bragged about?

"Are you okay, young man?" An older bald gentleman, who came up to Jack's neck, looked at him with concern in his blue eyes.

It took a few seconds for Jack's brain to make the connection. He hadn't seen this man in years. "Mr. D?"

The man laughed. "Of course. You're Beth's grandson. I never forget a face. Did you lose someone?"

"I lost my son." The words stuck in his throat. How could he lose his child? What kind of a total idiot was he?

"We'll find him. Where did you see him last?" Mr. D gripped his arm with force as if to share his confidence.

He filled in Mr. D with what he knew. Mr. D made a call and had two of his sons also out looking.

"Jack."

He whirled in the direction his name came from. The sky spun around him. Bailey ran across the street toward him, clutching her hat in one hand and a to-go bag in the other.

"Bailey, where is Luther?"

"What do you mean?" She gripped his shoulder in the same place as Mr. D. Except this time her heat seared him. "Hi, Mr. D."

"*Ciao*, Bailey. I'll start looking down the boardwalk." Mr. D hurried away.

"Why isn't he with you? Where is he?" He didn't care that he yelled or that now he had the attention of passersby. If yelling at a woman was the only way to get help finding Luther, he would yell all day long.

"He said he was coming back to you. He never did?"

"You allowed a kid to wander around on the beach by himself?" He had been foolish to trust this woman.

"He's not that little and he insisted that he knew where you were. I watched him until he blended in with the crowd. Your chair should have been right there."

"He's only ten. What do you know about taking care of a child? I can't believe I let you take him. What if he drowned? What if someone took him?" He didn't want to imagine the worst, but his mind raced ahead to all possibilities. How would he explain this to Sloane?

"Jack, let's take a deep breath. Panicking isn't going to help. Did you look everywhere?"

"Of course I did. What kind of a ridiculous question is that? I scoured the beach. He's not down there."

"Is there a chance he went back to the apartment or your grandmother's?"

"Not the apartment. He hates it there. I'll try my grandmother again. I can't my phone is dead. Can I use yours?" He hadn't considered Luther would walk back to Grammie's. He wouldn't know how to get there from here.

Bailey handed hers over. Jack punched the screen hard enough he dropped the phone.

Bailey retrieved it. "It's going to be okay."

"You don't know that."

"I do. You call your grandmother. I'm going to go back down on the sand and look again. Is your stuff still there?"

"Yes."

"Good. Maybe he's already at the towel." She squeezed his arm then dropped her to-go bag in the garbage.

He turned from her, unable to look her in the eye, his vision clouded by fury. Of all the mistakes he had made recently, the bad investment, wanting to sell his grandmother's store for money, allowing Luther's care to Bailey was his worst one.

"Hello, this is Beth. Is this thing on? Oh, phooey. If you can hear me, leave a message. You're not actually talking to me."

He waited for the beep. "Grammie, it's me. I'm calling from Bailey's phone. Please call back."

He leaned over the metal rails and searched from this vantage point. Some of the people had left the beach now that the dinner hour was upon them, leaving empty spots of sand where there were none before. But still no sign of Luther.

He couldn't tell Sloane he had lost their son. Tears pricked the corners of his eyes, but he swatted them away. He had no time for such emotion. He needed a minute to think. Should he call the police? Was he being unreasonable? Or was he wasting valuable time?

He saw her then. Bailey ran down the beach away from Serenity and toward Bradley Beach. Her arms were in the air, that silly but adorable hat clutched in one hand, waving like a flag.

Running toward her was the silhouette of a little boy. Jack's knees buckled. He gripped the rail to keep from falling.

He forced his feet to move, and he tore down the stairs to the sand and flew to his son. He brushed past Bailey and scooped Luther's warm body into his arms.

Luther wrapped his arms around Jack's neck. Hot tears seared his skin.

"Are you okay?" He couldn't manage another word but held his son in a viselike grip.

Bailey joined them. "I told you it was going to be okay."

Jack eased out of the embrace and gripped Luther by

the shoulders. "What happened? Why didn't you come back?"

"I got lost. I walked back to our spot. I thought it was our spot, but the volleyball game was over. I couldn't find you. I kept walking around and around. But every time I thought I knew where I was, you weren't there." Luther hiccupped between tears.

"It's okay now. Everything's okay." He smoothed Luther's hair, but it only bounced back to attention as if out of protest.

"I'm sorry," Luther said.

"Nothing to be sorry about. I'm glad you're okay." He placed a kiss on Luther's head.

Bailey's warm gaze raked over them both. Her smile spread wide. He imagined for someone like her, someone who seemed to float through life without a care in the world, today's events were no big deal now that they were over. But for him, the man who had become a father only hours ago, today was a nightmare.

"I never want to see you again," he said.

The smile fell from her face.

Chapter Thirteen

Bailey threw the marshmallow in the fire. Tears dripped from the corners of her eyes. Her sisters stared at her. They sat in Kassidy's backyard. Even though the humidity hadn't backed off, they had lit a fire to make s'mores.

She had raced over here after the confrontation with Jack, not knowing what to do or where else to go. She didn't dare return to Beth's.

Bailey had never meant to hurt Luther. She would never. The moment Jack's pain was evident while they stood on the boardwalk, a helplessness washed over her. Something she had never experienced before. She wanted to fix what was wrong and thankfully she had. But what if she hadn't?

When she had run down to the beach, something inside her had told her to keep walking away from Serenity. The neighboring beach hosted as many people as

Serenity did. Her gut had sensed Luther had missed Jack without realizing.

And he had. Luther had misjudged where Jack waited and walked onto the other town's section. Easy enough mistake. Anyone could make it, especially a ten-year-old who had never lived in Serenity before. Signs didn't exist on the beach to notify anyone they had passed the town border. She had misjudged her surroundings plenty of times as a kid. Her sisters always teased her for it.

When she had seen Luther walking farther away, she screamed his name. He and several other people had turned to her. Luther ran and she ran. Her dumb hat had lifted off her head. She had instinctively grabbed for it. She hadn't cared one little bit about it, not when Luther threw himself into her arms.

"I didn't mean to lose him. I watched him. I thought he had made it back. You should've seen the hatred in Jack's eyes." Bailey covered her face with her hands.

"Give him a little time." Her sister Maren sat beside her on the chaise lounge and squeezed her knee. Maren smelled of vanilla and beach wood. Her brown hair was pulled back in a low ponytail. "He was frightened because he thought he lost Luther. Any parent would overreact, especially one with no experience."

"He already hated me." Not that she was terribly fond of him either. She couldn't handle it when other people didn't like her. Probably because she grew up thinking if she could keep her mother happy, then her mother would love her. It took many years before Bailey

111

realized her mother's happiness was her own responsibility.

"I can't imagine how terrified I'd be if something happened to Emma," Kassidy said. "I wasn't prepared for the overwhelming love, guilt, and protectiveness for such a tiny person I hardly know."

"Every mother feels that. Well, most mothers." Maren poked a stick into another marshmallow and handed it to Bailey.

"Are you saying because I'm not a mother that I don't know how he feels?" She wiped her nose with the back of her hand.

"I'm not saying that at all." Maren stood. "I'm saying his reaction to what happened is normal. You were an easy place to put the blame. One time Dave left Peyton at the town fair. He thought I had her, and I thought he had her. She must've been around Luther's age. I got home first. When he walked into the house without her, every horrible scenario popped into my head. Thank God she was fine and with friends of ours, but I was mad at Dave for weeks."

"I'll apologize again tomorrow. We have to start getting along. We're supposed to work together." The words were out before she knew what she was saying. She hadn't told her sisters yet about working in the bookstore. She also still hadn't mentioned her little trip to Colorado.

They looked at her with confusion painted on their faces.

"Did you hire him as a client?" Kassidy smooshed her

toasted marshmallow between chocolate and graham crackers.

"No."

"Then why are you working with him?" Maren said.

"I'm helping out in the bookstore while Beth heals." She stuck her stick in the fire, giving herself something to look at besides her sisters.

"That's very nice of you," Maren said. "But what about your clients? Will you have time for them?"

She was no longer hungry for dessert. "Can we talk about something else? Maren, how's work?"

Maren worked at the local university with her partner Shane. She was the director of special events. Maren also had a side hustle planning parties for select clients. She had so much business, she turned people away. She also turned people away because Maren insisted on working with a certain type of client.

"Why don't you want to talk about the bookstore or your business?" Maren crossed her arms over her chest.

"There's nothing to talk about. Beth will be back at work in no time, and I'll go back to what I was doing." Which was leaving town and starting a new life with Mark. She wanted that life. She wanted a committed relationship and a family of her own.

"Something's up." Kassidy put down her s'more and wiped her hands on a napkin. "What aren't you telling us?"

"I don't know what you're talking about."

"Bailey, your foot has tapped this whole time. At first, I figured you were upset about earlier, but that's not all of it. Did Jack do or say something to you today that may have crossed a line?" Maren said.

"I've heard about his reputation for finding trouble," Kassidy said.

"Who's going around talking?" Of course, someone would have stirred up old news with Jack's return to town.

"Natalie Lowe. Who else?" Kassidy passed around the chocolate.

"I can't believe one of Beth's good friends would start rumors about him. Beth told me some of his history, but that's not any of Natalie's business."

"Is this one of those *the lady doth protest too much* times?" Maren said to Kassidy with a smirk on her face.

"I believe so." Kassidy wagged her eyebrows.

"Stop it, you two. I don't have any kind of feeling for Jack. I—" She almost slipped and said she loved Mark. She wasn't ready for that conversation, and even though she did love Mark, Jack was on repeat in her mind.

"You what?" Maren said.

"Nothing. I don't have feelings for Jack except maybe annoyance."

"Sounds like a crush to me." Maren stuck her marshmallow in the fire.

"Are you kidding? No way. Jack Billinger isn't even my type." He wasn't, but that swagger of his could turn many heads. It had turned hers a few times. He had an easy smile and when he wasn't trying to get rid of the bookstore, he kind of grew on her.

She preferred the man who wanted his hands in dirt,

didn't drive a motorcycle, and liked to have sex on the kitchen floor. Jack didn't strike her as a man who would do that. He seemed more like the expensive sheets kind of guy. Which had her wondering why had he moved into the apartment above the store.

"If you don't like him, then what is it? You're hiding something." Kassidy bit into a piece of chocolate.

"Why are you pushing this? Why do you push everything? You did it to Maren when she started seeing Shane because you thought he wasn't good enough for her. You're doing it now." She moved off the lounge and shoved her feet in her shoes.

"I'm just concerned."

"You know, you don't have to mother us."

"Why not? It's not as if any of us have the best mother. I don't mind it when you two look after me." Kassidy stood too.

"Things are getting heated. Why don't we all just forget it and enjoy the rest of the night together?" Maren said.

"I'm not heated. Do I look heated?" Her skin burned from the inside out.

"I think you do," Kassidy said. "But if you don't want to talk about Jack or how you're going to juggle your business and help out at the bookstore, then don't. You're right, it's none of my business."

She glanced from Kassidy to Maren. Her sisters were the reason she had returned to Serenity by the Sea. She had wanted a chance to be close to them. She had always felt like an outsider growing up. They were older than her and shared a mother.

Bailey was the product of her parents' affair. Her father had been married to Kassidy and Maren's mother when he got involved with her mother. Her mother had broken up Dad and Vanessa's marriage. Then Dad had married her mom, but they hadn't lasted either.

She had only wanted to find a place to belong. She didn't know where that was sometimes, but Mark had offered her another chance to have what she thought she wanted.

"I can handle two things at once. I'm not a hopeless case just because I'm a little unorganized." She fought the frustration out of her voice.

"Whoa, who said anything about hopeless? We were talking about you and Jack." Kassidy threw her hands in the air.

"No, you brought up me juggling two things at once. You aren't the only one who can handle the pressure." She bit her tongue on wanting to say that Kassidy couldn't handle the pressure because she had to lie to get help, but that would make Bailey the worst possible sister considering she was lying too.

Kassidy sat down and grabbed her iced tea. "I'm not trying to be mean, but you're late for everything, running from one event to another. You'll overextend yourself, helping Beth get around, helping at the store, helping with Sea Glass, and taking care of your clients. Your clients need to be your priority."

"Kassidy, for the hundredth time, I don't need you to

tell me what to do. I am a grown-ass woman who can take care of herself and have for a long time. Just because you're a mother now doesn't mean you have all the answers. If I want to swing from a chandelier, run off with a stranger, or close my business, that's for me to decide. Not you. Now, shut up."

She pushed past Maren and ran around the house to the street. Her sisters' voices traveled after her, but she didn't stop to catch them. She had left her car at the boardwalk and would have to walk back to it, but maybe that would give her some time to calm down.

She walked through the Topside Community. Residents sat on their front porches under their striped awnings. Bug zappers crackled with each win. Music drifted from someone's window. The air smelled like grilled hamburgers and her stomach growled. She hadn't eaten a real meal in hours.

Bailey's insides tangled from the stress of the day. All she had wanted was a few hours doing something she loved to help her deal with what had happened with Jack and Luther. Instead, she had started a brawl with her sisters because she was too afraid to tell them the whole truth.

Kassidy's street met Main Street and Bailey headed for the pizzeria on the boardwalk. It would still be open, and she could bring a pie back to Beth's. The salad she had craved earlier would no longer do the trick.

She glanced toward the bookstore. The windows were dark, but light spilled out from the upstairs windows, through the leaves of the cherry tree. The hummingbird was probably tucked in for the night.

Jack and Luther were up in the apartment, and she longed to knock on their door and apologize again. She would apologize forever if Jack would let her.

In the morning, she would stop by Bella Notte and buy some muffins and pastries. No one could stay angry when Mr. D's goodies were around. She'd stop by Jack's with her peace offering.

They did have to work together even if she disagreed with his desire to have his grandmother sell the store.

She would never hurt Luther. If it took her and Jack being cordial for Jack to believe that about her, then that's what it would take.

She would see to it.

Chapter Fourteen

B ailey poured hot water into two mugs for her and Beth. Morning sun streamed through the kitchen window dressed in yellow curtains. The old laminate countertop trimmed in a thin metal showed wear in spots. Scuff marks on the linoleum floor told years of stories.

Beth's home was well lived in but clean. Dust didn't stand a chance under Beth's touch. When Bailey had stumbled upon a spill in the refrigerator and sauce spatter on the stovetop, nothing short of surprise shook her.

She opened the window to let in the ocean breeze and chase away the mustiness. Today already promised to be a hot one.

Beth hadn't come downstairs yet. She was usually up early and floating around the kitchen by now. Bailey dropped a tea infuser into each mug and went to check on Beth.

"Good morning, sunshine." She knocked a couple of times. "Are you up?"

Silence met Bailey. Beth might still be asleep or just hadn't heard her. She tried again.

"Beth, it's me. I made tea. I can make you something to eat if you want before I run out." She hadn't mentioned anything about Luther when she had returned home late last night.

Cara had tucked Beth into bed and left a note for Bailey in a messy script that took her three times to figure out. Cara had written that Beth was tired and hadn't eaten much. Beth wasn't a big eater. Bailey wasn't concerned.

She hadn't wanted to burden Beth with the mishap yesterday, especially since everything worked out. She would talk to Beth when the time was right.

Still no answer. She tried the knob. "Beth, I'm coming in. Yell if you're not decent."

The shades were still drawn, but light slipped through the sides, coloring the room in grays. Beth was under the covers. Her chest rose and fell in a slow rhythm.

Bailey placed a hand on Beth's shoulder. "Bethy, it's me. Are you up?"

Beth shifted under her grip and Bailey pushed a thankful breath over her lips.

"Ooh, Bailey, dear. Did I oversleep?" Beth pushed herself to sit up with her good arm.

"It's still early. Do you want to go back to sleep?"

"Oh, no. Sleeping late is the devil's curse. Let me get

120

up and make you some breakfast." Beth shoved the covers away and swung her legs over the side of the bed. She held her forehead with her hand.

"Are you okay?"

"Fine, dear. Just sat up a tad too quickly. Give an old lady a hand." Beth held out her good hand.

Bailey slipped her hand around Beth's paper thin one. "I made some tea. I could bring it up to you."

"Nonsense. Now pull up those shades and let the light in. I'll throw on my robe and be down in a jiffy. Go on. Get moving." Beth swatted her toward the window.

"I could make some breakfast for you before I run out. I... I have a couple of errands this morning. I also wanted to check in at the store and see how Amy is doing."

"I'm the one making you breakfast. You're far too skinny. You need meat on those bones of yours." Beth struggled into her robe, the one side hanging limp over her bad arm.

"I would hardly call me skinny. My sister Maren is the skinny one." She rolled up the shades and flooded the room with morning light. "Thank you for—Beth, are you feeling okay?"

Beth's face was the color of water after paintbrushes had invaded it. Bruises hung under her eyes like a sick moon.

"I feel fine. My elbow is a little achy. Some aspirin will fix me right up. How about that breakfast?"

"Did you get much sleep?"

"Slept like I always do. Down for the count." Beth

hobbled toward the bedroom door, ending the conversation. "Are you coming?"

She followed Beth downstairs to the kitchen and watched as she shuffled around the room. Some of the color returned to her face and the circles blended into her skin, almost disappearing. Maybe she had a bad night and hadn't wanted to complain, but Beth's coloring had been off. Bailey hoped she wasn't trying to hide how much pain she was really experiencing.

She checked the time on her phone. If she planned to stop by the bakery, apologize to Jack once again, and make the meeting with the Lilacs, she needed to hurry. Kassidy was wrong. She wasn't always late.

"Beth, I have some errands to run this morning. Will you be okay by yourself for a few hours?"

"Run along, dear. I'm right as rain." The smile didn't reach Beth's eyes as she poured eggs into a pan.

"I can cancel my meeting if you'd rather I stay here with you. I should be the one making you breakfast anyway." She dumped her phone on the table. Jack could wait a few hours. She wanted to be here for Beth.

"Don't be silly. I'm fine. My other arm still works, and my legs might be a little stiff in the morning, but they'll warm up any second now. Go on. I need you at the store when it opens. As much as I love my grandson, I don't want him getting any ideas. You're in charge over there. Not him."

"Do you think you'll ever sell the store?" She regretted the words as soon as they left her lips. What Beth did with the store was none of her business. But the idea that beautiful store, holding thousands of lives and journeys, could be turned into another real estate office or salon put an ache in Bailey's heart.

Beth placed a plate on the table in the usual spot she took her meals. "As long as I'm breathing, I will not sell that store to anyone. It's my family's legacy. If Jack doesn't want it, then I'll give it to Luther."

"Luther won't be able to take it for at least eight years."

"Then I'll just have to live that long. Unless you want it?" Beth put toast in the toaster and looked over her shoulder at Bailey.

"Your bookstore? No, but thank you." The dream was not to be a shop owner, stuck in a small town forever. When she had returned to Serenity by the Sea, deep down she knew she would not stay till the end.

"I think you and it could be a good fit."

"I'm not family. I don't know anything about running a bookstore."

"You're like a granddaughter to me. You've been my best tenant ever. We share the same interests and values. You would take care of my store until Luther was old enough."

"What if Luther doesn't want it either? Or sells it somewhere down the line." She hated to admit how hard bookstores had it with online shopping putting everyone out of business. Bailey worried there would be no more local stores one day.

Beth pushed the eggs around with a spatula. "That would certainly break my heart."

"Jack isn't going to give up asking you. He's only looking at the numbers."

"I suppose not, but I don't hold that against him. He was raised by a man who valued money above all else. It was a shame my Priscilla took too long to see it."

She couldn't imagine a father like that. Her dad was sweet and kind. Lost sometimes, but he loved her and her sisters as they were.

"Do you think Jack is like his father?" Valuing money above all else would explain why he took the Louisa May Alcott book. Since he had such a strong fear of heights, climbing to get a rare, valuable item would seem worth it to him.

"He has a lot of my Priscilla in him. But he's used to things working out for him. He's charming and used to getting his way." Beth glanced at the clock above the sink. "Oh my. Look at the time. I promised Natalie I'd give her a call this morning and let her know how I'm doing. She wants to have some news at her morning coffee klatch. That woman is such a gossip."

"She's been telling people Jack is a troublemaker."

"That woman." Beth fisted her hands on her hips. She winced. "I will have words with her. Now go and enjoy your day, dear. I'll see you later." Beth shooed her from the kitchen.

Bailey left the house but stood by her car. She wasn't sure if she should leave Beth or not. But Beth did want her to be at the store today and that was the least Bailey could do for the woman who took her in and made a home for her.

She still didn't understand how Beth could remain friends with Natalie. Beth must see something Bailey did not.

She had an hour before her meeting with the Lilacs. That gave her enough time to buy pastries and walk down the street to Jack's.

Bailey found a place to park and used her parking app to pay for the spot. She missed the days when she didn't have to pay to park at all, but that was a long time ago when she was young, her dad was still alive, and Mark hadn't walked into the picture yet.

At this hour of the morning, Bella Notte burst at the seams. Tourists and year-rounders alike visited the bakery for its fresh bread and pastries. Some weekends the line to get in snaked down Main Street.

Inside, the few tables were full of people in deep conversation. A line from the pastry counter almost hit the door.

She stepped in line behind a man with arms like bright-red sticks poking out of his white t-shirt.

He turned and glanced at her. His nose matched his arms. Freckles dotted his cheeks.

"Hello," he said.

"Hi. Does that sunburn hurt?"

He glanced down at himself, then back at her. "It does. I haven't been to the beach in years. I forgot how easy it is to get sunburned."

"Be careful out there today."

"Thanks. Are you on vacation too?" He moved up in line.

"I live in Serenity."

"How lucky. I'd give anything to live at the beach, but my wife and I can't afford it. I bet you don't like living here, do you?"

"Such a strange thing to say. What would make you assume that?" She would always love Serenity. But she wanted a new chapter in her book of life. The time had come to fly.

"We often want what we don't have." His words startled her.

"Bailey." Someone called her name.

She searched for the owner of that voice. Sophia DeFazio waved her over from behind the counter. *"Vena ca."*

"Excuse me. Nice to meet you." She dashed away from the philosophical tourist whose advice left a tightness in her chest.

"Hi, Sophia. Big crowd today."

Sophia laughed. She was a petite woman with a big personality. Her hair had grayed, but she kept it long and pulled back when she worked at the bakery. She wore gold hoops and a large diamond on her ring finger.

"Everyone wants Gio's pastries. God bless. I'm going to be late to our meeting. I can't leave him with this crowd. Our boys are in the back baking. They can't come out and work the register. I'm the best on the register anyway. These men. Start without me, okay?"

"We can wait for you."

"No. You need to convince Cara to have that event. And tell her to stop putting ideas in Beth's head that she's sick. She's going to jinx that woman. What can I get you?"

"Get me? Oh. No, Sophia, I'll wait like everyone else."

Sophia pointed behind her. The line was now out the door. "Oh boy."

"You want something for yourself?" Sophia grabbed a white box from the shelf behind her.

"I was getting something for Jack and Luther. I need to apologize."

"About losing his son?" Sophia wagged a finger.

"Does everyone know?" She glanced over her shoulder as if the line of people all knew what a horrible mistake she had made.

"Nah. Gio told me last night about helping Jack look for Luther. You were the real hero."

"Not me. I'm the one who thought Luther had returned to Jack safely. Big mistake. Big."

"Ah. Easy accident. Anyone could have made it. Wait here. I'll put a box together. That will be apology enough." Sophia buzzed around behind the case, pushing Mr. D out of the way as she filled the white pastry box.

"Thank you. What do I owe you?" She scrounged for her wallet in her big bag.

"Pay me later. Go fatten up that man. He doesn't eat enough." Sophia winked.

"You're not very subtle, Sophia. Jack and I are barely friends."

"You don't see the way he looks at you."

"Sure I do. Like I have ten heads."

Sophia laughed again. "To be young again. I have to go check on my boys. Make sure they're filling the pastries the way I want."

"Thanks, Sophia." She raised the box that emitted mouthwatering scents of warm sugar, vanilla, and cream.

She still had plenty of time on the meter. She left her car and walked toward the store. People milled about on the street. Some held coffee cups and sat on benches. Others pumped their arms and speed walked around the meanders.

The hummingbird sang its morning greetings as she approached Tea and Tales. Bailey liked to think the bird actually knew it was her. She paused at the base of the tree and looked up.

"Good morning, bird."

A man carrying a beach chair on one arm and pulling a wagon filled with a child and beach necessities gave her a dirty look.

"What? You don't convene with nature? You're on your way to put your feet in the sand." She huffed past him and around the back of the store.

Jack had said he never wanted to see her again. She couldn't blame him. She was at fault yesterday and things could've turned out badly. She would've never forgiven herself if something had happened to Luther.

She climbed the stairs to the apartment as the sun rose higher in the sky and spread its heat over the town like an open oven door. She'd be sweating in no time.

Shifting the box from one hand to the other, she knocked on the door. If he wasn't home, she'd have to take the pastries to the store and put them in the mini fridge. Her apology would have to wait.

No one answered and she tried again. She'd count to ten before leaving.

"Jack, someone is at the door." Luther's voice came from the other side.

She sighed with relief and fear.

Jack swung open the door and halted. "Oh."

His hair stuck up in all the right places, but the ends were wet. He had shaved because of the fresh nick on his chin. The tiny spot of blood hadn't dried yet. His collared shirt hung over the top of carpenter shorts that exposed his toned legs. She sucked in a breath.

"Hi. I brought you something." She held out the box.

He stared at her but didn't move.

"They're pastries from Bella Notte. A peace offering." She held the box out again.

"I can't accept that."

"Please. I'm sorry for yesterday. Truly sorry."

"Cakes don't make it better. You lost my son." He crossed his arms over his chest. He wasn't going to make this easy on her.

"He's not lost. He's right inside." She pointed past Jack to Luther sitting on the couch. "Hi, Luther."

"Hi, Bailey." Luther waved.

She commanded her heart not to melt. The boy was beyond adorable with his chubby cheeks and infectious smile. His father was a grump.

"You're missing the point," Jack said.

"I don't think I am. We should be grateful for our blessings and not focus on what didn't happen."

"I can't have this conversation now." He started to close the door.

She put out a hand to stop it. "Why not?"

He lowered his voice. "He could've gone in the ocean or worse."

"He didn't. He didn't do anything except walk too far past you. He's fine. You're fine. Let's not dwell."

"It's that easy for you to just let everything that bothers you go?"

"I don't have time to waste getting stuck. Life is too short. I made a mistake. I'm sorry I didn't walk him straight to you. But I'm glad he's okay and that's what I want to focus on. If you want to keep score and hold it over my head, fine. Do it. You're the only one hurting here."

He shifted his weight from one leg to the other but didn't say anything. She should put the box on the stoop and walk away. He could do what he wanted with the pastries. She would make sure to pay Sophia when she saw her later because this was no longer a peace offering.

Luther joined Jack at the door. "What's in the box?"

"Pastries from Bella Notte."

"What's that?"

"Only the best bakery in the county. Want one?" She shot a glare, at least she hoped it was a glare, at Jack. She should have asked him if he minded whether Luther had a pastry, but he stood there with a scowl on his face as if he were determined to hold her mistake over her head.

She had made an honest mistake by not walking Luther all the way to him. She wasn't thinking it would be a problem. She had wandered the beach by herself as a kid all the time. Her father never came down. He was too busy working.

"Can I have one, Jack?" Luther looked up at Jack.

Jack glanced between the two of them. She silently dared him to say no to his kid who just found out who his father was and whose mother was sick.

"Just one." Jack slid his hand under the box and their fingers grazed.

Heat vibrated over her skin, and she forced her hand to stay in place and not drop the box. He handed the pastries over to Luther.

"Well, I'd better go. I have to get down to the store."

"Don't you want one too?" Luther said.

"Thanks, buddy, but those are for you and your dad. I'll see you soon."

"Wait. I want to show you the book I'm reading." Luther handed the box of pastries back to Jack and sprinted from the doorway and through the bedroom door in the corner.

"I can come in or I can go. It's up to you, Jack."

Chapter Fifteen

J ack closed the door behind Bailey. He was letting out the new A/C anyway. He had stayed up half the night fixing it.

The small apartment shrank with her in its space. She was too much life for this little room. He put the pastries on the counter to give himself something to do with his hands and some air to breathe.

Touching her a moment ago almost sent him straight through the roof. He couldn't remember a time when a woman's slight touch affected him to his core. Probably because none had in that way, definitely not Sloane.

Bailey wasn't like other women. She was full of life. Something he wasn't these days. He suspected passion ran through her veins like roaring rapids. Touching her again would sweep him away, lost to her power. He'd do himself well to keep his distance.

"I won't stay long." She turned in circles. Her short

white dress showed off her legs. He wondered if her skin was as smooth as it looked. "I love what you've done with the place."

Something like a laugh burst free of him. "I haven't changed a thing since you left."

"That was kind of my point. Are you going to stay mad at me? I just need to know what I'm dealing with." Her directness took him by surprise.

She had been right about him holding on too long to his anger. He'd done that far too much in his life and hadn't quite figured out how to lose the stranglehold. He could learn a thing or two from this woman, if he were willing to admit that to himself.

"Look, I'm new at this parent thing. I can't be the guy who loses his kid on day three. His mother took ten years to tell me I had a child. Imagine if I called her and said he was gone."

"I can't imagine it." She covered her face with her hands. She wore a silver ring on almost every finger except for the ring finger on her left hand. "I don't want to, but it all worked out. Can't we focus on that?"

"I guess so."

"Thank you. I wanted to ask you something."

He wasn't sure he wanted to hear the question. "Do I have a choice?"

"You always have choices, Jack. You just might not like them." Her smile brightened her hazel eyes. He liked when she smiled at him that way.

"Okay. Hit me with your question."

"It's actually two questions."

"Oh boy. Okay. Go ahead."

"Why are you living above the store? Your house must be nicer than this. Don't get me wrong, I enjoyed staying here, but it's small and stuffy. I know it's none of my business. My sisters are always telling me I'm nosy, but I am curious. Beth talks about your house all the time."

His grandmother had always been the proudest of him. "I sold the house. It was too big and needed too much attention. This is a temporary stop until I decide where to buy next." He skirted right up to the truth. She wouldn't be able to accuse him of lying to her when and if she actually found out he was broke.

"Makes sense now. Thank you for your honesty."

He nodded because speaking might push him over the lying line. "What's your next question?"

"What did you do with that Louisa May Alcott book?" She opened the pastry box as if her question was benign when it was actually a bomb he didn't have time to deactivate.

He hadn't told his grandmother what he'd done. Heat burned his cheeks. Ever since losing his life's savings on that scam, he had become someone he didn't recognize anymore. A month ago, the idea to see if his grandmother still kept that box of rare books wouldn't have crossed his mind.

He could try and justify his actions by asking what she was doing with books like that in a box anyway.

His grandmother had been lucky through the years with her business. She had built a community of readers who came regularly for their latest bestseller. She also offered summer events for the tourists. Her Afternoon Tea and History was a major draw.

He couldn't believe how many people attended. Those tickets kept the store afloat during the lean months, but that luck would not last. The economy's downturn affected current buying patterns.

Sweet smells mingled under his nose, distracting him from his runaway thoughts. Bailey waited for his answer. He could tell her about his money problems and the added stress now that he had Luther to take care of. She might understand.

"Here it is," Luther shouted from the bedroom, saving Jack from answering Bailey.

Luther propelled into the room like a speedboat and handed Bailey the book he had been reading while Jack had fixed the air-conditioning.

"This looks like fun." She took the book and inspected the cover.

"It's great. Do you want to read some with me? My mom and I read together before bed."

A darkness passed over her face but disappeared before he could be certain. She handed back the book. "I'd love to read with you, but I have to get downstairs to the store."

"Please. Just a page. I'm about to get to the part where the kids have to enter the magical forest."

"It sounds like a great story. How about if I come back another time?"

"Sure." Luther's gaze dropped to the floor. He slunk back to the bedroom.

"I'm sorry," Bailey said to him. "I have a busy morning."

He understood busy mornings. "He'll get over it."

"Are you sure about that? He looked pretty upset." Her gaze followed the direction Luther had gone.

"He's a kid. He's probably used to getting his way."

"Jack, try to remember what it was like to be a kid. Then think about how hard living with you and worrying about his mom is for Luther. If you're not doing anything today, maybe you can read with him for a bit."

"I tried last night when he told me Sloane always reads with him. He told me no."

Bailey closed the space between them and gripped his arm. Her heat seared his skin, and he wanted that heat everywhere.

"I'm sorry. This is probably hard for you too. You guys need some time to get to know each other. When that happens, he's going to love you."

"Thank you for saying that." He eased out of her grasp before he did something stupid like kiss her. Her words surprised him, that was all. Before now, he thought Bailey disliked him, maybe even hated him. The idea of Luther loving him... that would be something.

"Luther's a great kid. Hang in there." She tugged on the gold pendant around her neck that dangled between her breasts.

From the moment he met Bailey last September when she had tumbled into the bookstore one afternoon, her beauty had stuttered his breathing. But when she had scowled at him for suggesting the bookstore had overstayed its welcome in town, they had become adversaries. He wished he could take that moment back. She would've been a good ally to have.

He hadn't been able to move his grandmother on selling, but maybe if Bailey talked to her about the positive aspects of selling now, Grammie would agree. Logic had to win over this emotional desire to hang on to the past.

"Can I ask you something?" He checked to make sure the bedroom door was closed. Then to act as if this wasn't a personal question, he took a cannoli from the box and bit into it.

"I suppose." She ran her gaze over him. He wondered what she thought.

"Were you serious about coming back to read with Luther?"

She hesitated. "If I have the time, I will. I have to check my schedule."

"You don't have to make up for yesterday. I don't want you to promise something you would rather not do."

"What are you trying to say? That you don't want me around your kid because of yesterday? Because I don't make promises I can't keep." She took a step back. Her fingers still clung to her necklace.

"Then maybe it's me you don't want to be around."

"I'm standing here, aren't I? I brought pastries as a

way to say sorry again. I don't mind being around you even if I don't always understand your motives."

"Then why am I making you so uncomfortable?" He liked the banter between them. She never backed down from him.

"What makes you say that?" She laughed as if to show how ridiculous he was being.

"You're about to rip that necklace off."

She released the jewelry as if it were hot. "You don't know me, Jack. You don't know my tells."

He started to get a picture of her, and he enjoyed what he was learning. She may have moved the needle from two people who simply knew each other, to she might be interested in him a little. But her hesitation around Luther's request to read with him had some bells ringing in his head.

"So being here with me doesn't make you uncomfortable." He took a step closer, wanting to get a note of that nectar and honey scented perfume of hers.

She opened her mouth, then closed it again. Her fingers returned to her necklace, but she dropped her hand to her side. "How could you make me uncomfortable? I don't give you a second thought."

He almost believed her. "If that's the case, I hope you'll come back when you have time to read with Luther."

Her lips twitched into that smile again. "I would love to, but I actually do have plans tonight. I'll text you some dates."

"I understand." His gut doubted her statement. A time not so long ago, he would've trusted his gut without question. But now, since his debacle with the real estate investment and finding out he'd been a father for ten years and didn't know it, he wasn't sure any part of him could be trusted at all.

"I have to go. Please say goodbye to Luther for me." She opened the door and hurried through.

He wanted to run after her and explain about his financial crisis, how he wasn't sure how he was going to pay for groceries in a few weeks, how he feared he couldn't care for his son. Fathers were supposed to keep their children safe. He might fail at that too. Then his father would have another reason to believe Jack was nothing but the chump Sterling had always accused him of being.

"Where's Bailey?" Luther returned from his room. He grabbed a doughnut from the box, then poured himself a glass of milk.

"She had to go." The apartment expanded without her presence, and he could breathe again.

"Is she coming back?"

Jack stared off in the direction she went. She was like the wind, unable to contain it and ready to suck him up inside it.

"I don't know, pal. I hope so."

"What are we doing today?"

He hadn't given that much thought. He needed to give his grandmother some space about selling, but he would check in on her later. He needed to search for a job because working in the bookstore wouldn't give him enough money. And he wanted to see Bailey again.

"There's an old pinball game arcade in Asbury Park. Any interest?"

"Really? That's cool," Luther said with a milk mustache.

"I'll take that as a yes. Finish your breakfast, then grab your sneakers. I'll get my keys."

Chapter Sixteen

Bailey stopped outside Tea and Tales. She needed to pull herself together before her meeting with the Lilacs.

Bailey would have jumped at the chance this morning to spend more time with Luther. He was a great kid, and she wanted to prove to Jack she could be trusted with his son, but she could not read aloud to him unless she had time to practice the pages first. She wasn't ready to embarrass herself in front of Jack. He might be afraid of heights, but she was certain he hadn't meant for her to see that.

Amy had already turned the Open sign. Customers browsed some of the books near the door. No one was supposed to be there before ten, but if Amy had arrived to find customers—most likely tourists who didn't pay attention to store hours—waiting outside she would let them in the store. That had always been Beth's practice. She believed customers should not wait. Bailey agreed.

Maybe she could get a copy of the book Luther had and read it aloud to herself in the spare time she didn't have.

Humidity already thickened the morning with its stifling heat. Sweat dripped down her neck. She twisted her hair up and secured it with a clip from her bag. The cherry tree offered a slight breeze, but not enough to cool her fevered skin.

Being in such close space with Jack set her nerves on fire. She believed in instant attraction and soulmates. But she couldn't imagine a soulmate would also be the person who could set her teeth on edge.

The door to the store opened. Natalie Lowe stuck out her head. "Are you going to stand there all day?"

"I just got here." She checked her phone. She was only five minutes late.

"We're ready to start the meeting." Natalie clucked her tongue.

"I'll be right in." She wished she could sit under the tree a while longer and breathe in the salt air. She wasn't prepared for this day.

"Bailey," a female called from behind her.

She hesitated at the sound of her name. At least it wasn't Jack, but she didn't want to talk to Kassidy either after last night's argument.

Ducking into the store seemed juvenile, so without much choice, she turned to find Kassidy pushing sweet Emma in the stroller. Kassidy waved. She held up her hand in return.

"Do you have a minute?" Kassidy said.

"I do for my adorable niece." She tickled Emma's chubby feet. Her niece was picture perfect in her pink baseball cap, pink striped tee, and pink fleece shorts.

Emma rewarded her with a belly laugh and kicking legs. Her smile pressed dimples into her chubby cheeks. Emma reached up for Bailey with her pudgy arms.

"Can I hold her?" She needed the warmth and sweet smell right now. Emma was innocence and all that was good in the world. Ever since Bailey had realized Luther went missing, her nerves scraped her insides raw with thoughts of children being harmed. She couldn't imagine how Kassidy and Maren handled the worry that came with being a mother.

"Of course you can hold her. She wants you to pick her up."

Bailey scooped Emma out of the stroller and nuzzled her neck. She smelled like lavender and baby powder. Kassidy grabbed her phone and snapped a picture.

"I'll send that one to you. It's cute."

"Thanks. So, what's up?" She glanced in the store to find Natalie waving her hands, then pointing to her wrist.

"I wanted to apologize for last night." Kassidy played with the set of plastic rings attached to the stroller handle.

"Forget it. I shouldn't have told you to shut up." She had lost her cool as if they were kids again.

"It's not the first time." Kassidy smirked with mischief in her eyes.

"Yeah, but I'm not fifteen anymore."

"Sisters fight," Kassidy said.

"I think we fight more than some." They had spent years arguing over one thing or another. Sometimes Kassidy and Maren would gang up against her. She hated being the odd one out, the one with the different mother when they were kids.

"Maybe, but I wouldn't want any other sisters besides you and Maren."

"It's a good thing it's just the three of us. Another would upset the delicate balance we have."

"A delicate balance between the three of us? That's a good way to put it. Look, I am sorry about implying you couldn't handle all the things coming at you at the moment. I know I stick my nose in where it doesn't belong. I'm the pushy one." Kassidy pressed her lips in a thin line.

"You like things your way," she said.

"Don't we all?" Kassidy laughed.

"We don't all make up stories to get our way." Bailey referred to the story Kassidy had told after their father had passed away.

"It worked. You two stayed and we had a chance to get closer. I need my sisters around."

She debated on coming clean about the trip west and her confused feelings for Jack. If Kassidy could help her carry the heavy load she was under with taking care of Beth and the store, her stress wouldn't vibrate under her skin.

The door to the store swung open again. Natalie stepped outside. Her brown hair framed her face in short corkscrews.

Even at her age, somewhere close to eighty—and the youngest of the group—Natalie's skin was still smooth. Without any help from cosmetics or fillers, her lips were full. Natalie was a natural beauty with a penchant for talking.

"Bailey, we don't have all day, you know. Just because we're older doesn't mean we aren't busy. We should've started ten minutes ago. Even Sophia arrived before you and she was supposed to be late."

"Sophia didn't come past us." She would not have missed that woman. Sophia might be short, under five feet, but she was a tornado.

"The back door, child. Good morning, Kassidy. How is that precious little baby of yours?" Natalie waved to Emma who blew raspberries in return.

"She's just fine. Thank you." Kassidy's face beamed with the pride she carried for her daughter.

"Are you still allowing that sexy man of yours to leave his boots by the bed?" Natalie wagged her faded eyebrows.

Bailey stifled a laugh. Natalie might be the town gossip, but she was also the one who said what other people only thought. Rumor had it for a woman her age, she made the rounds. Though it was possible that Natalie had started that rumor herself.

"Are you referring to my husband, the father of my child?" Kassidy said.

"That's the one. Doesn't he have a brother?" Natalie tapped her cheek as if considering the answer.

"He does. Are you looking for a hookup? I can give

you his number." Kassidy made a show of looking through her bag.

This time Bailey set her laugh free, picturing Natalie with Grant's brother. She wasn't sure who would have it worse.

"Ooh, child." Natalie looked at Bailey and laughed too. Her large breasts bounced with each exhale. "I wouldn't know what to do with a man young enough to be my grandchild. But if he's in town, let me know. There are a few women looking for a date to the Afternoon Tea."

"I'm not sure Levi Hawkins could handle any of the women coming to the Afternoon Tea," Kassidy said.

"Natalie, I'll be inside in just a minute. I want to say goodbye to my sister."

"Hurry now." Natalie watched through the door as it closed.

"You'd better go. You shouldn't keep them waiting. It's rude." Kassidy took Emma from her arms. She began to cry.

"I wasn't late until you showed up." The words held a bite. She decided against telling Kassidy anything about her troubles. Her sister wouldn't understand. Kass was judging her from her spot as older, better sister.

"Then why didn't you say something? I could've come back."

"I don't know." Because she wanted a minute to gather her wits. Because she needed her sisters in her corner.

Emma started to cry. Bailey wanted to cry too.

"You need to focus. You're always jumping from one thing to another."

"We're all not like you. Some of us are less than perfect. We have messy lives." She didn't always like the fact she would start something and abandon it. If she could stay the course longer, maybe she'd have more to show for her life. But she also had many interests and had tried to pursue them, hoping the right thing would find her, and it had. She loved being a health and wellness coach. She had a chance to grow that business by working with Mark at his.

"I'm not perfect." Kassidy helped Emma into the stroller.

Emma screamed. A man walking his dog turned and stared. He gave Kassidy a dirty look.

"You're damn near it. You worked like a dog right beside Dad for years. You took care of him when he was sick, never asking for help."

"I did ask. You told me you couldn't come."

"You never said how bad it was." She hadn't wanted to see her father dying. That might make her a bad person, but he had been her hero—strong, resilient. The only parent always there for her. Her mother was like a kite lost in the wind. But Dad... Dad may have had his share of flaws, but he had been as constant as the ocean.

"Let's not bring up the past. What's done is done," Kassidy said.

Bailey couldn't grab on to the olive branch Kassidy held out to her. "I can't be you. I don't even want to. I like my less than perfect life."

"But do you? You don't have a home. You have a career that could crumble under you without much effort. You don't have a significant other."

"I don't like to be tied down." She wanted to scream the truth, but Natalie still glared at her from beyond the window. Now wasn't the time to start a conversation about moving and Mark.

"Or you're afraid."

Natalie banged on the store window.

"I have to go." She wrenched open the door without waiting for Kassidy to respond.

Cool air smacked into her, reminding her to slow down. Dim lighting was a stark contrast to the bright light outside. A couple of customers turned in her direction. She forced a smile and straightened her dress to give her a second to compose herself—again.

She inhaled the book smell and could breathe with ease for the first time since leaving Jack's. Peace existed between these walls and inside those covers. She needed to be knee-deep in a book.

The Lilacs sat in their circle by the window. Cara, wearing a bright yellow top, skirt, and high heels, sipped from a to-go cup. Her white hair fell straight to her shoulders. Natalie brushed something off her floral blouse. Sophia looked at her phone. She had traded her work clothes for black capri pants and a white sleeveless top.

Bailey's stomach growled. All the arguing this morning had worked up an appetite. She wished she had taken a pastry earlier.

"Hello, ladies. Thanks for coming." Her fingers

reached for her necklace, and she forced them back down. Jack had been right about her always pulling on it.

"Have you convinced Beth to cancel the event?" Cara said.

"We're having the event. The tickets are sold out." Sophia threw a hand in the air.

Bailey glanced around the store. Amy sat at the register with her book. Two women giggled over an open book. Walking away from all of this would be the best thing for her. Jack could take care of his grandmother. He was determined to live in that tiny apartment at least for the summer. Beth had her lady friends. Those women could help take care of her and fight it out about this event and any others.

Bailey could get in her car and drive away. She could be in Colorado in a few days. Why was she holding on to this? She didn't understand. No wonder why Mark didn't either.

"Well, Bailey, what did Beth say?" Cara's words dragged her attention back to the group.

"She wants the event. That splits your group down the middle. Two for it. Two against. I'm the deciding vote."

"What about Jack?" Natalie said.

"Jack doesn't get a say."

"Why not?" Cara put her cup down and smoothed her skirt.

"Because Beth put me in charge here, and I say we have the event." She almost couldn't believe the words coming out of her mouth. She wouldn't even be here when the event happened. The planning would have to be done by Beth and her friends. Jack would have to help too. She wasn't sure he could be trusted.

"Good for you." Sophia clapped her hands.

Cara pursed her lips and spun the ring on her finger. Natalie shook her head.

"Beth needs your help. All of you." She pointed her gaze at each one. Only Sophia smiled back.

"This is a mistake." Natalie gathered her things. "I have to be going. Tell Beth to call me when she needs something."

Cara stood too. "Wait for me, Natalie. I'll walk out with you."

The two women left the store without looking back. Bailey flopped down in one of the chairs. This nook was a great place to sit and read. It could use a little updating with more comfortable chairs and individual tables for readers to place a coffee or tea.

Tea was offered in the store decades ago, but Beth's father had done away with it, claiming no one wanted the tea, especially in the summer. Bailey wondered.

"Well, that went well," she said.

Sophia arched a brow. "They're just stubborn. They'll come around. They won't let Beth down."

"I don't know anything about this store and all its activities. I just know that Beth wants things to continue as is. She shouldn't be denied that because she hurt her elbow."

"Will you be here to see the Afternoon Tea? Beth mentioned you were planning a trip before her accident."

"Honestly, I don't know. I can only put it off for so long before I end up with regrets."

"Don't put off that trip. It could change your life. When Gio asked me to get on a boat and come to America, I thought my husband had lost his mind for good." Sophia chuckled. "I had told him no a thousand times, but he's a charmer. He convinced me to go. We made a good life here."

"This isn't that kind of trip." In some ways it was. She was leaving behind family and friends to start a new adventure with the man she cared for deeply.

Sophia stood and grabbed her oversized purse. "We only regret the things we don't do. Beth will understand when it's time for you to go."

"I hope so."

"Trust an old lady. I have to get back to Bella Notte. I promised Gio I would work for a few hours so he could go to the racetrack with the boys." Sophia shook her head. "That man has a wild streak that hasn't slowed with his age. I'll tell you that. Ciao."

"Ciao."

Mark did not have a wild streak. He planned everything down to the minute. She admired that about him, that and his drive to work hard. But he wasn't spontaneous or daring. Starting his own business was the riskiest thing he'd ever done. Even with that he had planned every detail.

Jack on the other hand... Beth had told her about his wild days. She would like to hear more. Imagining him sauntering into a room, commanding it, doing what he wanted made her sit up straighter. That motorcycle he drove was pretty daring and sexy if she had to admit it. Mark wouldn't even park near a motorcycle.

Mark. What was she going to do with him? He was offering her something she craved, and yet she was hesitant to take the leap, because the past had proved if she fell, he might not catch her.

Chapter Seventeen

"Just get in the car." Jack held open the door for Luther. The sun sat straight up in the sky and pounded his already throbbing head. This day gave him a whopper of a headache.

Luther slid into the back seat, set his jaw, then crossed his arms over his chest. Jack used control he didn't have to stop himself from slamming the door.

He closed his eyes and took a deep breath. The salt air did nothing to calm his nerves. The pinball arcade had been a mistake.

He pulled out his phone and shot a text to Aaron.

I can't do this dad thing. In two days, he'd lost his kid and had fought with him over a stupid game.

Aaron's response came right back.

Yes, you can.

How do you quit?

You don't.

Jack stared at his phone. He couldn't argue with that.

He wasn't a quitter, and he had to try to be a better father than Sterling.

He should've checked the arcade's hours before they left, but he hadn't. They arrived and the store wasn't open for thirty minutes. He had suggested getting bagels. Luther hated bagels.

They settled on waffles. The breakfast cost more than Jack wanted to spend at the moment, but he didn't see a way out, so he forked over the money.

Inside the arcade, Luther smiled, asked him to play a few games, but then out of nowhere, Luther wanted to leave. Jack had spent additional money on tokens to play the games. He wasn't leaving with a pocket full of tokens that wouldn't do him any good.

One thing led to another, and he found himself at one end of an argument with a ten-year-old. Which was bad enough until a mother who was there with four girls decided to give him some advice.

He yelled. She yelled. Luther cried and called Sloane before Jack could stop him.

Jack slid behind the steering wheel and kicked over the engine to get the air-conditioning going. His head hurt and he was hungry because Luther ate most of the waffles.

He glanced in the rearview mirror. Luther's bottom lip trembled. He had tucked his chin and curled in on himself.

Jack remembered doing that very same thing when Sterling had yelled at him as a kid. He had wanted to disappear so his father could never find him. He had wanted to be anyone else's son. He still did.

He turned to face Luther. "I'm sorry. I was out of line."

Luther only looked at him.

"I shouldn't have yelled or made you stay longer than you wanted. Truthfully, the arcade wasn't much fun for me either. I had spent a lot of money on those tokens and I... I... well, I don't have extra money right now." It hurt to admit that. He had been on top of his game for a long time, making investments, buying and selling. He had grown too cocky, too sure of himself, and he paid the price trying to invest in a development project that wasn't real.

Luther swiped at his face. "I want to go home."

"We can go back to the apartment after we check on Grammie."

"No, my home with my mom." Luther shook his head with force.

"Your mom isn't there, pal. You know that." Sloane had given him an earful when she had demanded to be put on the phone. *"Don't fuck this up, Jack. I don't have time to save you."*

"What about my aunt? Can I live with her in my house in Maryland?"

"I don't think so. Your mom wants us to get to know each other. While you're out of school you have to stay with me." Sloane had admitted that her sister didn't want Luther after all. She had rescinded her offer to take her nephew. Jack could never tell him that.

"I didn't say yes to living with you. I only wanted to meet you."

He wasn't all that keen on living with himself these days either. "It's only for another month or so. Then your mom will be back. It will go by fast." He hoped Sloane was ready to return. If she wasn't, he would enroll Luther in a local school here and they would struggle through the fall and into the winter.

"No, it won't." Luther crossed his arms over his chest again and looked out the window.

Jack took that as a sign Luther was done talking. He was too. He put the car in drive and traveled down Ocean Avenue until he made a right into Serenity by the Sea, then weaved his way through town to Grammie's.

Luther ran ahead of him up the walk and onto the porch.

"Don't knock. I don't want her to come to the door if she's upstairs." He jiggled the keys to make his point.

He inserted the key, but before he turned it, he looked at Luther. "I am sorry about earlier. I hope we can be friends."

"My mom says it's okay to make mistakes as long as you say sorry and mean it."

"I mean it."

"Okay." Luther stuck out his hand.

Jack forced himself not to laugh because having a ten-year-old try to act like a man had to be the cutest thing he'd ever seen. He was also impressed how quickly Luther had come around. Kids really were resilient.

He shook Luther's hand.

He let them into Grammie's small house. The structure wasn't more than an expanded ranch. His father never liked coming here. Jack never understood how Sterling could fall deeply in love with Jack's mother. Priscilla was his opposite. Sterling didn't like oppositions.

"Grammie, it's me and Luther."

Luther grabbed a picture frame on the coffee table. "Who is Grammie with?"

"That's my Grandpa Jack. I was named after him. That young woman was my mother. This picture was taken about a year before I was born."

"It looks old."

He found himself laughing again. "Well, pal, I am old."

"Where's your mom now?"

"She passed away when I was five."

"Oh. Wow."

"Yeah. I hardly remember her." He had some memories. They would be in the kitchen and one of her favorite songs would come on the radio. They would sing together. They would dance and she would spin him until he was dizzy and laughing on the floor.

"Where's Grammie?" Luther said.

"Good question. She might be upstairs napping. Why don't you go out back and play. The yard is fenced in."

"What am I supposed to play with?"

"Use your imagination."

Luther held up his phone.

"Fine. But do it in the sunshine and not in here on the couch."

Luther skipped out the back door.

He used to run in and out of that back door a thousand times every summer he came to visit his grandmother. This house had been his home away from home growing up, and not because he was here all the time. He only spent two weeks a summer in Serenity by the Sea. This house was a second home because his grandmother loved him in ways his father didn't seem to know how.

Here, in this house, love poured like water from an open spigot. His father's love always came with conditions.

"Grammie?"

She wasn't on the first floor. This floor had a bathroom and one extra room that she used as a bedroom. Bailey must be staying in this room. A suitcase was left open. Clothes in florals and patterns spilled over the side and puddled on the floor. Lacy underwear draped over the back of the chair.

He turned away, not wanting to think about Bailey's undergarments because then he would picture her wearing them. He should have kissed her this morning instead of debating her about everything.

He returned to the living room and glanced out the window. His grandmother's car was parked in the street. She hadn't mentioned plans with any of her friends. She had to be taking a nap.

He took the creaky wooden stairs to the second floor. At the top, he had to duck because of the low ceiling.

Someone in the eighty-plus years this house existed had raised the dormers to add the second floor and hadn't planned on taller people living here.

Two more bedrooms and a bathroom were upstairs. Grammie used one of the bedrooms as her craft and television room, but that room was empty too.

Her bedroom door was closed. He hated to wake her, but he wanted to see if she needed anything while he was here. He had no idea when Bailey would return, and he didn't want to be here when she did.

He eased the door open. "Grammie?"

The room was bright. The curtains were pulled back and the bed was made. The room smelled of dust and food. His gaze searched for her.

She was slumped in the wingback chair tucked in the corner by the old highboy dresser, her chin touching her chest. Her arm was still in the sling.

"Grammie." He lunged for her, needing her to wake up. He couldn't lose her. She was his world, the one person who loved him for who he was, flaws and all. She was the only relative left on his mother's side whom he spoke to. Great aunts and uncles had drifted away over the years, discouraged by his father's cold and dismissive demeanor.

He gripped her shoulder and gave her a slight shake. "Grammie. Wake up."

He didn't want Luther to find her like this. Jack didn't know what to do.

Grammie's head bobbed on her neck. She blinked a few times. "Jack?" Her voice cut his name in two.

He gripped the arm of the chair to keep from falling to the floor. "Did I wake you?" He couldn't very well tell her he had thought for a second she was gone.

"What time is it?" She twisted in the chair, struggling with her unusable arm. He helped her sit up straighter.

"It's afternoon. You must've fallen asleep." He could count on two hands the number of times his grandmother took a nap. She abhorred them.

"I came in here for something and needed to sit down. I think that was this morning. I didn't even realize I fell asleep." She placed her good hand on her forehead.

"It's probably the pain medicine. When did you take it last?"

"I haven't taken any of it. Did you pull back the drapes?" Her face twisted in confusion.

She hadn't taken any of her pills? What was making her so confused? "The curtains were already opened."

"I didn't sleep well last night. This arm makes it difficult to get comfortable, but I also had terrible indigestion." She pushed half-way to stand but sat back down.

"Would you like a soda or cup of tea? I could make you one." He took shallow breaths. His heart pounded in his head. He had thought he lost her.

What would he do without Grammie in his life? She deserved to be comfortable in her golden years. He could see to that for her if she would just let him. He could move her to a nicer house or assisted living. He could hire someone for her to take care of whatever she wanted, if she would sell that damn store.

"A cup of tea would be very nice. Let's go downstairs

and out into the fresh air. I think it will do me good." She pushed to stand again and stayed upright this time.

"Will it be too hot outside for you?"

"Oh. Well, it might. Maybe some tea in the kitchen, then."

She didn't argue with him about sitting outside and that had him more concerned than her sleeping the day away.

He followed her down the stairs. She held on to the railing, taking her time. He didn't rush her but maybe should have gone in front of her in case she lost her balance.

"What kind of tea would you like?"

Afternoon sun streamed through the kitchen window above the sink. Grammie had small plants along the sill that needed watering. He caught the glimmer of a suncatcher in her tree beyond the window. Luther sat under that tree with his nose to his phone. Jack would have to deal with that screen time problem later. He could find an old tire and hang it from the tree. Kids loved tire swings. Didn't they?

"I have a nice herbal tea with rose hips. Up there in the cabinet." She plopped into the kitchen chair.

"Grammie, are you feeling okay today?" He put the water on to boil, then searched for the box in her crowded cabinet. She had tea boxes tossed in with cans of tuna, cereal, and mixing bowls.

"I'm fine but thank you for asking. Where's Luther?" She glanced around the room as if expecting to see him.

"He's actually outside sitting under your weeping

willow." He found the mugs in the lower cabinets near the stove.

"Why don't you bring him inside?"

"I will, but I think he needs some time away from me right now."

"What did you do?" Grammie raised her brows.

He told her about the pinball arcade and his outburst.

"You're going to have to try and practice patience. I know that's not your best strength, but Luther needs a lot of it."

"I'm finding that out." He placed the empty mug in front of her and offered his best smile.

"You'll get your sea legs. You always do." She winked.

"Thank you for always believing in me."

"That's what Grammies are for, dear. Is your visit just to make sure an old lady didn't die in her sleep?"

"I wish you wouldn't talk like that." That little scare brought him too close to a reality he wasn't ready to handle.

"It's going to happen one day."

He refused to face the idea his grandmother would not always be here. She had been larger than life when he was growing up.

"I'd rather it not be anytime soon. Who's going to make my favorite dessert at Christmas?"

She glanced away and then back at him. "You know what? I think I'll teach Bailey how to make my rustic apple tart."

"Bailey? Does she even know how to turn on an oven?" He didn't see Bailey comfortable in a kitchen making desserts from scratch. Not because she wasn't capable, though it did seem as if she tended to forget details, but because she wasn't the homemaker type. Grass did not grow under her feet.

The teapot screamed to life. He poured the water for his grandmother.

"You don't give Bailey enough credit. She owns that restaurant with her sister. She can handle a simple recipe." Grammie dunked her teabag. The smell of rose-hips circled around him.

"If you say so." He wouldn't mind if Grammie baked for him, but he doubted Bailey would want to.

The phone on the wall rang. He always forgot Grammie still had a landline. She never wanted to get rid of it no matter what he tried to tell her about cost and convenience.

"I'll get that. It might be Sophia." She attempted to stand but banged into the table on the way up. The hot water sloshed over the side of the mug. "Oh my. Look what I've gone and done."

"I'll get it." He mopped up the mess with a towel.

By the time she shuffled to the phone, it had stopped ringing. "Oh well. They'll call back." She went to the window instead. "Oh, there's sweet Luther."

He joined her. "Do you want me to call him in?"

"Give him a few more minutes to himself." She heaved a big sigh. "The birds don't come to the feeder as much anymore. They must've found better accommodations. Everything changes."

"Change can be a good thing."

"Not always. When Priscilla passed, that was the worst day of my life. I didn't need to witness that kind of change. When my Jack passed, that wasn't change for the good either. But I'm glad he went before Priscilla. He wouldn't have survived losing her."

Jack couldn't meet her gaze. His grandmother had suffered more than her fair share. She hung on to that bookstore because it was her ties to people she loved, but love didn't pay the bills. For her sake, he wished it did.

Grammie sat back down and sipped her tea. More of the color drained out of her face. He didn't like what he was seeing.

"I'm tired."

"Do you need to go back to the doctor?" He would drive her and wait with her.

"I have a follow-up visit for my elbow in a couple of weeks."

"Is there something else?" He leaned closer.

"You're turning into a worrier." She patted his cheek. "I'm fine. Really."

"You would tell me if you weren't well, wouldn't you? No secrets, right?"

"Is anybody home?" A female voice dove into the kitchen, stopping the conversation in its tracks.

Bailey drifted into the room with a wide smile on her face that dropped. She looked between the two of them.

"I can come back later if I'm interrupting something."

"Stay, dear. We weren't discussing anything important."

His grandmother had dismissed his concern for her.

He shouldn't be annoyed, but he was. She had acted as if he were still a child who hadn't lived the life he'd lived. He actually knew a thing or two and something was going on with his grandmother that scared him.

"Except that she isn't feeling well." He kept his gaze on Bailey's.

"Jack Billinger, that is not true." Grammie slapped the table with her good hand.

"You just told me you were tired."

"Tired does not equal on death's door."

"She has a point," Bailey said.

"I didn't say you were dying. You know what? Never mind. You are both the most stubborn women I have ever met."

"Why is everyone fighting?" Luther stood just inside the back door with a look of confusion painted across his face.

"Hello, Luther, dear." Grammie punched the air with her good arm. "Come on over here and give Grammie a big hug."

"But I heard yelling."

"Don't you worry yourself about us adults. Even we don't always know what we're doing or saying." She eyed him over Luther's head.

He needed some fresh air. He turned to Bailey. "Would you join me on the front porch?"

"Uh... okay?"

She followed him through the living room and outside. The heat met him like an unwanted visitor.

"What's up, Jack?"

"Have you noticed anything different about my grandmother?"

"Like what?"

"Is she sleeping a lot? Complaining about not feeling well maybe."

"You're starting to sound like Natalie and Cara. Beth is fine, except for the elbow. People her age get tired. She's pretty active. I think that's good for her."

"In other words, I should stop worrying." But he couldn't shake the sinking feeling.

"Put your attention on Luther instead."

He took a seat on the step. Bailey sat beside him and graced him with her honey scent.

"Yesterday, when Luther went missing and I yelled at you, I should have considered your feelings."

"Pardon me?"

"I got angry at you, but I should've realized you might have been frightened too. I'm sorry. I don't know what I'm doing these days." And it drove him crazy. He wanted his old life back. That life made sense to him. He went to work. Made great money. Worked out. Saw friends on weekends. Met women. Now he watched the world by standing on his head.

"You don't have to apologize to me."

"I'd like to make it up to you, if you'll allow me." He wanted to be near her all the time now. When she was around, the world straightened out some.

"I don't understand."

"May I cook you dinner?" Asking her to share a meal with him was dangerous. He risked his pride that had taken a big beating. He wasn't sure if he could handle another rejection. Before he lost his job, he wouldn't have thought twice about asking her to dinner, except his offer would have included the best oceanfront restaurant on the Jersey Shore. Before getting ripped off by a professional scammer, before Luther entered his life, he may not have bothered to ask Bailey to dinner at all.

"Me?"

He couldn't help but laugh. "Yes, you. Is that such a strange request? You do eat, don't you?"

"I love to eat, but we could just go out and grab something."

"I'd prefer to cook here."

"You don't have to cook for me. That's a lot of work. Let's take Luther to Max's. I bet he'd love the giant hot dogs."

Dinner out would cost him too much money. He couldn't believe he was about to do this. "Bailey, I haven't told anyone this yet, but I lost my job. I'd prefer to cook here than go to a restaurant."

She studied him for a minute. "I'm sorry you lost your job. Can I ask what happened?"

That answer he didn't have the strength for after this morning. "I'll tell you another time. It's a long story. So, what do you say? Dinner?"

"I'm not sure that's a good idea." She looked away.

"Why not? Luther and my grandmother can be there so you don't have to worry."

"I'm not worried. I don't want you to get the wrong idea." Her fingers toyed with her necklace.

He envied that necklace. "What idea would that be?"

"That we could be anything more than friends."

"Being friends suits me just fine." He hoped he hid the disappointment from his voice. He hadn't been thinking they could start up a lifetime affair or anything, but he didn't want to be out of the running before he even had a chance to start.

Her smile brightened. His stomach dropped. She was pushing him into the friend zone.

"When were you thinking... for this dinner?"

"Will tomorrow night work?"

She didn't answer him. His confession might not have convinced her that a night with him was worth her while. He didn't have a lot to offer any longer. Someone like Bailey would at least expect the man asking her out, friend or not, to have a job.

"What can I bring?"

Chapter Eighteen

Bailey struggled to put the key in the lock. Her hand shook and she didn't understand why. Except maybe this moment was the first time she had let herself into Tea and Tales as if she were the owner. Owning a bookstore, running a bookstore was never the dream. This was the place she came to escape, to forget about the real world for a while.

When she was younger, her father would give her money to come up here and pick out one book. That book could last her weeks with her dyslexia, but she didn't care that it took her longer to read than her friends or her sisters. She treasured that book because it represented the time she spent with her father, Maren, and Kassidy. Her family.

The family she was running away from to start another business in Colorado when she had her coaching business and now the bookstore to keep her busy right in Serenity.

Amy was off today, and Beth hadn't felt up to coming into the store. Bailey was concerned about Beth. She hadn't been forthcoming with Jack earlier about her worries. She hadn't wanted to alarm him.

But Beth's pale complexion and poor appetite might lend itself to something more than that elbow. She also continued to complain about the indigestion. Bailey saw her chew down three antacids last night.

The sun yawned and stretched its way into the morning, still too tired to recolor the faded blue sky. Sleep had evaded her. Jack's dinner invitation whirled around in her head all night long.

Beth had wanted to sleep in this morning and one of the Lilacs was coming over for brunch. Bailey had decided to take advantage of the opportunity and arrived hours before the store opened.

She didn't want to have dinner with Jack and Luther. Even though she had said she only wanted to be friends, she might be leading him on, and she didn't want to do that.

She liked him and that had her insides buzzing. Last night when he revealed the truth about losing his job, she witnessed that vulnerability she'd only seen when he had hugged Luther in front of her. That softer side endeared her every time.

But Mark was her soulmate. Twin flames. So why was it Jack who she continued to think about and Mark's calls that she avoided? Answers she did not want to touch. At least, not now.

Luther was another reason she couldn't be in a relationship with Jack. They would never make it as a couple, too different. She couldn't risk Luther becoming too attached to her. She had been the child who became attached to her mother's boyfriends, some of them good guys, only to learn that they had left and would never return. Luther didn't need that kind of heartbreak. If she and Jack were only friends, she could be one to Luther too.

Bailey walked down the fiction aisle and ran her fingers across the spines, making note of the authors, some in alphabetical order, some not. The store's dim lighting covered her like a favorite blanket. Darkness didn't scare her or try to hide her.

She also wanted to talk to her sisters about this invitation to dinner with Jack Billinger without revealing her plans to be with Mark.

This bookstore, her place, smelled like home. The building creaked around her, greeting her. She loved it here. Beth and her sisters knew how much.

She had declared the store belonged in town. This store should not be replaced by some homogenized retail establishment. Locals and even the tourists—they needed the tourists—deserved a spot where they could find a story, buy a book, and sit on a bench facing the ocean with a whole world in their hands, waiting to be explored.

Beth couldn't sell it, but what if Jack were right? What if it was time for Beth to pass on her legacy to someone else? Modern and new always risked tradition and history. She and her sisters changed their father's history for the better. Could that be done to this store too?

She placed her things behind the register. Beth had mentioned some inventory was due to arrive today. Bailey also wanted to dig through the details of this summer event. But for a few minutes, she wanted to sip her coffee and look out onto the store.

Coming in this morning was like entering Tea and Tales for the first time. If Bailey had her way, she would change the carpet and expand the sitting area. She would put in a coffee station and more comfortable chairs to read in after the cracks in the plaster were fixed, but she won't have her way. She wasn't staying around to see major projects through. Beth would be back in no time and in her rightful place as owner and she would be in Colorado.

Jack would argue over every idea Bailey had anyway. He didn't want to see this place grow. She understood better why he would want Beth to sell the store. In this town, prime real estate held its value and then some. He would also benefit by the sale.

She'd been broke multiple times in her life. Needing money scared most people with plenty of good reasons. Someone like him—accomplished, wealthy—would struggle more with an uncertain future.

She left her coffee and went over to the children's section. On the bottom shelf was one copy of the book Luther had shown her. Bailey held it in her hands and wished the words could seep into her fingers and travel up to her brain. She didn't want to struggle to read.

Someone like Jack might think her stupid if he heard her stumble over simple words, her mouth working against her, giving her away.

Beth bragged about Jack's career at Billinger and Associates all the time. Even if she wasn't terribly fond of her son-in-law as person, she couldn't argue that Sterling Billinger had built a financial empire, and Jack had benefited until recently.

She left the book by her purse and went outside. The street was still quiet. Even the hummingbird hadn't woken yet. Sitting still held no appeal to her, but if she went for a walk, she'd have to lock up the store again.

Instead, she pulled up Maren's number in her favorites list and hit the call button. The phone rang, but Maren wasn't answering. Bailey was about to give up.

"Bailey? Are you okay?" Maren's groggy voice came across the line.

"Hi. I'm fine. I couldn't sleep and came to the bookstore. I know it's early, but would you want to come down here and have coffee with me?"

"Is she all right?" Shane's voice, muted in the background, came through.

Rustling sounded in the phone. Maren must've moved it. "She's fine. Go back to sleep."

"I'm sorry I woke you guys."

"It's not a problem, but it's only a little after six. What are you doing at the store at this hour?" A door closed in the background.

"I had to get out of the house. I didn't know where else to go."

"Are you sure everything's all right?" Maren's voice grew louder through the sentence as if she had moved away from Shane and their bedroom, no longer worried about waking him.

"I need some advice." Bailey picked at the wood on the doorframe.

"Do you want to talk now, or do you need me to come to the store? I'll do either."

When she spent the summers with her father and sisters, Maren stepped in like a mother figure with her care and concern for Bailey's feelings. Kassidy was closer in age and that often led to typical sibling arguments. Kassidy just wanted to boss Bailey around because when she was around, Kassidy wasn't the youngest anymore and now had a little sister she could torment.

"Do you have any chocolate?"

"I don't, but I could stop at Bella Notte and get a chocolate croissant or muffin."

"You're the best sister. But don't tell Kassidy I said that."

Maren ended the call, laughing.

"What do you need advice on?" Maren sipped from her coffee. She had arrived as promised with two chocolate croissants, two coffees, and a *Buongiorno* from Mr. D.

Funny how everyone called Mr. D's wife Sophia, but they all referred to him as Mr. D. Bailey never put that together until now.

"Someone asked me to dinner tonight and I don't know if I should go." The buttery flakes melted in her mouth. She had been blessed and cursed with a sweet tooth which was why she had started with s'mores for her sisters get-together and not something more adult like margaritas.

"Okay. First, who?" Maren shifted to face her.

"Your smile is going to wrap around your head. It's not like that."

"It's like something; otherwise, you would have just said no to this person, or you wouldn't be asking me if you should go."

She should be telling Maren about Mark first and then reveal her dinner companion was Jack. Maren would have a million questions. Bailey wasn't sure if she was ready for that, but she had started this ball rolling. She had better see it through.

"When I say who, don't get how you get." She tried to hide behind her muffin.

"How do I get?" Maren fisted a hand on her hip.

"You know. All busybody mom like. It's not always a bad thing." But it would be soon.

"That's Kassidy. She's the mom one. Tell me." Maren sipped her coffee.

She forced her gaze to meet Maren's. "Jack."

"Jack who?"

"Jack Billinger. Beth's grandson." She hitched her thumb toward the store.

"The guy you don't like because he wants his grandmother to get rid of the store?"

"One and the same." She had complained to Maren last fall when she had first found out Jack didn't think the store was worth keeping. But now she had more information. He was desperate for money.

"I don't understand."

"I don't either." These new feelings for Jack made no sense to her because they were unexpected and somehow refreshing like a cool breeze after a humid day.

"Then why go? Why did he ask you? Do you still hate him?" Maren dished out the questions at top speed.

"I never hated him."

Maren arched a brow.

"Okay, okay. I may have said I didn't like him intensely. But that's changed a bit. He's very sweet to his son." He had also been kind to her when he said he was sorry for not considering her feelings. She couldn't remember the last time a man had said that to her.

"What about his grandmother?"

"He's good to her. He cares about her. He just thinks it's time for her to sell the store so he can get a good deal on it for her. He's some kind of financial whiz."

"That's not what I heard."

"What do you mean?"

"It would just be rumors. You know how rumors are, but I was in Rumson the other day organizing a sweet sixteen party for a very lucky young lady whose parents have more money than God. The mother of the birthday girl and the mother's sister were talking while I was going over directions with the decorating crew. The sister did not have an inside voice."

"I know the type. They're on the phone somewhere like the train, screaming to their friend about their mammogram so the whole car can hear."

"Yes, exactly like that. Anyway, the sister's husband works at Billinger and Associates. When I heard the name, my ears perked up."

"It's not nice to eavesdrop, Maren." She wagged a finger at her sister.

"I know, but since Billinger has a connection to Serenity by the Sea, you, and the bookstore, I thought maybe this would be worth listening to."

"Me?"

"I saw the way your face lit up when you talked about Jack."

"It did not."

"It did too. Now, let me finish my story. Unless you don't want to hear it."

"Finish." She broke off another piece of muffin.

"The mother's sister goes on to say that her husband told her the chairman, Sterling Billinger the eleventh or twelfth—whatever—fired his son. His own son. The sister was shocked beyond words when her husband shared this information. She couldn't imagine a father getting rid of his child. Unless maybe if there was a crime."

"Was there?"

"I don't think so. The sister never mentioned a crime, only that Sterling was a very difficult man who expected perfection from his employees, including Jack. She had said her own husband had tangled with Sterling on occasion."

"Did she say anything else?"

"They went on to talk about the sister's children and the birthday girl, and then Gerard needed me, so I didn't hear the end of the conversation."

"That can't be true." Jack losing his job was true, but his father firing him? She couldn't imagine what Jack might have done to be fired by his father. Bailey didn't know Sterling Billinger at all, but from what Beth had told her over the years, he was focused on earning as much money as possible at any cost.

"There must be some truth to it. His getting fired would explain why he wants his grandmother to sell. Maybe you don't want to go to dinner with him. He might not be the right guy for you."

She stood and paced. Mark was supposed to be the right guy for her, but... Jack. *Jack.* She was in big trouble.

"There has to be a reason why Jack's dad fired him. Are you sure those women were talking about Jack's dad?"

"I definitely heard Sterling Billinger."

"If I go to dinner, then I could ask him straight up what happened. He's living in the apartment and that isn't exactly luxury housing." He had said why he lost his job was a long story. He might tell her everything if she pushed, but did she want to hear it? What if he had embezzled money? Or stole from clients?

"Can I ask you something?" Maren said.

"Sure."

"Why do you care so much about this store staying with Beth? She's a wonderful woman, but she's getting up there. She has to be tired from running this place and bookstores like this one struggle all the time. It's a miracle it survived this long."

She sat down and grabbed Maren's hand. "This store has been in her family since the 1920s. It's been a bookstore for over a century. She wants to hand it down and now she has Luther to give it to."

Her phone vibrated in her pocket. She debated on checking, but at this hour it could be Beth. Mark's name scrolled across the screen. She ignored it. He could leave a message.

"I can appreciate all of that, but it's just a small business that may have overstayed its welcome. I'm sure plenty of people come to the beach with a book already in hand or could grab one at the drugstore out on Route 71. If they're staying long enough, several online retailers have overnight delivery."

"Tea and Tales is not about the cheap sale. It's about community, having a place to meet up and share the love of stories. In this store, someone will help you find the perfect book for you. Who's going to do that in a drugstore?"

"How many books do they even sell? Do you know?"

She didn't. She hadn't looked at the accounting books yet. "Enough to stay open year after year and Beth puts on those events that make her money."

Maren arched a brow. "What if Beth isn't up for running the store and events any longer?"

"She says she is." But Bailey worried about the recent lack of energy or interest in food. This unfamiliar version of Beth acted as if the broken elbow had bruised some of her spirit too.

"Maybe she is just fine, and she'll go on running the place until she's a hundred. But if she can't, or doesn't want to, wouldn't it make sense to have Jack help her sell it? He can make the best financial decisions for her."

Maren stood and smoothed down her thin jogger capris. "If it were me, I'd sell the building. If Kassidy hadn't wanted The Blue Dot when Dad got sick, I would've suggested he sell to me. I would've turned around and sold it to a developer."

"Aren't you glad you didn't do that?"

"With hindsight, absolutely. My life is much better than I could have ever expected because that nasty old tavern had a place in Kassidy's heart. So, what are you going to do about this dinner?"

"I have to go. I need to find out why his father fired him." And what kind of man Jack Billinger really was.

Chapter Nineteen

"Where are you going?" Bailey followed Beth to the front door. She had just announced that she wouldn't be home for the dinner Jack was cooking.

"Cara is picking me up. I'm going to her house for a few hours. The Lilacs are meeting there. We need to do a deep dive on the second half of *Little Women*."

"Beth, how many more times can you talk about that book?"

Beth glared at her as if she had committed a sacrilege. "How can you say something like that? You love the book."

"I do love it. I've read it countless times, but I don't want to talk about it all the time." And she didn't want to be left alone with Jack.

Beth shook her head. "You and Jack can have the house to yourselves without worrying about an old woman."

"He's bringing Luther and you're not old." She wanted Beth at dinner to be another layer of buffering, but Bailey would not be able to ask Jack why he was fired if Beth was around.

"Actually, he's not bringing Luther. Jemma Klein is babysitting. Her older daughter Hazel and Luther are around the same age. Luther needs some friends in town." Beth grabbed her beaded purse by the front door.

"Jemma Klein? From the chocolate store? How did that happen?" Jemma was a nice person, even if the woman believed she had life completely figured out. Bailey didn't have anything figured out and there was Jemma in her perfect outfits, taking perfect pictures of her perfect children and husband. Even her chocolate was perfect.

Beth tapped the side of her head and smiled.

"You arranged it? How could you?"

A horn beeped outside. "Enjoy your evening, dear. I won't be back late." And just like that, Bailey stood in the living room alone.

She hadn't planned on being with Jack without someone to distract them. She should have, though. She wanted the truth from him, and he wasn't likely to give it with an audience. The evening was now hers to play as she saw fit. So, why was she worried?

Because being alone with Jack unnerved her. Until a few days ago, she had barely noticed him as anything other than Beth's grandson. Now, she found herself thinking about his blue eyes or the swagger in his walk like he owned the room once he entered it.

She had to stop. Tonight wasn't a real date anyway. They were just friends.

Being friends didn't stop her from going into her room to change into a black skirt that came mid-thigh and floated around her legs when she walked.

She should be ashamed of herself. She picked up the phone to call Mark back. The call went to voicemail. "Hey, babe. It's me. Sorry I missed your call this morning. You're probably out on a hike. Hope you're having a good day. Miss you. Call me back." She ended the call on a disappointed breath, then shoved her phone in her pocket.

"Bailey, are you here?"

She jumped. He must've let himself in. With a final look in the mirror—not much she could do about the wild tilt to her curls—she peered around the corner.

He waited for her just inside the door. He held a brown paper bag filled with groceries in one hand and a bouquet of sunflowers in the other.

Okay, maybe this was a date. Nothing would happen. He was just being nice.

He smiled and her body responded. She might need an escape route, but there was nowhere for her to go. She was stuck for now.

On a deep breath, she stood before him. "Hi."

"Hi. You look nice." His smile spread wider.

"Thank you. So do you."

He was handsome in his green collared shirt and pressed khaki shorts. She had never expected to be attracted to a man who was more country club than shaggy surfer. Her usual type could talk to her about chakras and daydreaming. Jack would never understand the things that made her tick, yet she admired the way his shirt draped over his pecs and flowed away from his abs.

"Please forgive my manners. These are for you." He held out the sunflowers and she took them.

"They're beautiful. My favorites." She held them to her nose and inhaled their magical scent.

"I thought they might be." That smile pressed dimples in his cheeks.

"How?"

"They're happy like you." He shrugged. "I brought chicken to throw on the grill with some tomatoes, lettuce, and avocado."

"Nothing beats a Jersey tomato."

Jack held one up. "That is very true. I also have a bunch of vegetables. I realized I don't know if you eat meat. If you don't, that's okay. I prepped a pasta salad earlier."

She paused for a second. He had her favorite flower without knowing and had considered she might be vegetarian, which she wasn't. She needed to keep her head on straight tonight. She only wanted information. Not another date.

"Why don't we start cooking? I can help." She went into the kitchen, and he followed.

"You don't have to help. I offered to cook for you." He unloaded the bag.

"I don't have to sit around and watch either." Helping

out would give her something else to focus on besides his butt in those shorts.

"How about a glass of wine for each of us?" He produced a white wine from the bag. "It's chilled. I think there's an opener in that top cabinet."

She busied herself with the wine and pouring two glasses in mason jars because Beth didn't have wine-glasses. Jack fired up the grill. He cut and sliced zucchini, tomatoes, and the avocado, then he went to work basting the chicken.

She leaned on the deck's railing. The trees pushed around a warm breeze that did little to cool her. The sun refused to give up its heat for the day as if it might not get the chance to burn hot and bright again tomorrow.

"Do you like to cook?" Starting with small talk was a safe place to begin. She and Jack had barely held conversations that lasted long or weren't centered around his grandmother and the bookstore.

"I do. I don't get a lot of time to do it, though. So, thank you for giving me an opportunity." He flipped the chicken and zucchini over the open flame.

"Tonight was your idea."

"It was because I don't want you to dislike me any longer." One side of his lip curled up and something fluttered low in her belly.

"I don't dislike you." She'd come a little too far off the dislike button.

"Really? Tonight might be the first time you haven't looked at me like you want to burn me in my spot."

"I don't look at you that way." She turned away before he could read something else in her face.

"If you say so." He turned his gaze back to the food. Looked as if he couldn't make eye contact either.

"I do say so." She paused with the glass by her lips. "Okay, I have looked at you a few times like I wanted to personally send you to Hades. I'm sorry." She was. He wasn't all bad. He cared for his son, probably loved him if she had to guess. He loved his grandmother very much. He was cooking her dinner. He had great legs. She wanted to give him some grace.

"At least we have some honesty."

"I can admit it. I was wrong about you."

"Really? How so?" His eyebrows shot up to his hairline.

"You're softer than I thought." She regarded him a moment. She had assumed that a man with his position in finance and a fancy family pedigree would mean he didn't think about anyone but himself. He had a hard shell, one she wasn't sure anyone could penetrate, but from time to time he peeked around it. She liked that man, the one who didn't feel as if he had to protect himself from the world.

"Softer? I'm not sure that's a compliment." He plated the food and brought it to the patio table.

The outside table was perfect with a single white candle in a vase and two places set with blue and white gingham napkins beside white plates. Beth must've set the table before she left. Bailey hadn't noticed until now, a few missed details with so much on her mind.

"Would it be better if I said you're less uptight than I thought?" She pushed a playfulness into her voice and hoped he heard it.

"You really don't like me." He pulled out the chair for her. "Is this okay or are you too independent for a man to hold the chair for you?"

She took the seat and covered her lap with a napkin. "I'm very confident in my femininity, thank you. A man holding a chair or a door for me doesn't threaten that in any way. Thank you for doing it."

"That's refreshing. At work, I don't know if I should open the door for a woman who's coming into the building at the same time I am or not. If I do, sometimes they growl at me that they can open their own door. As if I don't know that. Or if I decide I had better not hold the dreaded door, then someone yells that chivalry isn't dead."

She fought back a laugh. "Always choose kindness."

"Is that one of the things you tell your clients?" He took the chair opposite her.

The smell of the grilled food drifted between them. Her mouth watered. She hadn't eaten all day, but her throat closed around the idea that she would have to talk about her work. She didn't want to spoil the spell this night whirled.

"I tell my clients what they need to be motivated to take care of their health." She had some new workshops planned for Mark's hiking clients to help them sustain energy during their climb. *Mark's clients.* Those words again.

Why hadn't she thought about that before now? Because she was wrapped up in the idea that their time had finally come. All the years waiting for him to figure out he loved her best had paid off. But she was uprooting her life to get to him. Any of her clients that weren't online she would lose, and she had built up some locals after being in Serenity for a few years now.

"How did you become a life coach?" His question startled her back to the present.

"Can we talk about something else? My job is boring." She wouldn't be able to look him in the eye and lie about her intentions to move.

"Not any less boring than being a risk manager." He cut his chicken into equal size pieces and topped it with the avocado.

"How did you become one?" She ditched the fork and ate the zucchini with her fingers.

"That's an even less exciting story. My father told me that was my role in the family business, so I went to school for that. Do you always eat with your fingers?" He leaned in closer. He licked his bottom lip.

She squirmed in her seat or risked leaning even closer to him. Close enough if she dared, she would be able to taste the vegetables on his lips. She leaned back to give herself some air. "There's something primal about eating with your hands."

He whistled. Heat burned her cheeks.

She needed to get the subject on safer ground because she was afraid to trust herself to behave. "Do you do everything your father tells you?"

"Now that's a subject I'd rather not talk about. Tonight is lovely, let's not ruin it with conversations about my family."

"Okay, no shoptalk for either one of us. Can we talk about the bookstore?" She grabbed another zucchini.

His top lip curled up. "Why? So you can go back to hating me? I think we're making great progress, don't you?"

"Okay. No shoptalk. No family talk. No bookstore talk. What's left?" She still wanted to know why he was fired. She would have to bide her time.

"Can I ask you something?" He dropped his hands in his lap.

"I guess so. I mean, I'm a pretty open book."

"Have you ever made a really stupid mistake you wish you could take back?"

She wasn't expecting that and wondered how to answer him. He had appreciated her honesty a moment ago. She often said what was on her mind, much like Kassidy did, but not everyone appreciated the straight answer that could sting. Did she want to tell him the truth about the dumber things she had done in her life?

"Yes." She had a few. The one she always regretted was breaking up with Mark the first time. He had been in Serenity for a family vacation. It was supposed to be a summer fling for her. Her sisters weren't particularly fond of him, always bragging about this or that. Her father hadn't liked him much either. Said Mark had no future. She broke up with him but had immediately regretted it.

By the time she had worked up the courage to tell him, he had begun dating someone else. It took four years before their paths would cross again. They hadn't lasted that time either. If she had never broken up with him in the first place, if she had been brave and defended him against her family, they would still be together.

Or would they? He had rushed right into someone else's arms, and he wouldn't leave that new woman even though he had only dated her for a month.

"I made a truly bad investment. The worst kind because I should have known better."

"Those kinds of mistakes happen." Sometimes numbers jumbled up on her. One time, she had forgotten to track down a client who hadn't paid because she'd realized all her accounting was wrong.

"That investment cost me my life savings and my job." He pushed his plate away.

Maren was right. Jack had been fired by his father. "That had to hurt."

"Which part? The part where I don't have employment or the part where my father was the one who took my job away because I looked bad to the clients?"

"Both. I'm sorry." She placed her hand on his. He didn't pull away. "You didn't deserve that."

She understood why he wouldn't want to talk about being under his father's thumb. If Jack had made a mistake at work, then his father hadn't stood beside him the way a father should.

"Don't be sorry. I'm sorry. I hadn't wanted to talk about my father, and I went ahead and did it anyway. I'm sure there are other topics of conversation more suitable for a first dinner together."

"I don't mind you talking about your dad, especially if it helps you. It's not the same, but I miss mine. I never miss a chance to say that."

"I'm sorry you lost your father. I knew him a little and he was a nice man. Everyone in town liked him. My grandmother said as much."

"Thanks. I think everyone liked him too."

He stood and gathered his plate. "Are you finished?"

She pushed out of the chair. "I can help clean up."

"It's not necessary."

"Maybe, but I want to." They went inside and stacked the dishes in the sink. Beth didn't have a dishwasher.

Jack filled the sink with sudsy water. "I'll wash if you'll dry."

"I can do that." She grabbed a kitchen towel. "You want to sell the bookstore because you need the money."

Jack fixed his gaze on hers. His mouth opened and closed before he spoke. "I want my grandmother to sell the bookstore, so she doesn't have to worry about getting the best deal for her valuable building and property. I can take care of the entire thing for her. She won't have to work another day."

"How can you guarantee that?" She took the dish he handed her and dried it.

"Because I know what I'm doing." His gaze returned to the sink.

"No disrespect because numbers aren't exactly my

thing, but if you just made a bad investment that made your father fire you, are you the best person to sell the bookstore?" She looked at him until he turned to her.

"Just because I made a mistake doesn't mean I don't know what I'm doing. I'm sure you've made mistakes at work that don't sum you up as a businessperson."

"I'm sure you do know what you're doing. I was just asking a question."

"Or you were pointing out that I failed in my position; therefore, I would fail in taking good care of my grandmother. Is that where you were going with your point?" He dropped the dish back into the water. Suds splattered against his green shirt.

"Jack, I don't know if you would fail or not. I want to understand why you want your grandmother to give up her store for you. Is it really just to protect her? Why does she have to sell now, anyway?"

"Do you want the store?" He turned to her and dried his hands on another towel.

"Me? No. Why would I want the store?"

"Because you've moved in here and taken over." His hard gaze held hers.

"Hang on a second. Beth came and got me the other night. I was ready to leave town." She wanted those words back in the worst way.

He took two steps back as if she shoved him. "Leave town? Where were you going?"

"It doesn't matter." She tossed the towel on the counter.

"It does to me. When were you planning on saying you were leaving for good?"

"I wasn't. Not to you, anyway." Not to anyone until it was too late to turn around. "But I don't know now. After Beth fell, things changed for me."

"Just like that?"

"Yes, Jack. Just. Like. That." Frustration bubbled inside her like a blister.

"Why didn't you want to read to Luther the other day?"

"What?" The unexpected change in direction made her head spin.

"Luther asked you to read to him. You said no."

"I said I was busy." She hoped her face didn't turn red. Jack had noticed her hesitation the other day, and she wasn't ready to share her disability with him.

"I saw your face. It wasn't just busy."

"Why do you care? I said I'd come back." She had meant it. She had even started reading the middle grade book earlier today.

"You're not telling the whole truth."

"What did you do with that Louisa May Alcott book?" She wanted the conversation away from her and asking him about the book was the best way to do it.

He gripped the side of the sink and stared into the water.

"Jack, answer me. What did you do with it?"

"I sold it, okay." He slapped the counter.

She flinched from his outburst.

193

"I sold it to buy a car because I couldn't drive Luther around on a motorcycle. Which, by the way, I also need to sell to help pay for the insurance on the car." He hung his head.

She went to him as if her legs had a mind of their own. She placed a hand on his arm. His wet gaze met hers.

"I should go," he said.

"Not while you're upset."

He straightened his shoulders. "I'm fine."

"Please don't go." She had pushed too hard and wanted to reverse the evening.

"Why?"

"Well, for one, you're leaving me doing the dishes." She hoped her smile would break the tension. He rewarded her with a deep laugh.

"I don't know what it is about you, but I've never felt the way I do about a woman when I'm with you. You're different from anyone I've ever met."

"Please don't say that." She couldn't allow this to go anywhere, but she wanted to see where the road with Jack would take her. She tried to pull up her feelings for Mark, but they dimmed.

"Why?"

"Because you don't mean them. How could you?"

"I never say anything I don't mean. You are an incredible woman. I want to spend more time with you, get to know you."

"I will always think Beth should keep the bookstore. That could be a problem for us."

"I'm out of options, Bailey, and I'm almost out of time." He walked to the window and looked out.

"What about jobs other than finance?" She had recreated herself more than once. Enough times she wore a chameleon's skin.

"Like what? Work at a fast-food place?"

"There has to be other things you can do."

He stepped away from the window and sat on the arm of the couch. "I interviewed for a couple of accounting jobs. I'm overqualified. They won't hire me, knowing I'd leave the second something that paid more came along. I would too. I haven't worked as hard as I have to sit in a cubicle and do taxes."

"Why don't you work in the bookstore?" They could work together, growing the store. That idea startled her as if it had jumped out of nowhere when in fact, it had lingered in the shadows.

"I can't make a living there, not one that would allow me to give Luther all the things he deserves."

"He would be happy without things."

"I was thinking more like college."

"College. I get that." She hadn't finished college. The scene hadn't been for her. "You see selling that bookstore as your only option."

"It's the option that allows my grandmother to live out her last years as comfortably as possible and gives me a year or two to figure myself out. Maybe start a whole new career. Maybe build my own financial company."

He wiped a hand over his face. She understood the depth of helplessness. She sat in it herself these days.

"Something will work out."

"I've ruined a perfectly good evening. Please know this wasn't what I had in mind for us."

"I have dyslexia."

"I'm not following."

"The reason why I didn't read with Luther on the spot is I have dyslexia. I don't like to read out loud and I didn't want you to think I'm dumb or something." If he could be vulnerable, she could too.

"I would never think you were anything except the smart, amazing woman you are. But thank you for telling me."

When the night started, she had no intention of being anything more than a friend to Jack, but his admission about the book, his ability to share something personal with her, that had to cut him, but now... Now the only thing she wanted was to press her lips to his.

Chapter Twenty

J ack waited for Bailey to turn on her heel and march straight into the room she was using, but she only stood in his grandmother's living room and stared at him.

He couldn't fathom what she thought of him, but her opinion had to lie somewhere near disgust. Though she had just revealed she suffered with dyslexia. But she also thought he would judge her for it.

She didn't trust him. How could she?

In addition to being a financial risk manager at the top of his game, falling prey to a scam any computer savvy teenager would have picked up, he had revealed he had sold that book to buy a crappy car. He was a fool. His father was right.

He needed to leave and spare himself any further embarrassment. "Thank you for a nice night."

She cleared the space between them. He pushed off

the sofa's arm and expected her to either slap him or spit in his face.

At this close distance, he noticed the tiny scar above her eyebrow and wanted to slide his hand into her hair to see if it was as soft as he expected. She was beautiful with her hazel eyes and skin like cream.

He wanted a chance to show her the ways she affected him. He wanted to be the kind of man she deserved. He needed to knock off the sentimental stuff. He was starting to sound like a Louisa May Alcott book.

Bailey pressed up on her toes and placed a soft kiss on his lips. She stared up at him, working her bottom lip under her teeth.

"Say something, Jack."

Words escaped him. Instead, he cupped her cheeks with both hands and kissed her. She tasted like wildfire. Her heat scorched him, and he didn't know if he could withstand it.

She kissed him back with the fierceness he saw in her eyes when she became determined to do something, like save the store.

He didn't want to think about the store while he kissed the most incredible woman he'd ever met. He shoved the thoughts away, but they returned. He eased out of the embrace.

"You didn't like it." She didn't ask.

"Quite the opposite." He liked it too much.

"But you don't want to keep doing it."

He wanted to continue kissing her and more, but not tonight. He needed to be careful in this uncharted territory of wild emotions. He had Luther to think about and their precarious future. What could he possibly offer Bailey? Not a life above the bookstore in that seven-hundred-square-foot apartment.

"It's not about want."

"What else is there?"

He reached for her hand. She jerked away.

"Bailey, please try to understand—"

"I understand just fine. Good night, Jack." She turned and walked out the door.

He wanted to run after her, but he stayed in his spot as if cemented there. He would have to leave eventually so she could return. This was practically her house too and his grandmother would not want Bailey feeling as if she couldn't stay here because of him.

He returned to the kitchen and finished washing the dishes. Maybe in another life, the one where he had an occupation, a full bank account, and no desire for selling his grandmother's store, he and Bailey would have a chance.

Bailey parked outside Kassidy's house. She hesitated for only a second before hurrying up the front walk and banging on the door. She should have sent a text. Emma might be asleep, and Bailey would be waking her up with her noise.

Grant opened the front door and startled her. She hadn't expected her brother-in-law to be home. She thought he had a gig playing at a fundraiser. She must have the dates wrong. Why wouldn't she? She always got the details wrong.

Bailey understood what drew Kassidy to Grant. His eyes held a soulfulness that looked right through her. He was a good man who took care of his family, a standup guy. Solid like the jetties. The kind of man Bailey would want. Maybe a man like Jack. Mark. She meant Mark.

"Uh-oh. Looks like this might be a s'mores night." Grant held the door wider. His appearance was nothing like Jack's. Grant was flannel shirts and boots to Jack's starched dress shirts and wingtip shoes.

"How can you tell?" She brushed past him.

"All you Russo women have the same look when life has snuck up and bit you like a rattler and nothing but a talk with each other over chocolate and melted marsh-mallows can fix it."

"If Kassidy didn't love you to pieces, I might have to hit on you."

Red blotches colored his face. "I couldn't handle you."

She laughed for the first time that day. "What does that mean?"

He arched a brow. "You're the wild one."

"Am I?" Wild wasn't exactly the way she'd describe herself, but she liked the ring to it.

"I'll get Kassidy. Make yourself at home. The s'mores kit is in the pantry." Grant jogged up the stairs, leaving her alone.

She made her way to the kitchen. The light above the

stove cast a small glow in the neat and tidy kitchen. Kassidy and Grant had expanded the back of the house when they renovated her beach cottage. Now, the kitchen stretched out like a content cat, offering plenty of space for everything.

The fixings for s'mores were easy to locate. Kassidy's pantry was practically alphabetized. Bailey grabbed what she needed.

The night wouldn't be complete if Maren wasn't with them. She spoke into her phone for a quick text. "S'mores night. 911. Come now."

She should never have kissed Jack. She didn't know what she was thinking. Well, she actually did know what she had been thinking. He had looked at her as if he could devour her on the spot. Mark had never looked at her that way and for just one second, she wanted to know what it was like to kiss a man whose desire was evident.

He had kissed her with a determination, as if he had to prove himself, and he had. When he had placed his hands on her face, she shivered from her head to her toes. That man could kiss. Not that it mattered. He didn't want her. Oh, and the Mark thing again.

"Hey, I wasn't expecting you." Kassidy stood in the doorway. Her hair was piled on the top of her head. She wore loose blue shorts and a Giuffria concert t-shirt.

"I'm calling an emergency s'mores meeting. I need advice. Maren should be here any second."

As if on cue, Maren barreled through the front door. "The screen door wasn't locked. I let myself in."

"Could you keep your voice down? Emma is asleep."
Kassidy turned on Maren.

"Oops. Sorry. Sometimes I forget you're a mom."

"Gee, thanks."

"Can we get this party started?" Bailey gathered the supplies and pushed through the door to the back patio.

One of the other upgrades on the house was a gas firepit for this exact thing. Grant had suggested they install one and tap into the natural gas line, so Kassidy and her sisters didn't have to mess with real wood.

Yet another of Grant's glowing qualities. He always had Kassidy's back. Her sister had really struck the motherload. Bailey was glad her sister finally had happiness.

Maren slid onto the chaise lounge. "I left Shane just as he was about to get out of his underwear. What's the emergency?"

"Eww," Kassidy said.

"Please don't give me a visual of the two of you together." Shane had plenty going for him too, especially his athletic body, but Bailey did not want to picture her sister with a man.

"I can share the details, if you want."

"No," she and Kassidy said together.

Maren burst out laughing. "Like I would tell you. Okay, Bailey, you have the floor. What's going on?"

She handed each sister a stick with a marshmallow. Kassidy took the seat beside her. The flames danced in the night breeze. Storms were on the way and might hit overnight. A wind warning had been issued.

"I kissed Jack."

"Jack Billinger?" Maren sat up straight.

"Is there any other Jack I might kiss at the moment?"

"Was he a bad kisser? He's a nice guy, but I could see him not being a great kisser." Kassidy stuck her marshmallow too far into the fire. Her sister never got the art of how to make the sweet snack the perfect golden color.

"He was a great kisser."

"Really?" Kassidy stared at her with wide eyes.

"Yes, really, Kass. Just because he's not a rock star like Grant doesn't mean the man doesn't know what to do with his mouth." He was a better kisser than Mark. And her troubles continued to grow.

"So, what's the problem? Is it because he has a son?" Maren blew the flame out on her marshmallow.

"No, Luther is great. It's something else."

Her sisters stared at her, waiting.

"Go on," Kassidy said.

She had to come clean about the entire fib. They would be mad at her for leaving them out of her decision. She should have included them when she was debating on the move, but she had been afraid to tell them. Because deep down she knew she was making a mistake.

"I have something to tell you both."

"I'm not sure I like the sound of this," Maren said.

"I was planning on moving to Colorado."

"What? When?" Kassidy put out the flame on her marshmallow with her hand.

"The night of the storm. I was supposed to go, but the storm had come in—"

"Wait a second," Maren cut her off. "You decided to move to another state and not tell us? Who does that?"

She did. She couldn't look them in the eyes. "I knew you'd think it was a bad idea."

"Of course, we do," Kassidy said. "We're all each other has. Why in the world would you move across the country by yourself? Did we do something to you?"

She pulled her knees up to her chest to give herself some kind of a shield. "I wasn't going alone. Well, I was driving alone, but I wouldn't be alone once I arrived. I was meeting Mark."

"Mark?" Maren stood. Her voice echoed in the trees.

"*The* Mark?" Kassidy shook her head as if she already knew the answer. And she did.

"Yes. We've been talking for months. I thought things were going to be different this time. I wanted a life with him, but then Beth fell and broke her elbow and now I have feelings for Jack."

Maren put her hands on top of her head. "I don't understand. What does Beth falling have to do with your feelings for Jack? And what about Mark?"

"It's a mess. I know. I thought Mark and I were soulmates."

Kassidy snorted. "You can't be serious."

"Why not?"

"This is Mark we're talking about. The man who wouldn't get back together with you because he had started dating someone else in a nanosecond of your breakup and decided he had to be a good guy for her.

Bailey, how many years has it been since you've spoken to him?"

Too many. "I don't know. Six."

"Try ten," Maren said. "Ten years ago, you drove to my house in Candlewood Falls and cried at my kitchen table for three days straight. I remember because Peyton had an elementary school show and Dave had to take her."

"How did you two even hook back up?" Kassidy reached for another marshmallow.

"He found me on social media, then private messaged me."

"And now you're going to start a life with him and leave us behind," Maren said.

"It sounds horrible when you put it that way." She wasn't trying to leave anyone behind; she wanted a little of what her sisters had—a family of her own.

"And what about Jack?" Kassidy said. "Are you leading him on?"

"No. Well, I had started out saying we had to be just friends, but then I kissed him." She slapped her hands over her face. She couldn't look at her sisters.

"What happened when you kissed him?" Maren stuck another marshmallow in the fire. No one had made a single s'more yet.

"He told me he could never be with me." She flopped back on the grass and covered her face again. "I'm so embarrassed."

Each sister lay in the grass beside her. Kassidy took

her left hand and Maren her right. They all stared up at the cloud-covered sky.

"Boys suck." Maren gave her hand a squeeze.

"Were those his exact words?" Kassidy said.

"I don't know. Something like that. I had to get out of there. I never planned on liking him. I wanted to keep hating him, but I couldn't. And now I don't know what to do about Mark. He's expecting me to show up and merge my business with his."

"Do you want to go to Colorado or not?" Kassidy said.

"I don't think so."

"I'm sorry you thought you couldn't tell us about Mark." Maren sat up and looked at her. "We aren't always the best sisters, are we?"

"Of course you are." She gripped Maren in a bear hug. Maren hugged her back. "You two are the best older sisters. You're just kind of judgy." She planted a kiss on Kassidy's cheek.

Kassidy gave her shoulder a little shove. "We aren't judgy—much."

"Listen, Bailey, we'll support you no matter what you do," Maren said.

"Thanks. I'm glad I have the two of you. You know, crazy as all this sounds, part of me wants the adventure of driving across country and growing my business in Colorado. I've never been there."

"We're finally living in the same town again. We get to spend time together. We're a family again," Kassidy said.

Kassidy had worked hard to get the three of them in one place and Bailey had been glad to live the last few years in Serenity, but was there more for her than this small beach town? How would she face Jack anyway?

"We'll always be a family. I might need to spread my wings for a while."

"But if you leave, you might not come back," Kassidy said.

"If I go, I won't be gone forever."

Maren looked between her and Kassidy but didn't say anything.

"How long would you be gone for?" Kassidy tossed her stick on the table.

"I don't know, but I'd have to give the business a chance. Three, four years probably." Her heart was torn in two. Mark was waiting for her, but Jack had her attention even if he wasn't sure he wanted it.

"I'll just miss you. I want us to be close by so we can have nights like these. You know, just a phone call away and we can come running," Kassidy said.

"I like our s'mores nights," Maren said. "I didn't at first. I'll be honest. I thought they were just a time suck, but then I realized I needed them. I craved them. If you leave, Bailey, it won't be the same."

"I don't know how to settle down." And yet Serenity was a huge part of her. She had always had an undercurrent pushing her forward. From the age of five, she wanted to swim out to the horizon to see if she could do it.

"Boys suck," Maren said again.

"Will you stop with the boys suck." Kassidy glared at Maren.

"They do."

"Not all of them. Do I have to remind you that Shane doesn't suck?" Kassidy stood and brushed some grass off her pants.

"He did for a long time until he didn't anymore."

"Truth," Bailey said.

"So, there's hope," Maren said. "You should kiss Jack again and tell Mark you're not coming."

"I can't."

"Why not?" Kassidy grabbed a graham cracker and snapped it in half.

"Because it's bad enough that Jack rejected me after he said I was amazing. Something must've scared him and that had to be me. And how do I call Mark and say I was wrong about loving him? I mean, I did—even still do —love him. He's an important part of my past." Bailey pulled out pieces of grass.

"Past being the operative word," Maren said.

"Please help me understand, Bailey. You spring on us you're leaving town, but you also kissed Jack Billinger. You want to go and stay. Do you want to be a part of our family or not?" Kassidy marched across the yard.

"Kass, come back," Bailey said.

"Yeah, come back," Maren chimed in too.

Kassidy went into the house. The door slid shut with a bang.

"She's mad," Bailey said.

"She needs some time. Will you at least stay until Beth is back at the bookstore?"

"I will. I can't leave her while she's not feeling well."

"What will you tell Mark if you decide to stay?"

"The truth. It wasn't meant to be." She would leave Jack out of it. He didn't want her. The kiss had been one of those life mistakes.

"Did you ever find out if Jack's money and work troubles were true?" Maren returned to the chaise, then stared up at the sky.

She didn't want to confirm the rumor that Maren heard. Bailey knew her sisters wouldn't gossip, but Jack's financial problems and his problems with his father were his stories to tell, not hers.

"I don't know. The subject didn't come up before the kiss." This small, white lie would protect Jack. Bailey expected her sisters would do the same for their men.

"If he convinces his grandmother to sell, where would that leave you?"

"Stuck in the undertow with no lifeguard."

Chapter Twenty-One

Bailey let herself into Beth's house. The rooms were dark and quiet, asleep for the night like she wanted to be soon. Jack must've left sometime after she had. She had half expected to find him still here, waiting for her.

The kitchen appeared as if no one had made a single meal in it tonight. Even from the small light above the sink the counters were visibly clean and void of the plates and pots he used to cook with.

She peeked outside in the backyard. He had even recovered the grill and pushed in all the patio chairs. He was a man of order. Jack would probably hate her disorganization. She wasn't one to separate her kitchen utensils in the drawer or pair her socks ahead of time. She imagined Jack as someone who folded his underwear.

The fireflies' green swoosh painted the darkness with quick strokes. When she was little, she loved running through the damp grass in her bare feet,

210

chasing the lightning bugs and yelling for her sisters to follow her. If she caught a bug, she'd cup the tiny creature with both hands. Its glow would seep through the space between her fingers, and then she would set it free. She used to imagine she was a lightning bug.

She hoped Kassidy wouldn't stay mad at her for long. Bailey hated fighting with her sisters. She looked at her phone, about to text them the lightning bug memory, but stopped. If she was going to leave town, she would need to remember how to be alone.

Soft voices drifted down the steps from Beth's bedroom. The door was cracked open an inch and a blue light flicked in the space between the door and the molding.

Bailey approached the door and knocked, hoping not to wake Beth if she had fallen asleep, but if she had, Bailey would turn off the television.

"Come in, dear." Beth's voice was a whisper.

"Did I wake you?"

"Not at all. Come in." Beth waved her over. She was propped up on several pillows. Her pink nightgown with the white scalloped collar stuck out from the crocheted blanket. The room wasn't cold, but Beth must be. She held the TV remote in one hand and pointed it to lower the volume. The room smelled of baby powder and hair spray.

A gold and glass vanity sat in the corner covered in perfumes and cosmetics. The hardwood floor creaked under Bailey's feet.

"Did you have a nice night?" She sat on the edge of the bed.

"We will never agree on whether or not Jo was a lesbian. I say she was. But Natalie says she was just a tomboy. That woman can't fathom a modern concept." Beth shook her head.

"Do you think Natalie is a closet lesbian?" She laughed because she couldn't imagine Natalie getting busy with anyone.

"Natalie? She's not hip enough." Beth laughed too. The laugh turned into a hacking cough that bent Beth in half, turned her face red and watered her eyes.

"Are you okay? Do you need something to drink?" She gave a quick glance around the room but didn't see a water glass on any of the tabletops.

The coughing subsided. Beth sat still again. "I'm fine. Just a tickle. How was your evening with Jack? I had expected to find you both here when I returned."

She wasn't about to tell Beth about kissing her grandson. That was inappropriate and she had enough of that conversation with her sisters.

"We had a nice time." She played with a piece of yarn that had come loose from the blanket.

"Bailey, dear, let's have the truth. He was a horse's ass, wasn't he?"

"Beth." Surprise tightened her throat around the word and squeezed Beth's name free in a high-pitched squeak.

"It's okay. I love him dearly, but that father of his turned my joyous grandson into a competitive, inflexible man. If my Priscilla had lived, maybe Jack and his father would have learned to enjoy life a little. At least that's what I like to believe." Her eyes watered again, but Bailey guessed it was for a different reason this time.

She wanted to tell Beth about Jack's problems, but again, it wasn't her place. Jack was competitive before everything that happened these past weeks, and he liked to live a life filled with busy weekends. Beth had told her, but now he was hurting.

"I think Luther will help Jack be the best person he can. He really wants to do what's right for his son."

"Let's thank our lucky stars for that. Luther is a sweet boy who might be the reason Jack stays on the straight and narrow for a change."

"Jack has been through a lot in his life." Everyone carried around something. She could sympathize with Jack more now that they'd shared parts of themselves.

"Losing his mother at such a young age is a hardship for anyone. Sterling's parenting style was to withhold love. I had insisted every summer Jack spend some time with me. Sterling was all too willing, wanting Jack out from under him for a few weeks."

"He was lucky to have you." Bailey never had a female role model like Beth, except maybe for her Aunt Joanna, her dad's sister. Aunt Joanna led a busy and full life, but she did make time for her nieces. She had come out to Serenity when Emma was born.

"He would've been luckier for him to have his mother and me my daughter."

"I'm so sorry you lost her."

"I think you two would've liked each other." Beth gave her a watery smile.

"I bet we would have. Can I ask you something personal?" She pulled on the blanket string to give her something else to look at.

"Of course, dear."

"Is the reason you don't want to sell the store that you can't let it go? I mean, the building does need a lot of repairs." She and her sisters were faced with that very question about their father's tavern not all that long ago.

"I'm not ready to retire just yet."

"You can tell me to mind my own business, but is there more to it? Are you worried what he'll do once the building sells?"

"I might be old, but I'm not stupid, dear. Jack has money problems. He hasn't said as much, but it doesn't take an Albert Einstein to figure out he's living above the store because doesn't have anywhere else to go. Plus, I checked online and saw his house in Rumson sold."

"You did?"

"Sure. I'm a pro at surfing the net." Beth tugged on her collar with a smile on her face.

Bailey laughed. "You are one feisty woman. I hope I'm like you when I'm your age."

"You're already better than I am. You don't need to be like me."

"Thank you for being so kind to me these past months. I've been struggling myself with certain things. Your bright spirit has made my troubles better." She patted Beth's papery hand.

"I haven't done anything. You have taken care of yourself. I just rented you an apartment."

"It's more than that. You've invited me into your life. Allowed me to be a part of your book club. Now you're giving me a place to stay. I've only had my sisters and my dad in my life for so long."

"No special man?"

Images of Mark jumped in her head like film falling off the end of the reel. He had been special for a while. They loved to hike and picnic. They had shared a community garden. They shared dreams that only floated away in the end. She had wanted to believe that he had loved her, but in the end, she had needed him more than he needed her. He had left her after all. She had never asked him why he wanted to come back now. He had said he missed her, but she had not pushed for more.

"Since losing my dad a few years ago, I only have Kassidy and Maren now. Well, and my aunt, but I don't get to see her often. I'm grateful to have you here too."

Beth coughed again. She spit into a tissue. Bailey was concerned with the sound of that cough and the lack of color in her thin skin. Beth's eyelids hung heavy too.

"You belong here, in my house, in my store, and in this town." Beth grabbed her hand and squeezed with a strength Bailey didn't know she had.

"I'm trying to figure out where I belong." A few weeks ago, where she belonged seemed clear, but maybe she had it all wrong.

"I see you with deep roots in this town. Your sisters need you. I need you."

"Me? For what?"

"To keep Jack in line when I'm not here."

"Oh, please. You're going to outlive us all." Bailey waved away the notion.

"I don't want to outlive any of you. That's not the order of things. When I go, Jack is going to need you."

"Jack doesn't want me in his life."

"He does. He's struggling to accept his situation. He's not used to having money problems and now he has Luther. He doesn't shift easily. Another thing that father of his ruined in him."

"Did you ever tell your daughter how you felt about her husband?"

"I wanted to keep Priscilla in my life. I chose to stay quiet on most things. But on their wedding day as I helped her with her headpiece, it had a long veil that went to the floor... she was such a beautiful bride... I asked her if she was sure Sterling was the right man for her."

"What did she say?"

"She said yes, of course. I just wanted to give her a chance to back out if she wanted it. Unfortunately, I think she realized she wanted a different life after Jack was born. That was why she named Jack after her father." The words seemed to cost Beth. What little color was left in her cheeks had washed away. Beth pressed the tissue to her lips again, as if waiting for another cough to come along and shake her.

"That's sad."

"Promise me you'll help Jack if anything happens to me."

"Beth, I'd be happy to help him if he wants it and I'm still in town. For now, I just want to continue to work in the store if that's okay with you."

"You can work in that store for as long as you like. The summer crowd needs you. We have the Afternoon Tea to finalize, and right after Labor Day, we'll start thinking about holiday shopping. Your bright smile will bring the customers into us."

"Let's start with the next few weeks or so, just until I figure out my next move." She needed to call Mark tonight and tell him she wasn't coming. That much she had figured out.

Beth sat up and pounded her palm on her chest.

"Beth, are you sure you're okay?"

"Fine, dear. Cara made some spicy food tonight. I just ate a little too much. An antacid will fix me right up."

"Can I make you a cup of tea?

"No, no. I'll get up if I want any."

"All right, then. I should let you get some sleep." She stood and smoothed the blanket in place. "I'll see you in the morning."

"Pleasant dreams." Beth waved as Bailey walked out the door.

Bailey sat up in bed. Early morning brightened outside the windows but kept the rest of the room in shadows.

Sunrise would arrive soon. She hadn't been down to the beach at this early hour in a while. If she hurried, she could catch the sun as it rose, taking the pale sky and twisting it into waves of pinks and yellows. She might even find some sea glass. Luther might like a piece or two to add to his collection.

She had to stop thinking about Jack and Luther. Jack made himself known. He wasn't interested in anything from her except that she go along with Beth selling. As long as Beth said she wanted to keep the store, then Bailey would back her friend.

She padded down the hall, but the kitchen was empty. Beth usually woke early and had coffee ready, but the coffee maker sat idle. The room was as she left it last night before heading upstairs to speak with Beth. Not even a cup in the dish drain. Beth must still be asleep.

Bailey could handle an at-home coffee maker, unlike the one at Sea Glass that she periodically broke, and got to work making some for her and Beth.

She would head over to the store before it opened and get familiar with the daily procedures. Excitement built inside her like buzzing bees with the idea of working there. She would stay through the summer maybe. July was half over. August would fly by, and then it would be Labor Day.

The tourists would leave their town and maybe she would too, not Colorado, not to Mark. She had tried to reach him last night but got his voicemail again. She left another message and sent a text, but he hadn't replied.

Beth, Amy, and Jack could handle the store if she did leave town. At some point Jack had to understand that store needed to stay in the family.

Bailey grabbed both mugs of coffee. She'd bring Beth hers. The woman deserved to lounge a little. She had earned some relaxation even if Beth fought it at all turns.

The wooden steps creaked and groaned like old joints as she climbed each one. The rich smell of coffee floated below her nose; the mugs heavy in each hand. Rays of gold streamed through the small window near the top of the stairs. Today promised some heat again. Another hot day on the sand. She'd take her straw hat this time.

She would drop off the coffee, ask Beth if she needed anything else, then hurry over to look for sea glass. Maybe she would call her sisters as a way to apologize. They could join her and together they could scour the surf for a colorful find of something once broken but now renewed and beautiful.

She wanted to be like sea glass.

Beth's door was closed. Bailey placed her mug down on the floor, then shifted Beth's mug in her hand. Her fingers cramped around the small handle. The bookstore could use roomy mugs for tea. She'd shop for some in a thrift store. She'd been lucky plenty of times thrifting. Different mugs would give an eclectic feel to the tea service.

She knocked on the door. Beth didn't respond. Bailey turned to see if the bathroom door in the hall was closed, but it was wide open. Beth wasn't in the bathroom.

Bailey knocked again. "Beth?"

Her hand began to sweat. She shifted the mug to the other hand, then wiped the sweat on her shorts.

"Beth?"

Her hand shook. She stilled the mug and stared at the closed door. Beth was usually up by now. She wasn't answering. Bailey wanted to go back downstairs and return to the moment when she noticed the sunlight through the window. In that moment, this morning held possibilities.

Now it held dread. Beth had been not feeling well for a while. Bailey turned the knob and pushed open the door. She dropped the mug. Coffee ran over her feet.

Beth sat propped against the pillows just as Bailey had left her last night. Her chin rested on her chest. Her eyes were closed.

Bailey didn't have to go any farther into the room to know the horrible truth. Beth's pallor was a plastic white. Her chest didn't rise and fall with the even rhythm of sleep. The television still flickered in the corner on mute.

Her knees hit the coffee puddle. Tears poured down her cheeks. She needed to get to Jack.

Jack hated this apartment. It was more like a prison cell than living quarters. The metal bar in the sofa bed had dug into his back all night and the air conditioner was on the fritz again. He and Luther needed a better place to live. If his grandmother was determined to keep that store, then he would need to find a job that paid more than minimum wage.

"Jack, it's so hot in here." Luther yanked off his shirt and tossed it on the floor.

"I know. I'll fix it again." He would need some parts this time and didn't have the extra cash. He'd have to put the purchase on his credit card because he would not ask his grandmother for money. He didn't care that she owned the building.

"Can we go to the beach? We can jump the waves to cool off."

"Not right now, pal. I've got to stay here and fix the air conditioner." Also find a job and another place to live that will let him rent on his good looks.

"I hate it here."

His words exactly. "It's temporary."

"Let's go to Grammie's. She has air-conditioning."

He wasn't ready to face his grandmother. By now Bailey would have told her about their bad date and if she hadn't, which he hoped, then Grammie would do her own detective work. He also risked running into Bailey this morning at the house. He'd rather sweat to death.

"Can I go outside?"

"Not without me." The store didn't have much of a backyard and was on a corner lot. Too many cars and strangers passing by for a kid to be out alone. He knew that much.

"Can we go to the bookstore?"

"After I fix the air conditioner." He didn't want Luther running around the store bothering the customers. And again, Jack might run into Bailey.

"I want to go home." Luther stamped his foot.

"For the tenth time, you can't go back to Maryland. No one is there. You're going to have to get used to me because I might be all that you have."

Luther's face crumpled.

"I'm sorry. I didn't mean you won't have your mom."

"Is my mom going to die?" Tears poured down his face.

Jack lunged for him and pulled Luther against him. "No, pal. She's going to be fine. I'm sorry. I didn't mean what I said to sound like that. I just meant while she was in Europe, I'm all you've got."

Luther sobbed into his shoulder, wetting his shirt.

"Hey, can you look at me?" Jack eased out of the embrace and held Luther by the shoulders. He shouldn't have promised Sloane would be okay, because that was anyone's guess. He didn't want Luther to be upset any longer.

Luther sniffled and hiccupped. Jack handed him a napkin. Luther blew his nose.

"A little better?"

Luther only shrugged.

"I know that I'm not such a great dad. I don't know what I'm doing yet, but I'll get better if you can give me some time." He would need a long time to get up to speed. He couldn't even ask his own father what to do. But he could ask Grammie how to be a father. He would take her out to lunch, well worth the money, and ask her to tell him everything she knew about being a parent.

Luther nodded.

"Yeah?"

"Okay."

"I'm glad you're here. I'm glad I found out about you. I want us to get along. And when your mom comes back, I want you to come and visit me. Would you do that for me?"

"Can we go to the beach when I do?"

"You bet."

Luther smiled. Jack's heart reset. Crisis averted. His phone vibrated against the counter.

"Let me see who that is." He grabbed his phone.

A text from Jemma Klein popped up on the screen.

I'm taking the girls to the beach. Hazel wanted to know if Luther would like to come. She had fun. I can pick him up. Be back around dinnertime. LMK.

"Hey, Luther, do you want to go to the beach with Hazel?"

"Really?"

"Mrs. Klein just sent a text." He held up the phone.

"Are you coming too?"

"Nah. I'll stay here and take care of that air conditioner."

"Okay. I'll get ready." He ran off to the bedroom.

He wrote back. *That would be good. Thanks.*

Great! Be there in five. Can you bring him outside?

Five minutes later, Jack piled Luther into Jemma's

car. He had the day to himself which he would fill with handyman and job searching stuff.

His phone vibrated with a call. Bailey. He debated on sending her straight to voicemail, but the part of him that wanted to kiss her again answered.

"Hey," he said.

"Jack, something terrible has happened."

Chapter Twenty-Two

Bailey stood on the front porch, holding Jack's cold hand as the hearse drove away with Beth inside. The police and ambulance had left a few minutes ago. Some of the neighbors who had come outside to see what was happening on their quiet street turned back toward their houses, leaving her and Jack alone.

She had called 911 immediately, knowing there was no reason for them to rush. Beth had been gone for hours. She had most likely suffered a heart attack. At least that was what the EMT had said.

Right after the 911 call, she had called Jack. She hated making that call and at the same time, he was exactly the person she wanted with her. It had taken her three tries to get the call through. Her hands had shaken enough to send the phone to the floor each time.

"What now?" His face was drawn and his eyes filled with a deep sadness.

"The funeral home will be in touch. You'll have to make arrangements."

"I don't know what she wanted. We never talked about that."

"Maybe one of the Lilacs has an idea." Beth had never discussed anything like her last wishes with Bailey. Beth was full of life, her dying seemed like an impossibility.

"What do I tell Luther?"

"The truth."

"But his mom is sick and he's worried Sloane might die. This is going to hit him hard."

"He's going to be sad, but in the end he'll be okay. He has you." She squeezed his hand.

"And you. He really likes you. I think better than he likes me." Jack offered her a thin smile.

"He loves you. I can tell just by looking at him. Kids are great that way. They're free to give their affection. They just want to be loved without conditions in return."

"I hope you're right."

"I am."

"I wasn't ready to lose my grandmother. I wanted her to show me how to be a good dad."

"I know. I wasn't ready to lose my dad. Each day gets a little easier. If you need anything, just ask me. Don't try to do this all alone." Jack would have his hands full with tying up the loose ends of Beth's life. Something like that could take months or longer. But he was stronger than he knew. He'd be able to handle what was thrown at him.

"Thank you. I might take you up on that, if you're going to be around."

"I'll stay until you get on your feet." She couldn't leave him like this. He would need help with Luther and selling the bookstore. Bailey's heart ached for the loss of the store too. Not as much as losing Beth. She would gladly see the store go if Beth could live longer. No one wanted to lose the people they loved.

"Where are you going, anyway?"

"I had a business opportunity, but I don't want it any longer. Things have changed a lot for me." She glanced down the street at the homes with their green lawns, some with white picket fences. Many had flowers hanging from porches. "Serenity by the Sea is a pretty town, isn't she?"

Jack followed her gaze. "I guess so. At least people take care of their lawns. It keeps house values up." He turned back to her. "What's changed for you?"

She took him in. His jaw was dusted with a day-old beard. His clothes were wrinkled as if he had slept in them. The crease between his brow deepened this morning. But even with all that, he was still the most handsome man she had ever seen.

"You."

"Me?"

"Yup. You. Crazy, right?" They had been adversaries, but now she wanted to help him, be with him.

"I'd say. I'm not really worth your time at the moment."

"Let me be the judge of that. Besides, being on hard times doesn't measure you as a man."

"It doesn't?" He smirked. "That's not how it works in my world."

"Give yourself a break, Jack. Life happens and sometimes it drives a bus right over our heads."

"I'll say. I already miss Grammie." He sat on the step.

"Me too." She sat beside him.

"I wanted her to tell me how to be a parent. I have so many more things to ask her. It can't be over yet." Tears filled his eyes.

She pulled him into a hug. He gripped her back. "When you're not sure what to do, think about how she would handle the situation. That's the way she can still guide you. She's in your heart. Her love is going to be the thing that keeps you afloat."

"You're a wise woman."

"Ah, it's all the life coaching classes I took to get certified."

"You're special." He placed a kiss on her lips.

He tasted sweet. She wanted more, but now wasn't the time. Instead, she cupped his cheek and hoped he understood if things were different, she would kiss him a thousand times.

"Can I make you some coffee? You'll have a hectic day ahead of you." She needed to stay busy before too many thoughts of losing Beth weighed her down. She'd have to tell her sisters, the Lilacs, and Amy from the store.

"Coffee will be great. Thanks."

"I can also be out of the house by the end of the day. You and Luther should live here. Maren has a lot of space at her place. I can hang with her for now." She'd have to put up with the lovebirds, but Peyton was coming back in August. She'd have her niece as a distraction. They could make sea glass art together.

"Stay here at the house. You belong here. Luther and I will make it work in the apartment."

"Not a chance. Luther needs a yard to play in and you need to sleep on something other than that uncomfortable couch."

"It is pretty bad." He shoved a hand into his low back. "Then stay with us. There's plenty of space. I'll take Grammie's room. After I get a new mattress. Was that wrong to say?" He wiped a hand over his face.

"Not at all. Human, but not wrong. I'll think about it, okay?" She wasn't sure if staying in the same house with Jack was a good idea. If she did, she'd need to tell Mark. She might be second guessing her decision to move, but they were still together. At least she thought they were.

He hadn't returned any of her calls or texts. She should be concerned, but he was probably on a weeklong adventure hike where he had no service. Though, it might've been nice if he had mentioned such a hike.

"Okay. But don't think too long. You do belong here, and Grammie would insist you stay."

Beth had insisted that Bailey get out of the apartment that night. She wouldn't take no for an answer and had played matchmaker the night of Bailey and Jack's dinner date. She was probably playing matchmaker from beyond, if Bailey knew her at all. Beth would want her to stay in the house to help Jack figure himself out and for them to have a chance to grow their relationship.

How had she found herself in a love triangle? She didn't think this kind of thing happened in real life. If she wasn't before, she was now convinced a person could love two people at once.

"I'll stay."

"You will?"

"Yes, Jack." She laughed at his surprise. "I'd like to stay in the house. As friends."

"Just friends." It wasn't a question.

"Can you handle that?"

"I don't know. I want to kiss you again."

May the Universe help her. She wanted to kiss him too. "Just once." Then she would call Mark later today and tell him they were breaking up.

Jack leaned in to kiss her.

She met him partway before her phone interrupted them.

Chapter Twenty-Three

"I'm sorry. I need to take this." Bailey pushed off the porch with some reluctance. She would much rather taste Jack again instead of answering her phone.

"No problem. I'll start that coffee for us and make some calls." Jack looked back once before he opened the front door.

She moved to the end of the walk, then answered. "Hi, Mark."

"Hey. I'm glad I caught you. Do you have a minute?"

She glanced back at the house. She loved the beige stone and white siding. This was a sweet house to raise a family in. Jack and Luther belonged here. She'd like a house similar to this one for herself someday, filled to the brim with a husband and children. She had always wanted a family but had put that dream aside for a number of reasons. One of them had been the man on the other end of the phone. He had never wanted children.

He wanted the freedom to roam the world, hike the mountains, swim the seas without the worry.

"Bailey, are you still there?" Mark's voice interrupted her thoughts.

"Yes. Sorry. I didn't hear what you said."

"I need to talk to you about something important."

"I do too." She needed to tell him about Beth and that she wouldn't be coming out to him. Even though she was pretty sure she knew who she wanted, she needed to sit with these new emotions and untangle herself from the ones involving Mark. He deserved a proper conversation about the end of things.

"Would it be okay if I went first? I've been trying to find the best way to explain myself."

Warning signals went off in her head. This path looked strangely familiar. "Explain yourself about what?"

"I screwed up."

Not again. She had promised herself she would not be on the other end of this conversation again. She would not allow herself to fall back in love with this man so he could smash her heart into pieces. She had said as much to him, but her heart had made her a fool again. She didn't even have to hear what he had to say to know that truth.

"What did you do this time?"

He cleared his throat. "I was seeing someone here."

"What?" She had heard him just fine. She couldn't believe what she was hearing.

"I'm sorry. It wasn't anything serious. You and I had just started talking again. I didn't know where we were headed at the time. But as things became serious between you and me again, I had ended it. I swear."

"Don't waste your breath swearing. I don't believe you." She paced the sidewalk and pulled at her necklace.

"I love you."

A sarcastic burst of laughter broke free. "Please. You don't expect me to think you're serious, do you? You love me. That's a good one."

A man walked his small, yappy dog on the other side of the street. He glanced up at her loud guffaw and scowled at her. She shot him a dirty look back. He scurried away with his mangy mutt.

"I do. I've always loved you."

"How much could you love me if you were seeing someone?" This man made her a clown on too many occasions because she had wanted to believe that he was the one for her the way a zealous religious person believed in their faith.

"I stopped seeing her the minute I realized how I felt about you."

"How long ago?" Her footsteps matched the pounding of her heart.

He didn't answer her.

"Mark, how long ago did you stop seeing her?"

"Two and half months."

They had already been deep in plans for her to move out there by then. She couldn't believe how stupid she'd been. She had believed every word he had told her.

"Why did you wait until now to tell me you loved me?" She had prompted him many times to see if he'd say it. She hadn't wanted to be the first one to declare it this time. The first time they were together, years ago, he had said it to her under the pier. The water had swirled around their ankles. The moon had glowed full and fat in the sky. She had never forgotten that moment. But this time, on the phone with the miles stretched out between them and no way to be together except a video call, he circled the words as if saying them would burn him in irreparable ways.

"Because I want you to know how I feel about you. I want the life we planned. I want you out here with me. I've been lost without you."

"If you're so lost, why haven't you answered any of my calls or texts?"

He didn't respond again. She wanted to scream.

"Mark?"

He let out a loud breath. "I had to get to the bottom of something before I could call you back."

"The bottom of what?"

"I swear things were over with her. But she's pregnant and she's keeping it. I want her to keep it. I want this child. We can raise him or her together."

She stared down the street. The road lengthened before her, as if someone grabbed the corner and stretched it like a rubber band. The cars parked along the sidewalk lengthened and blurred. Traffic sounds, people chattering, music playing faded away into some abyss. She was swallowed by a slow-motion tunnel. Her phone fell to the ground.

"Bailey?"

With the effort of moving a truck with her arms, she turned in the direction of her name. Jack stood on the porch. A look of concern twisted his features.

"Are you okay?"

"No."

Jack ran to Bailey. Something had upset her enough to cause her to scream. At first, he thought she had been hit by a car, but when he looked out the window her phone had tumbled out of her hands, then she covered her face. Not a single vehicle drove down the street.

He gripped her shoulders so she would look at him. "Are you sick? Is someone hurt?"

Her gaze dropped to her phone. He grabbed it. A call was still going.

"Hello? This is Jack Billinger. Who am I speaking with?"

"Who the hell are you?" An angry man barked in his ear.

"That's my question for you. What did you say to Bailey?" He couldn't imagine what her conversation was about, but Jack would not allow a man to speak to Bailey with disrespect.

"None of your business. Put her back on the phone."

Bailey had dropped to the sidewalk and held her head in her hands. "She can't come to the phone right now."

"Put her on the phone."

"Pal, you're lucky you're not standing in front of me. Anyone who speaks to a woman the way you're speaking to me right now deserves his throat punched. Stay away from Bailey or you'll have to deal with me." He ended the call before the guy could say another word.

He sat beside Bailey and put an arm around her. She rested her head on his shoulder. He would do anything to protect her. She could take care of herself, but he wanted to be the person who made her feel safe.

"Do you want to talk about it?"

"Not right now."

"Did that man hurt you?" He braced himself for the answer. If this guy had, Jack would hunt him down.

"Yes. But just my heart. And maybe my pride."

He stiffened. "Do you want me to beat him up for you?"

She rewarded him with a laugh. "He's in Colorado. He's not worth the trip."

"What did he do to you?"

"Made a fool of me—again." She let out a deep breath but kept her head on his shoulder.

"Is he the reason you were leaving town?"

"He was supposed to be."

He could stay like this forever if she wanted to, but now he understood a little better. "You have a partner in Colorado that you were moving in with. That's why you told me you could only be friends with me."

She eased away and he regretted sharing his deduction.

She placed a hand on his leg. "The night the air

236

conditioner went out and Beth asked me to stay here, I was getting ready to leave, believing he was the right person for me. We had a history. But then I saw you in a way I hadn't before and what was once dull was now in bright colors. You turned the world into high definition. I started having feelings for you and questioning the ones for him."

"You don't have to explain." He removed her hand with effort. He wanted her touching him, but not now, not like this.

"But I do."

"Let's talk about it later, okay? It's been a shit day for everyone. I have to go over to the funeral home. They called while I was inside. I need to focus on my grandmother and Luther for the next few days. We can talk about us after. Would that be okay?"

He didn't want to hear about another man she had feelings for. Feelings so strong that she was willing to relocate and start a life with. Whatever the jerk had said to her had to be big for her strong reaction. That had to mean her feelings for this jerk ran as deep as the ocean.

He had wanted to believe what was happening between them was real and had a chance to become the kind of thing he always wanted, but how could it be if she was about to move across the country? He really was an idiot. Add mistaking her feelings for him to the list of other mistakes of late.

"Yes. Of course. I'm sorry. I wasn't thinking. He just... it doesn't matter. Beth matters." She shifted farther away from him.

"Could I ask a favor?" He shouldn't ask, but he didn't know who else he could count on at the moment.

"Anything."

"I've texted Jemma and told her what happened, but not to say anything to Luther. I asked her to drop him here when they were done at the beach. Could you be here when he arrives? I might not be back yet. You don't have to say anything about what happened. I just don't want him to be alone."

"Sure. I'll be here. What time?"

"Around three."

"I'll be back then. And if you're here, I won't stay. You two will need some time together."

He wanted her to stay, to be there holding his hand like she had when they took Grammie away. When Bailey was around, he could handle the crap in his life. Relying on her this afternoon could be a mistake. Her loyalties were compromised, but she didn't strike him as someone who would let down Luther.

"Thanks for everything." He stood to give himself a little room to regroup.

"You don't have to thank me." She stood too. "You know, I think it's better if I move out tomorrow after all. Things will be better that way."

He wanted to argue with her. But he didn't.

Chapter Twenty-Four

Bailey banged on Maren's door. She poked the doorbell hard enough to break a nail. "Maren, it's me." She looked through the smoked glass but couldn't make out anything because the afternoon sun stood at her back as if it followed her over here.

The door swung open. A short man with wavy dark hair and thick eyebrows stood on the other side. His sudden appearance became a bucket of cold water in her face.

"Lordy Lord. It's the wild one." He turned toward the interior. "Maren, darling, your youngest sister is here causing a ruckus."

"Hi, Gerard."

"Hello, beautiful." He kissed the air beside each of her cheeks. "You need a date with a caffeine eye patch. Who has you going without sleep and does he have a brother?" Gerard worked with Maren on the events she planned, taking care of the photography. He was incredibly talented and a lot of fun to be around.

She laughed in spite of the horrible day. "Aren't you seeing Arnold?"

He wiped the air with his hand. "We broke up. He was an old hag. I have to run. Maren's inside somewhere."

"See you around."

Gerard waved over his head as he hurried to his car. She went inside and closed the door, stopping inside the hallway to allow the cool air to wash over her. The house smelled like apples and blueberries. Maren's home was decorated in a beach chic design with lots of whites and soft blues and greens. Maren had picked every detail out herself because her sister had a good eye for style.

"Maren?" Bailey went into the kitchen. Everything in here gleamed in whites and stainless steel. Only the walls had a hint of gray on them to coordinate with the gray veins in the countertop.

Maren came inside from the backyard whistling. "Hey. When did you get here?" The smile fell from her face. "What happened?"

She burst into hot, messy tears. Maren ran to her and wrapped her arms around her. Maren, as the oldest, was a stand-in mother for her on so many occasions. Her own mother was not often available for Bailey's emotional outbursts. Even now her mother was on some world cruise, unreachable. Beth had also been a stand-in for her. Now, she didn't have Beth to be the pillar of strength, the one with sage advice, the soft place to land.

"Bailey, please tell me." Maren rubbed her back.

She pulled away from Maren and wiped her face with the back of her hand. Maren pulled out iced tea from the refrigerator then poured two glasses.

"I've had the worst day possible." She told Maren everything from finding Beth to Mark's confession and Jack's rejection.

"I'm sorry about Beth. Is there anything I can do?"

"Not right now. I already called Sophia and asked her to tell the other Lilacs. I also spoke with Amy from the store. I didn't want Jack to have to do all that. I'm sure I'm forgetting a few people, but between Sophia, Cara, and Natalie, they will cover it."

"Do you want to move in here for the time being?" Maren handed her another napkin.

"How did you know I was going to ask that?"

"Sister's hunch." Maren pressed her lips into a thin line.

"Just temporarily. I can't live with Jack right now, not even as roommates. My head isn't on straight."

"Forgive me for saying this, but I think your head might be on straight for the very first time."

"How can that be? Not all that long ago I was planning on starting a new life with Mark and now I have feelings for Jack, not to mention I'm pretty upset that Mark got someone pregnant while he was supposed to be with me. If I didn't love him, why would I care so much?"

"There has never been a man who has turned your head from Mark. Sure, you've dated other guys. Some for a while even, but no one has ever tied you up in knots like

Jack. Maybe you and Mark aren't the soulmates you think you are." Maren drank her tea.

The weight of the day became too much to carry. She flopped into a nearby chair and held her heavy head in her hands.

Maybe Maren was right, and Mark wasn't her soulmate. Jack had invaded her thoughts when she hadn't paid attention. Jack had become the man she longed to connect with. But her heart still stung from Mark's betrayal. Life was confusing.

She needed to pull herself together soon. She had to get back to the house to wait for Luther. Jack had better be there by the time she returned. Distracting Luther from asking about Beth would only work for so long.

"You know what, I'm too tired to keep talking about Jack and Mark. I'll give Jack his space to grieve his grandmother and I'll decide what to do about Mark. I should be focused on Beth anyway." She didn't think she could forgive Mark for what he did, but she didn't want to be like her mother, always jumping from one man to another.

"You can't do much for Beth at this point. Jack has to take care of the details. What do you think will happen with the bookstore now?"

"He'll sell it as soon as he can." He needed the money in the worst way, and it was his right to do what he wished with the building. If he invested the money well, he and Luther would be okay, and Jack could find the new career he needed.

"It will be a shame to see it turn into something

generic." Maren poured more iced tea for herself. Bailey's glass was still full.

"I've thought the same thing, but we can't stop it now unless someone who has always dreamed of owning a bookstore happens to come along."

"I know you don't want to talk about Mark, but do you think you'll still go out there?"

"I don't know." Too many thoughts spun in her head. She couldn't sort any of them out.

"He cheated on you." Maren held her gaze.

She didn't dare look away or she would be agreeing with what her sister was implying. "He says it happened before we were serious. And how can I judge him when I kissed Jack more than once knowing I should have been in Colorado?"

"Kissing someone isn't exactly the same as putting a baby in someone."

"Would you feel that way about Shane?"

Bailey wanted to justify her actions with Jack. The kiss was harmless by itself, but it was what was underneath that said all she couldn't. Yet if she gave up her plans with Mark, she would be alone, and she had been alone for too long.

Jack couldn't possibly be in a place for a relationship with anyone. He didn't have a job. He now had a son he didn't know how to raise. She didn't even understand Jack well enough to discern if he would stick it out with her.

"Shane and I are in a committed relationship and have been living together for almost a year. It's not the same thing as you and Mark. He's been leading you on for years. He's never made a full commitment to you."

"You forgave Shane for his past mistakes."

"Bailey, if you want to forgive Mark and make a life with him and his baby, that's your choice. But this isn't the first time he's turned to another woman when you were only arm's length away."

Maren's words rattled her. "Can you just be supportive?"

"I am being supportive. I just said if you want to be with him, then do it."

"But you don't think I should be with him."

"Being supportive doesn't mean I have to agree with you."

Jack didn't want Bailey to leave. He didn't know what to say to her to make her change her mind. She was determined to do things her way without giving him a chance to make up for pushing her away earlier.

This other guy, the rude one on the phone, had a hold on her that Jack didn't understand. She wouldn't give him any more details.

"When you kissed me, did that mean anything to you?" He had to know.

"I shouldn't have kissed you."

His legs didn't want to hold him up after that. He dropped down onto the arm of the upholstered chair in Grammie's living room.

She had packed her things before he could get back from the funeral home. He had never done anything so difficult as make choices for his grandmother's burial. The funeral director had spoken about countless options, but Jack had barely heard him. Grammie had life insurance that would cover her needs. Jack had picked the things that fit the budget. He had only wanted to get back to the house and never wanted to do anything like that again.

"Stay tonight. It's late now. Go to your sister's tomorrow."

The day had washed away into the deep ink of night. The heat remained stuck to everything outside. Only a good thunderstorm would lift the oppression. For the oppression inside him, only Bailey staying would lift that.

She stared at him with wide eyes. She had pulled her hair up in a knot and changed into sweat shorts and an oversized tee. Her long necklace hung beneath the shirt, out of reach.

"You and Luther need some time. I'm just a call away. I'll come right back if you need me to."

"Luther is finally asleep. Let's have a beer or some wine and sit outside. The fireflies are in full force. We don't have to talk." Jack had told Luther about Grammie the minute he returned from making the arrangements.

Luther had cried. Jack had tried to console him, but he wasn't sure he had done a good job of it. Luther had wanted to call Sloane. They had spoken for an hour. Jack had overheard Luther telling Sloane about Beth. By the time the call had ended, Luther had settled down. Jack's inabilities as a parent had flashed before him in neon. He couldn't do what Sloane had.

"I need time too. I think it will be easier to figure out what we both want if I'm not in this house. I also don't want to confuse Luther." She dragged her sticker-covered suitcase into the living room.

"You're still thinking about going away."

She was right about them, but he hated it. He needed time to get his act together. There had to be a therapist or two who would tell him that starting a serious relationship now was a bad idea. It wouldn't survive.

"I don't know what I'm doing besides staying with Maren and Shane."

"Will you help out in the bookstore a little longer?" He couldn't run that store by himself and find a way to sell it. Bailey working there would give him an excuse to talk with her.

He glanced around the living room. Grammie had left a copy of *Little Women* on the table beside the sofa. Her reading glasses were on top of the book.

The blanket she had crocheted when he was in college was draped over the back of her rocking chair. She had picked the colors of his school to make the blanket with. She had made a duplicate one for him. He had it in a box somewhere. He would dig it out and give it to Luther.

She was everywhere. He wasn't ready to remove all traces of her. Packing up her things would break him in two. He had thought seeing the bookstore go would be easy. Now he wasn't so sure.

"I can go to the store every day if you need me to. I can work with my clients from there during the slow times."

"Do you like being a health and wellness coach?"

She tilted her head and regarded him. "That's a strange question now."

"I guess. It popped into my head. Do you?" He wanted any reason to keep her in the house and talking to him.

"For now. People want to feel good. I help them do that. It's an honor to be trusted."

"Does the bookstore make people feel good?"

"You have to ask that question?" She grabbed her big duffel bag and plopped it by the door.

"You know, I've never actually watched the customers. I've only looked at the financial records, the state of the building, the value of the property. I'm a numbers guy. Black and white are my favorite colors."

She rewarded him with her honeysuckle laugh. "You're missing out. But it doesn't matter now. You'll be able to sell the store. Your money problems will be over."

"What can I do to convince you to stay here?" If she asked him not to sell the store, he would consider it. Without the sale, he would have few options and none of them viable, but he couldn't lose her too.

"You can't. We'll still be friends, and if we're meant to be, then we will be." She looped her duffel over her arm and dragged her suitcase over the threshold, banging into the doorframe as she went.

Leaving him alone.

Chapter Twenty-Five

Bailey flopped onto the bed and stared at the tray ceiling. Maren and Shane stood in the bedroom doorway.

"There are clean towels under the cabinet in the bathroom." Maren pointed to the adjoining bath.

They had graciously allowed her to use the second master bedroom. The room was decorated in neutrals like the rest of the house with clean lines and windows that opened wide to allow in an ocean breeze.

They had the extra space for overnight guests which they had plenty of since Shane was a former major league baseball player and manager. He knew a lot of people.

"If you need anything, just yell," Shane said.

Maren glanced up at the man she was engaged to and flashed her brightest smile. Shane had a formidable presence with big biceps and plenty of height. He used to be able to smack a baseball clear into the bleachers of almost every stadium in his day. He had broken records that other players still couldn't touch. Even Bailey was impressed, and she didn't even like baseball.

But for her, he didn't hold a candle to Jack. Jack made her insides light up. He could make her laugh. He tried to fix his problems any way he could, especially if those problems affected someone else as well. Only Jack wasn't ready to be in a relationship.

"Thanks, guys. I appreciate you letting me crash for the time being."

"Have you spoken to Kassidy?"

"Not yet. I'll call her."

"She misses you."

"I miss her too." Kassidy had sent a text when she had heard about Beth, but Bailey hadn't spoken to her sister since their last argument.

"Good night," Shane said and disappeared into the hallway.

Maren gave her a quick hug. "Sleep well."

"You too."

"It's going to be okay."

"Everything works out exactly as it should, right?" She forced herself to smile.

Maren looked over her shoulder in the direction Shane went. "It does."

Maren closed the door, and she was finally alone. She would call Kassidy first thing in the morning. They had a lot to catch up on. She would have to tell her sister about Mark's newest drama. Kassidy would say she had told her so. Kassidy would be right, but that didn't change much. Bailey might want to try and move forward with him.

She opened the window to let the salt air in the room. She slept better with the fresh air. The curtains blew with the breeze. The children's book she had purchased was in her bag and calling her name. She wanted to practice some of the pages and read along with Luther next time she was at the house. Purchasing that book seemed like a lifetime ago.

She climbed into bed and opened the book. Her phone rang, startling her.

Mark was calling. She debated on answering, but in the end, she found herself swiping the button on her screen.

"Hi, Mark." She put the book aside.

"I wasn't sure you'd pick up." His voice was low, as if he might be whispering.

"Well, I did. It's late. What can I do for you?" Answering was a mistake. She wasn't ready to talk to him about their relationship.

"How are you?"

"I'm fine." She wouldn't ask the same of him. Right now, she didn't care how he was doing. He had slept with a woman while they were trying to get reacquainted. He claimed it was over, but what if it wasn't? What if she did go to Colorado and he cheated on her again?

"I'm glad you're doing okay. Losing Beth must be difficult."

"Mark, could you get to the point? I was about to go to bed."

"I forgot about the time change. Listen, Bailey, there's

something you should know. I don't want to drag this out any longer. My timing is bad, but it can't be helped."

"Just say it." Then she could read for a little while and hopefully get some sleep.

"I'm sorry. It's not you, but it's over between us. I'm going to stay with Naomi. We're going to get married and have the baby."

"Naomi? Your marketing person? That's who you slept with?" She looked at the phone as if the screen would clear up the confusion in her head. "You're going to get married and have a family?"

"I know I always said I didn't want a family, but now that it's happening, I'm glad. Naomi and I think the baby should have parents who are together. Two households, shared custody isn't good for a child. You have to agree with that."

Her childhood had been a challenge, but not because her parents were divorced. Her mother was having an affair with her father when Bailey was conceived. She sucked in a breath. Much like Mark and his baby momma. Bailey and her mother couldn't always be a part of Bailey's dad's life. When his first wife left him, and Bailey could finally live together with her parents and her two sisters, Mom and Dad fought all the time.

"You said you loved me only hours ago." She wanted to be the one to say things between them were over—not him.

"I'll always love you. We have a special connection, but this is different. Naomi and I are meant to be together. You understand that. You say all the time things will be the way they were meant to be."

"So, that's it? What about the business?" She had spent hours planning the transition for her work, and now he decided to erase everything she had put together. *He decided.*

"We both know you weren't going to last out here. Those wings of yours would have started flapping in a year or two and you'd be off."

"I was serious about growing your business together. Making it our business." But there was truth to his words. In the back of her mind, she always had an escape plan if they didn't work out. That alone should have told her this thing between them was not real.

"How serious could you have been? The second something detoured you from leaving, you didn't come. I always thought that was a possibility. You're flighty. Which I think is cute, but that doesn't make a life partner. I didn't really know that until I found out I was going to be a dad. My child needs stability. Naomi is that kind of woman."

She didn't argue about her not leaving Jersey when she had the chance. Beth had stopped her from going and she had allowed the interruption, blaming it on a storm and then on Beth's elbow. Bailey wouldn't leave now for any reason, not before Beth's funeral or until Jack sold the store. Beth had asked her to be there for Jack if she didn't make it, as if she knew what was coming.

Bailey looked up at the ceiling. Tears burned her eyes. Mark had lied to her again, had chosen another woman over her like before. He wanted a family with this woman but had never wanted a child with her because she was too wild.

"The wild one," Maren's friend Gerard had said.

Maybe she was. But she didn't want to be any other way.

"Bailey, are you still there?"

"Yeah, I'm here."

"I'm really sorry. I hope you're okay and we can be friends."

"You're not sorry. You know you shouldn't have been lying to me. Boy, am I glad I didn't get in the car to come to you. I'm glad I didn't shut down my business like you had asked. I was foolish to believe you still cared for me. I had wanted us to have one of those great romances we could talk about for decades. Soulmates. Twin flames. But we aren't that. You're just a lying coward and I dodged a bullet. Shove it, Mark."

She ended the call and tossed the phone. Her breath came in short spurts. She couldn't sit still. Her skin itched and her legs needed to move, but it was after ten. Where was she going to go that wasn't filled with tourists?

Jack would be awake and maybe happy to see her. Right now, all she wanted was someone who cared about her the way she was, flaws and all.

She sent him a text.

Are you up?

His answer came right back. *Can't sleep. Too wired.*

Do you want company?

How fast can you get here?

Chapter Twenty-Six

Jack waited on the front porch. He couldn't sit inside another second with the walls closing in on him. He had checked on Luther who was fast asleep and then came out front to wait for Bailey.

Her text had come through while he was thinking about her.

Now she was on her way over here and he couldn't wait.

Her car turned down the street and parked in front of Grammie's neighbor's house. His neighbor's house now. He had to get used to that. At least he and Luther wouldn't be homeless until the property taxes were due. That nut would choke him.

Bailey jumped from the driver's side and ran to him. He didn't know what happened that changed her mind about being here with him, but he didn't give a damn what had her running up the sidewalk.

He jogged down the steps to meet her. She jumped into his arms, almost knocking them both to the ground. She wrapped her legs around his waist. He pulled her to him.

She ran her fingers through his hair. "I love the way the front of your hair spikes up like that."

"Good to know." He held her with one arm and pushed her soft hair away from her face. "No one has ever greeted me this way before."

"Too much?" She hopped down.

"You are never too much. You are full of life. You remind me to live." He gripped her hips and tugged her closer. "Should I ask what has you running over here at this hour?"

"I wanted to see you."

"Cool, but you wanted your space earlier."

"I did. But something happened and you were the first person I wanted to talk to even though you probably don't want to hear about it."

"The other guy?"

"Yeah. It's over between us. For good."

"Was that your idea?"

"I realized how wrong he was for me. Something I should've seen sooner, but I'm stubborn when it comes to admitting I'm wrong. My sisters will attest to that."

He tucked a curl behind her ear. "I want to kiss you again, but I won't if you think there's any chance you'll go back with this guy. My heart can't take it."

"Your heart?"

"Yes, beautiful Bailey. My callous heart that only

cares about money and having a good time won't withstand you breaking it. How's that for honesty?"

"I like your underside. It's very sexy."

"Don't go telling too many people I have one. Especially your brother-in-law Shane. That guy is a man's man."

She laughed. "They're not married yet."

"Doesn't matter. If I have to look him in the eye, I don't want to be emasculated."

"It's a deal. Your secret is safe with me."

"So, if I kiss you, will I live to regret it?"

"You might, but not for the thing you're worried about."

He cupped her soft cheeks. She looked at him with desire in her eyes. He leaned in and kissed her.

Jack's kiss turned on every nerve in her body until she shuddered with anticipation. Her skin tingled as his tongue swept her mouth. She wrapped her arms around his neck to pull him closer. She was like a woman stuck in the undertow, not wanting to be saved from the force of the ocean. He turned her into the wind and earth and sand as he ravished her mouth.

He gripped her bottom and pulled her against his intentions for this evening. He may have a soft side, but there was nothing weak about him now. She wanted to rip off his clothes on the front lawn. *The wild one.* Yes, she was, and he fed that description with his kiss.

"Should we go inside?" She licked his taste from her lips.

"Will you spend the night?"

"What about Luther?"

Jack smacked his head. "I should have thought about him first. I'm still getting the hang of this father thing. You have to be gone before he gets up. Then you can move back into the house and take the extra room."

"One thing at a time, cowboy. Let's focus on tonight. Tomorrow is a new day, and we don't know what it promises."

He held out his hand and she slipped her smaller one into his. He led her into the house and to the room she had used during her stay here.

"Are you okay with this?" He closed the bedroom door, then locked it.

The room was how she had left it. A queen-size bed made up in a floral bedspread, so like the previous owner of this house, and a simple wood dresser and desk. He hadn't moved in here which meant he occupied one of the rooms upstairs. She was grateful he hadn't taken her to Beth's room.

"This is perfect."

He kissed her again and the rest of the world went away.

Chapter Twenty-Seven

Bailey let herself back into Maren's house. The sun hadn't crested the horizon yet but had brightened the sky, giving her enough light to see. Maren and Shane should still be asleep. She kicked off her shoes by the door, then tiptoed down the hall. Her bedroom was off the family room at the back of the house. She'd get a quick shower, and no one would be the wiser she had been at Jack's.

She still couldn't believe how the night had ended. He had made love to her with an urgency and a tenderness twisted in one. His every touch had sent her to madness until he delivered her to the exquisite end that had him swallowing her cries with his kisses.

"What are you smiling about?"

She shrieked from Shane's unexpected question and slapped a hand over her mouth. He stood by the sink with a coffee mug in one hand and a smug look on his face.

"You're up early," she said, stating the obvious.

Jack yanked off his tie as he stood in Grammie's bedroom that still smelled of her powdery perfume. He had waited to rip off that tie all day. He hadn't worn a suit in weeks and hadn't missed them. He was tired of the confines of a stiff dress shirt and wingtip shoes day in and out as he commuted into the city for work. He didn't miss that commute on the train either. He did, however, miss his grandmother.

The funeral had dragged on for what seemed like hours. Many of her friends had wanted to say something about her. Customers had come from all over the county to share their condolences and tell him stories about his family, stories he had never heard before. A couple of his mother's friends from high school had shown up and told tales about her antics as a young woman. Seemed he got some of his wild side from his mother since his high school days had been filled with a lot of drinking and a few suspensions for fighting.

The sun had pounded on them at the cemetery without any help from a single white cloud. Natalie Lowe had run to the shade because she almost passed out. The other Lilac ladies had taken care of her as the minister droned on about life after death.

He didn't know what he believed about the afterlife. Sometimes he liked to think his mother was somewhere watching out for him. If there was a place where the people who loved him met up, made all their favorite meals, grew gardens and played cards, then Grammie was back with Grandpa and Mom. He hoped they were happy wherever they were.

The funeral attendees had all hugged him, even when he had preferred not to, saying he could call on them anytime and inquired how long the store would remain open for their book club meetings.

He didn't have an answer for that. He had to finalize his grandmother's estate before he could sell the building, and he didn't know how long that would even take. Mr. West, the local attorney, had found him at the services to tell him there would be a reading of the will. Jack had asked if there were other beneficiaries. Mr. West wouldn't say, but Jack guessed his grandmother wanted to leave a little something to her Lilac club.

All he wanted to think about now was getting in some shorts and holding Bailey. They hadn't spent any more time together since the night they had made love. Every time he thought about her underneath him, a pleasant shiver racked him. He couldn't wait to be with her again like that. She also hadn't returned to the house either, insisting the space was best.

She was right. He wanted to toss right aside and make love to her now. Instead, he yanked a t-shirt over his head, shoved his legs into a pair of shorts, and went out to check on Luther.

Jack's father had been at the funeral too. They hadn't spoken since the last phone call, but Jack was glad Sterling could find a spot in his heart that still beat with warmth. They had shaken hands but didn't say much. Luther and Sterling shared a moment at the restaurant afterward, but Jack wasn't a part of the conversation. If

Sterling wanted a relationship with his grandson, it would be on him.

"Hey, pal, how's it going?"

Luther had set up the video console the other day and was sitting on the couch playing a racing game.

"I'm winning."

"Good for you. Are you hungry?"

"Nah. Is Bailey coming over?" Luther kept his gaze on the television.

"I don't know. She's got a lot going on right now."

A knock came at the door. Jack hoped it was Bailey. But when he opened the door, Mr. West, with his full head of white hair, stood on the porch.

"Hey, Mr. West. What brings you by?" He couldn't fathom what Mr. West would have to tell him only hours after seeing him.

"Could you come outside, Jack?" Concern shone in his eyes.

"Sure. Luther, I'll be right back." Jack followed Mr. West onto the front walk, far enough away from the door that Luther couldn't hear them.

"Is everything all right?" Jack searched his face for some kind of answer.

"I've debated for days about how to handle this. After speaking with you earlier, I decided to come straight over here. What I'm doing is unethical, but I don't want you to be blindsided at our meeting. You've had enough surprises for one summer."

"What's going on?"

"Your grandmother left the bookstore to Bailey Russo."

Chapter Twenty-Eight

"She did what?" Bailey stared at Mr. West, standing in Maren's kitchen.

She, Maren, and Shane had just finished up dinner and Bailey was finally shaking off some of the stress of the funeral. She had stood beside Jack and Luther most of the time to help them through whatever they needed. She had also held Sophia's hand when the poor woman cried hard enough she couldn't get up out of the pew.

Natalie almost passed out when the cemetery caretakers began to lower the casket. Bailey had run to get the woman water while the other Lilacs fanned her with tissues from their purses.

"I realize it's unusual for me to bring this kind of news to you instead of telling you in my office." He wrung his hands.

"I'd say."

"Beth came to me months ago, right around the New

Year, and made the change to the will. I had tried to talk her out of it—no offense."

"None taken." She wasn't the least bit upset by his comment. She didn't want the bookstore in the first place, and if she had any idea what Beth had been up to, she would have talked that woman right out of her plans.

"But she had insisted that Jack couldn't own the building or he would sell it and she wanted the building to stay in the family."

"But I'm not family."

"You were to her," Maren said. She had stood off to the side of the kitchen near the ovens. Maren had wanted to give them privacy, but Bailey wanted her sister present. "You were like the granddaughter she never had. She's been close to you since you came back to Serenity. Beth was a smart cookie. She wouldn't make this decision lightly."

"We've been talking books for years. I even sat in with the Lilacs several times. I just don't want the book-store. Jack's right about it, you know. The building needs work and there isn't much profit in selling books. I already have a job." She couldn't believe this was happening. What had Beth been thinking?

"You can't sell it for a year," Mr. West said.

"That's allowed?" Maren said.

"Can I sell it to Jack?" Beth couldn't have meant Jack. She might have been frustrated with him, but she wouldn't cut him out like this.

"Jack can't afford to buy it," Mr. West said.

"For a dollar. I can sell it to him for a dollar." Jack needed that store to get back on his feet.

"Bailey, Beth put in her will that you could not sell it to Jack ever. Not even a year from now. You can, however, put it in trust to Luther. If you put it in trust now, Jack will be in charge of the trust. Then he can do what he wants with the building, claiming it's in Luther's best interest. Or you can state that the building can't be sold until Luther is of legal age."

"Or you can keep it," Maren said.

"This is a mess. Does Jack know?"

"He does. I just left there. I had to tell you both before the meeting. Jack didn't deserve to be hit in the head with this and if he knew, you needed to know too. I'm sorry to bring the bad news. I'll leave you to your evening."

"I'll show you out." Maren led Mr. West out of the kitchen.

Bailey dropped into a chair. She was going to be the owner of the bookstore. She didn't want to own it. She only wanted to see it stay there. If she owned it, she would take away Jack's chance to succeed.

A month ago, she would have been fine keeping the store from him, justified in her decision. But now... Everything had changed between them. She cared about him in ways that still surprised her, and she loved Luther. If Luther had to live full-time with Jack, how would they get from one week to the next?

"Thanks a lot, Beth," Bailey said to the ceiling.

"Well, this is a pickle," Maren said, coming back into

the kitchen. She went to the fridge and pulled out two beers. "These are Shane's favorites. I think the occasion calls for them."

"Thanks." She downed some of the expensive cold beer. "I can't hold on to the store for a year."

"Looks like you'll have to. A year goes by quickly. Jack will be okay until then."

"No, he won't. He needs to sell that building. Or he'll have to sell the house. This is all my fault. I had been telling her for months that her grandson shouldn't have the power to take away her legacy." Bailey threw her arms in the air. "I should learn to keep my mouth shut."

"It's not your fault. Beth made the decision months ago without your influence. She didn't want Jack to have the power to sell and she couldn't know you two would end up together."

"Or she hoped we would. She had been playing matchmaker weeks ago. She was probably hoping I'd change Jack's mind."

"Can you?"

"Maren, keeping that store doesn't make sense."

"Sometimes family and tradition are more important than money."

"On a practical level, that is not true." But on a personal one, Maren's opinion was spot-on. That building had been in Beth's family for generations. Working there had helped her through her grief when her daughter had died. That bookstore built a community, turned strangers into friends. Beth had opened the doors on holidays when locals didn't have anyone to share them with, providing them a way to ward off the loneliness. If the bookstore was gone, there'd be nothing left but memories. Eventually, those would go too as time turned its hourglass.

But if she kept it, allowed the bookstore to continue to be a second home to some, knowing Jack needed to sell it, she would destroy anything between them.

"I need something stronger than a beer."

"Looks like a trip to Sea Glass is in order." Maren checked her watch. "It's still open."

On the ride over to Sea Glass, Bailey debated on texting Jack, but she didn't know what to say to him. She could tell him she didn't want the store. That would be true, but if Beth wanted her to have it, how did she go against that?

With Beth gone, did what she had asked for months ago even matter now?

Last wishes would matter to Bailey. She turned to Maren who drove them over to Sea Glass. "Would you honor my last wishes no matter what I asked or would you do what you think is best?"

Maren glanced at her with a frown, then turned back to the road. "First of all, I'd rather not think about you going at all, but if the worst case happened, I would do whatever you asked."

"What if it was totally weird?"

"I expect whatever you decide to be weird." Maren smiled.

"I haven't given it much thought, but I don't want to be buried in the ground. That's too confining and all that dirt. Yuck."

"A mausoleum, then?"

"Oh, no. That's like condo living for the deceased. Too crowded for me. Find a pretty forest and spread my ashes around trees. I want to go back to Mother Earth."

"You don't want your ashes placed in the ocean?" Maren made a left turn.

"Can you do that?"

"I don't know. That's what I would want. Stand on the edge of the jetty right here in Serenity and let me fly." Maren pulled into Sea Glass's parking lot.

Even at this late hour, the place was still packed. Sometimes she still couldn't believe they had turned around that old dark tavern. Now she was faced with another old worn-out building to deal with. Only this time, she was on her own to decide.

She met Maren around the back of the car. "I'm buying the first round," Maren said.

"And I will let you."

They found a table outside on the patio tucked in the corner. No band played tonight, making it easier to have conversation. The evening was warm with a balmy breeze. They ordered two old fashioneds from the new server working there.

"To starting over." Maren clinked her whiskey glass to hers.

"Starting over." She had started over plenty of times. Starting over didn't scare her. What scared her was never sticking around long enough to see something all the way to the end. For years, she had no desire to sit still. The world called. But lately... She was the plus side of forty now and slowing down. She wanted that family but might have missed her chance because she had been too busy pining over Mark.

"Let me ask you something." She sipped her drink.

"I'm ready." Maren flipped her hair and straightened her shoulders.

"Am I difficult?"

"Ooh. That's a loaded question."

"I'm serious. Did I keep Mark away because I was too difficult. Should I have been... I don't know... not me?"

Maren reached across the table and grabbed her hand. "You are amazing exactly like you are. Don't you change for anyone. If Mark couldn't see how lucky he was to have you, wanted to swap you out for another person, that is on him. Not you. You want a man who loves you for you. Not who he wants to change you into. And for the record, Mark is a dickhead." Maren raised her glass.

Bailey was lucky to have such great sisters. "I don't know what I would do without you."

"Looks like you don't have to find out. I'm not going to lie. I'm glad you aren't going to Colorado. I didn't want to stop you, but I wanted you here. You remind me to live my life and let go of the responsibilities from time to time. You remind me to laugh."

"And you remind me to set a reminder on my phone because my dyslexia screws with the details. You never judged me for not being able to read as well as you."

"I used to read to you when we were kids because I knew how hard you struggled, and your mother never took the time."

"Dad had horrible taste in women."

"No truer words." Maren raised her glass again. "This drink is already going to my head."

"Lightweight." They shared a laugh.

A commotion by the door interrupted them.

"Uh-oh." Maren pointed to two male employees, Hank the head chef and Brock who worked the line, along with Kenny from Beach Rhythms music store, trying to escort a disorderly patron off the patio and into the parking lot.

She recognized the customer with his light-brown hair that swooped up in the front and his thin, but muscular frame. The men outweighed him, but Jack was wiry and most likely drunk and giving them a run for their money.

"I'll be right back." She hurried over. "Hey guys, can I help?"

Brock, with his signature bandana, smiled and shook his head. "We've got it, Bailey."

"Bailey?" Jack turned his glassy-eyed gaze on her.

"Hey, Jack."

"Bailey." Jack threw his arms into the air, then around her, pulling her to him. She bounced off his chest. He smelled like booze. "What are you doing here? Oh, wait, you own this place too."

"I'll take it from here, guys."

"Are you sure?" Hank asked. "He was being a real pain in the backside, singing and spilling his drink everywhere."

"Yeah. Not the first time I've dealt with a drunk and stupid man." She looped Jack's arm around her shoulders and eased him away from the men.

Maren appeared at her side. "I'll follow you."

"Thanks. Jack, where are your keys? I'll drive you home." Then she would dump him on the sofa before going back to Maren's. Bailey was relieved she had waited to text him earlier.

"In my front pocket. You want to go after them?" He wagged his eyebrows.

"No, thanks. I have to ask. Where's Luther?" She held out her hand.

Jack fished out his keys, then dropped them on the ground. "Luther is having a sleepover at Jemma Klein's. She had called and asked if it was okay right after I learned my grandmother hates me." He leaned forward on wobbly legs, trying to pick up his keys, but he tripped over his own feet.

She gripped his shoulders and propped him up on the side of his old beat-up car. The car he had bought with that Louisa May Alcott book. As far as she knew, Beth had never found out about that transaction. If Beth had, she would have been more convinced she had made the right decision to leave the store to her.

"Let's get you home." She helped him into the passenger seat. "Can you belt yourself?"

"I'm not that drunk."

"Drunk enough." She closed the door.

Maren pulled her car up to Jack's. "I'll meet you at Beth's."

"Thank you." She slid behind the wheel. The car reeked of booze too. She checked for an open bottle, but didn't find one. "Did you drink before you got to Sea Glass?"

"I might be a first-class loser, but I'm not that stupid."

"You're not a loser." He was hurting. She wished she could take away his pain.

"Sure I am. I lost my life savings on a bad real estate investment. I'm a damn financial risk manager and I missed the scam. My own father doesn't want me in his life because I've been a disappointment to him my entire life. I find out I've had a son for ten years, but the mother didn't want to tell me because she thought I wouldn't stick around. My grandmother, the one person in the world I thought loved me, stabs me in the back from the afterlife." He held his head in his hands.

"Are you going to be sick?" She gripped his shoulder.

He shrugged off her hand. "No. Even you were afraid to get involved with me. We've made love and you stayed away from me."

"Jack, you're in no position to have a deep conversation. In the morning, things will look different." All she had thought about since that night was going back to him. She wanted his arms around her, keeping her safe.

Because that was how she felt when she was with him. But Beth had just died and she still hurt from Mark's betrayal even if she never wanted to see him again. She had wanted a little time and knew Jack needed some too.

"In the morning, my life will look exactly like it does now. I'll be broke, unemployed, and alone."

She turned onto his street. Maren was already parked a house down. Bailey found a spot out front. She put the car in park and turned to Jack. "I'm going to help you inside. You need to sleep this off. Luther needs you on your game. I'm sorry life hasn't turned out the way you had hoped, but you can't change the past. You have to decide how you want to create your future."

She walked him to the door. Inside, he stumbled over the coffee table and landed on the sofa. At least he had made it to the couch. She wasn't sure she could pick him up off the floor. She took the blanket off the back of the rocking chair and covered him. The room was dark except for one small lamp on the side table casting a soft glow. The darkness hid some of the pain and suffering.

Jack gripped her wrist. "Please don't go. I don't want to be alone."

"I'll stay until you fall asleep." That shouldn't take very long. She didn't want to make Maren wait and she didn't want to have to walk back.

"Please be here in the morning." He pulled the blanket up closer to his chin.

"I'm not sure that's a good idea." She would like nothing more than to climb onto the couch with him and spoon, but she still didn't know what to do about the bookstore. Keeping it would destroy him. Or she could leave it in trust to Luther now and Jack would take charge of that trust.

"Why is you staying a bad idea? Because you're going to keep the bookstore?"

"Jack, you're in no shape to talk about the bookstore."

"Why did she do it? Why did my grandmother hate me?" Tears filled his eyes. One slipped free and ran down his cheek.

She wiped it away. He took her hand and held it against his chest. Her heart ached for this man and all the loss he suffered in his life.

"She didn't hate you. She loved you very much. And in a short time, she loved Luther. But she also loved that store."

"It's a building. How could she pick it over her own grandson?"

"Families are complicated." She wished she could ask Beth what she was truly thinking. Didn't she realize how hard Jack would take this? He had to see it as a betrayal from the one person he thought he could trust above all else.

"Tell me about it. But I thought she was on my side."

"She was. You have to believe that. She was probably doing what she thought was best for you. She must've hoped that maybe one day, you'll change your mind and want the store."

"By then I'll be living under the pier with that old guy who thinks he's a surfer and it's still 1969."

Even Serenity by the Sea had a homeless person. The old surfer dude was Beard. No one knew his real name or if that was his real name. He was harmless so the police and the locals left him alone. He never bothered the tourists. Mr. D fed him day-old pastries and bread that he couldn't sell and the local church gave him shelter when the weather was too bad for him to stay under the pier. He disappeared in the winter. But he returned every summer.

"You aren't going to end up like Beard. You have friends. Can't Aaron help you find a job?"

"Not in finance. I told you. I was blackballed."

"You're good with your hands. What about construction work?"

"You know what? You're right. Let's talk about it in the morning. I want to get some sleep."

Finally.

"And Bailey?"

"Yes?"

"Thank you for saving me tonight." He closed his eyes and in a flash, he was out cold.

She snuck outside and waved Maren down.

Maren lowered the passenger window. "Well, how's mister drunk and dumb?"

"Passed out. Listen, I don't think he should be left alone. He might puke. I'll sleep on the chair and keep an eye on him."

Maren arched a brow.

"He shouldn't be alone, Maren. He thinks Beth hated him."

"Yowza. Okay. Call me in the morning. I'll come back and get you."

"You're the best. Love you."

"Love you madly."

Bailey went inside and locked the door. Jack was still asleep. She grabbed another blanket out of her old room and went back into the living room. The chair was upright and stiff, but it was better than the floor.

Jack's eyes were closed, but he lifted his blanket like an invitation.

The offer was tempting.

"I promise I won't make any moves," he said. "You won't have to feel guilty for taking advantage of a drunk guy."

She laughed in spite of the situation.

"Well, Ms. Russo? Will you sleep next to me?"

Without a word, she slipped onto the couch and tucked her back into his front. He pulled the blanket over both of them, then wrapped his arm around her middle.

He let out a long sigh. "Finally."

Chapter Twenty-Nine

J ack was dreaming. Somehow, he was lying on the sofa with Bailey's back pressed into his front. His body was primed and ready to take off her clothes and make love to her all morning.

Morning. Outside the window, the day brightened. Last night came flooding back to him. He stifled a groan. He had made a fool of himself at Sea Glass and had been thrown out when Bailey had appeared like an angel and saved him from being dropped on his ass in the parking lot. If she hadn't been there to save him, he might have woken up on the asphalt instead of his house.

After Mr. West had left, the anger inside his veins threatened to explode like a baked potato in the microwave. He didn't know what to do with all that emotion and didn't want them inside him anymore. He would've hopped on his motorcycle any other time and drove with the wind on his face until he couldn't feel anymore. But his bike was gone, and he had Luther to think about.

Luther had stared at him after Mr. West had left. "What's the matter, Jack? Your face is really red."

He hadn't explained. He had gotten a lucky break when Jemma Klein had called and asked if Luther would like to come to Hazel's impromptu camping sleepover. Some of the kids in the neighborhood, boys included, were going to camp out in Jemma's backyard. Luther couldn't get ready fast enough. The long, lonely night had stretched out in front of Jack and the only thing he could think to do to blur the pain was drink. And drink he had.

Now, Bailey was pressed against him, not because she had wanted him but because she had felt sorry for him. She smelled like honey, and he stuck his nose in her hair. He didn't want her to ever leave even if she was the new owner of the very building he had wanted to sell.

"Did you just sniff me?" she said.

"Guilty. Good morning." He held her close.

She didn't stir. He took that as a good sign. "Morning. How are you feeling?"

"Besides humiliated?" He couldn't believe he had gotten himself good and pissed. All he had wanted to do after he had dropped off Luther was drink until he could forget how his grandmother had betrayed him.

Bailey eased out of the embrace, then sat up and looked at him. Her hair curled around her face in wild screws. He wanted his hands in it, tangling his fingers through her curls while she was under him. He wiped a hand over his face. He needed to stop thinking about sex.

"I mean, do you have a hangover or anything?"

"You mean that train that's running across my brain right now?" His body ached right along with his head.

She stood and took the blanket with her. "Time to get up, cowboy."

He sat up but that made the pounding worse. "You know I'm no cowboy, right?"

She kissed the top of his head. "You're a mess, Jack Billinger. That's what you are. I'm going to make you some strong coffee, then I'm going to call my sister to come and get me. You have to figure out what your next move is and I'm sure you have to retrieve Luther at some point."

"You're not going to sell me the store, are you?"

She stopped folding and stared at him. "Mr. West didn't tell you?"

He pushed to stand because he needed solid ground under him. "Tell me what?"

She pressed her lips in a thin line. "I can't sell you the store. Not ever."

"There has to be a loophole." There was always a loophole. He would reach out to one of the lawyers at Billinger and Associates. If Sterling wasn't aware of the call, one of the legal team might talk to him and not charge for their time.

"Mr. West said Beth didn't want you to own the store ever."

He flopped down and leaned his head on the back of

the sofa. "She wins. My grandmother wins. I can't fight this any longer. I'm too tired. I'm out of money. I'll just sell the house. I'll have to find a job at the local home improvement center or something."

"Another career isn't the worst thing." She placed the blanket on the rocking chair.

He couldn't watch her tidy up. He didn't need her to tidy up his life. "A new career for you who floats around like a leaf in the breeze isn't a problem. I'm a Billinger. I wasn't supposed to be floating in the wind. I was supposed to be on top of the world, running it." He had swerved so far off track and had no idea how to get back in the lane.

"Wow. Okay. Well, I'm going to head out now."

"Bailey, wait. I shouldn't have said that." He reached for her.

She sidestepped him. "Nope, you shouldn't have, but you did. I feel bad for you. I really do. I can't imagine what you're going through. But you can't take it out on me. I didn't ask to be put in this position."

"Bailey, please let me—"

"Shove it, Jack." She pushed through the front door. It slammed shut on her exit.

He deserved that.

The wind grabbed Bailey's baseball cap. She shoved it back on her head. A crowd packed the beach. Almost every inch of sand was covered with towels, chairs, and umbrellas. Music blasted from different spots. People swam in the ocean. A lifeguard blew her whistle and waved some kids closer. The undertow was rough today. Yellow warning flags flapped in the wind.

Her life was stuck in its own undertow, and she didn't know how to get to shore. Jack's words about her being a floater had stung. She had believed that he understood her in ways no one else did. But he wasn't much different than Mark in that area. Mark hadn't wanted a life with her because she wasn't grounded in a way he thought proper. Jack didn't understand her. He was New Jersey royalty. She was the child of an affair with no permanent address. He had never acted as if he were better than her before today. Deep down he must've always been the person to judge others. She shouldn't have expected anything else.

She walked the beach, searching for sea glass. She hadn't found any yet. She wasn't expecting much of a find, but hoping the search and the walk on the cool, wet sand with the waves at her feet would help soothe the ache in her heart.

Losing Beth hurt her too and Jack hadn't thought about that for a second. She had no right to expect him to think about her. He was dealing with his own grief, but she didn't need to be the target of it.

She had terrible taste in men just like her father who couldn't pick a good woman. Maren and Kassidy's mother had left them too. No wonder Bailey couldn't create a good relationship with men. She had no role model in that department.

She did love listening to Beth talk about her Jack. They had been in love. They were married in January, and he had to carry her from the church to the car after the ceremony because it had snowed, and she couldn't walk in her heels.

Bailey had wanted a love that lit her up, one where the man treated her like a queen, like Kassidy and Maren had. That kind of relationship wasn't in the cards for her.

Beard the surfer was under the pier. She turned around before she got to him. He looked as if he might be standing guard today and she wasn't in the mood.

Something white glimmered in the sand. She wiped the small rocks away and pulled out a piece of sea glass with ridges. A nice find. She stuck it in her pocket, deciding she would give it to Luther.

She should get back to Maren's and shower. She needed to go over to the bookstore and check on how Amy was doing with the plans for the Afternoon Tea and History event. That was coming up in a few weeks. She also needed to figure out what to do with the store. Keep it or put it in trust for Luther.

Someone waved to her. With the sun in her eyes, she could only make a silhouette but kept toward the person.

"Bailey, is that you?" Natalie Lowe waved again. She wore a big sun hat with a floral scarf around the top and tied under her chin. Instead of a bathing suit, Natalie had on what a woman from her time would call pedal pushers and a white tank top.

"Hey, Natalie. I didn't think you came down on the sand."

"Not usually, but my grandbabies are in town, and they begged me to come. I saw you walking this way and wanted to see how you were doing."

"I'm okay. How about you?"

"Oh, I've had better days. The grandchildren help. They're so precious and innocent. They're about the living and the present. Makes an old girl like me forget for a second or two about loss and tired bones."

Bailey would never know what it was to have grandchildren. She could only hope Peyton, and someday Emma, would keep her in their lives as their favorite spinster aunt. Today's walk on the beach did not help ease her suffering.

"You're not old. You're full of life and a lot of town news," Bailey teased her a little.

"Don't forget to read my blog." Natalie's oversized chest shook when she laughed. "I wanted to invite you to the Under the Lilacs book club meeting on Tuesday. We need a fourth and well, we all thought you might need us too."

"Thank you, but I don't know. Without Beth—"

Natalie put up a hand to stop her. "I know we're all old enough to be your grandmother, and you probably have a busy life, but we're a lot of fun and we could all use the distraction. No one wants to notice Beth's absence. Please come."

"You make a strong case. I'll come."

"Wonderful." Natalie clapped. "I'll let the ladies know."

"Enjoy your family."

"Bailey, you're our family too."

"That's sweet." Even if it wasn't true.

"It's a fact. We're here for you if you need us. I know losing Beth left a hole in you too. And if you don't mind me saying, that momma of yours has her head on backwards. That's not your fault. With your daddy gone, you only have your sisters. Let us be a part of that family too. You hear me?"

"I hear you."

"I hope you do, child. I hope you do."

Chapter Thirty

J ack would not allow the ladder to beat him. Someone had put that box of rare books on the top shelf again. He was almost positive there was an early copy of *Oliver Twist* in there and he thought Luther would like to have it. Jack didn't think Bailey would mind and technically ownership hadn't changed hands yet.

He could ask her for the book, explain it was for Luther, but he didn't want to see the disappointment in her eyes. He wouldn't sell any more books for the money even if he needed it.

He had reached out to a headhunter this morning and submitted his resume. Jack doubted there would be a job for him in New York City or even Jersey City, but maybe his skills could work in another industry. He'd see. If a new job didn't come along soon, he'd have to sell his grandmother's house. He'd get a decent price for it, though not enough to buy something else in Serenity by the Sea without having a mortgage that could choke an orca. Banks would think he was too high a risk for a hefty mortgage.

He gripped the ladder and took the first step. Sweat broke out on his forehead. He could do this. It was only a few rungs. The next step was easier, but by the third one, he made the mistake of looking down.

The room spun. His stomach flipped inside out. He forced himself not to throw up all over the bookshelf.

"Just take slow breaths," he said to himself.

If he had the courage to reach up, his fingers would graze the box. He was almost there, but he couldn't take another step. He also couldn't take a step down.

He was stuck. Again. And this time Bailey wasn't there to prod him along. He would count to fifty. When he got there, he would go down and forget the book.

"Jack Billinger, what are you doing on that ladder again?"

He wished the floor would open up and suck him to hell. "Hi, Bailey."

She could not believe what was in front of her. Jack could not be stuck on that ladder again, trying to get to that box. She had put it up on the top shelf, hoping he'd stay away from it.

She had dug through the books that were in there.

Some were very old, but none of them were rare or worth what he thought. His friend Aaron had either been fooled or knew what he was looking at and had just given that junky car to Jack because Aaron had felt sorry for him. She would thank Aaron someday for being a good friend to Jack.

"Do you need my help to get down?"

"I'm fine." He kept his gaze on the shelf in front of him.

"You don't look fine."

"I'm good. Just hanging out."

"You know, after what you said to me the other day, I should leave you on that ladder until your legs give out or you give yourself a coronary from panicking."

"You'd really do that to me?"

"It's tempting."

"I'm sorry. I shouldn't have spoken to you that way."

"No, you should not have, and I won't take it anymore."

"I understand. But would you mind not yelling at me for a minute? I'm trying to get off this stupid ladder."

"You're so stubborn." She put her hands on his waist and tried to ignore the heat running off his body. She wanted to keep touching him until she was done with him.

He shook his leg, trying to find the next rung.

"A little lower," she said.

He found his footing and made it down the next three steps.

"Thank you." He dropped his gaze to the floor.

She put a hand on his shoulder. "You don't have to be embarrassed. Fears happen."

"When I was about fourteen, I was on a high dive at camp with some buddies. They were horsing around, pushing and shoving like kids do. My friend Lucas fell from the high dive and got hurt pretty bad."

"Oh, Jack. That's horrible. I'm sorry."

"I was so upset. I thought it was my fault. My father heard me crying and told me to stop. He grabbed me by the collar of my shirt and dragged me to the car. He drove me to the town pool and made me climb the high dive. I couldn't do it. I just held on to the ladder and cried. He told me I was a weakling and left me there."

"Can I punch your father?"

He choked out a laugh. "He's not worth it."

"Is that why you haven't said anything to him about the way he treats you?"

"I've already wasted enough energy on that man. I should've left the business sooner. If I had, I'd most likely still have a job. But I wasn't brave enough to go. I think I was hoping he'd see what I could accomplish and change."

She gripped him in a hug. She wanted to protect this man who didn't need any protecting. He was standing up to his demons every day and winning. He didn't always realize it.

"Excuse me, Bailey." Amy cleared her throat. "Sorry to interrupt."

She eased away from Jack, but he continued to hold her hand. She didn't let go. "What's up?"

"There's someone here to see you."

"Who is it?"

"Says his name is Mark."

Chapter Thirty-One

"**W**hat are you doing here?"

Mark stood before her and yet she still wondered if he was a ghost or her mind had splintered.

He was shorter than Jack, but every ounce of Mark was muscle earned by hiking and climbing the Rockies. He always had a tan because of the hours outdoors. If he wasn't on the mountain, he was in a lake or on the rapids. His skin resembled leather, but it gave him a tough and rugged look that she had always loved. Jack was cleaner cut with his suits and stylish hair. She never thought she'd prefer that over Mark.

"I wanted to see you." He wore his dark hair cut close to his head. The spot by his temples had started to gray.

"I don't understand. You made yourself pretty clear on the phone the other day." She willed herself to feel something for this man, some old memory that could make her swoon, but her body did not crave his.

"I made a mistake, and I had to see you right away to tell you before it was too late." He took a step closer.

She took a step back and bumped into Jack. "Too late for what?"

His presence gave her the courage to stand strong against whatever lies Mark would tell. She couldn't believe she had trusted this man again. What was that old saying? *Fool me once...*

"Too late to get you back. Can we take this conversation someplace more private?" His eyebrows shot to his hairline.

"How did you even know I was here?" She was not about to leave the store and go anywhere with him.

"Kassidy's husband. I stopped by her house when I got to town. You didn't mention she was married to Grant Hawkins. You only said her husband's name was Grant."

"Because him being Grant Hawkins doesn't matter. Mark, just say what you're going to say." Figures Grant would tell Mark. Grant didn't know the whole story and bless her sister, she had never told Grant all of Bailey's foolish mistakes.

"I wish he'd get on with it too," Jack said.

"Please go somewhere with me. This is between us." Mark glared at Jack. Neither man had bothered to say hello.

"Whatever you have to say you can say here. The store is slow right now."

"You've got some bodyguard dude behind you." Mark pointed at Jack.

"The lady said she didn't want to leave with you."

"Wait, is this the guy on the phone? Man, you're like a bad penny."

"Just spill it, Mark. I'm not leaving with you."

He ran a hand over the top of his head. "Fine. I deserve this anyway. I know I can be a prick. I'm sorry. I was wrong. You're the only woman for me. I realized that and I have to get you to forgive me. Come with me to Colorado and live the life we planned. I'll spend my life trying to make it up to you."

"What brought on this *come to Jesus* moment?" She had never heard him say things like that before. He was always stingy with his affection.

He looked at the floor, then looked at her. She couldn't read his face.

"The other woman dumped you," Jack said.

She spun around to look at him. Jack put up his palms. "I know guys."

"Is he right?" she said to Mark.

"Let me explain." Mark held up his hands in surrender.

"Oh my God. You tell me that you don't want a relationship with me because I'm too flighty or whatever dumb word you used. Then when your baby momma dumps you, you come out to New Jersey, to my perfect little town that is not tarnished by you at all and tell me you made a mistake only because you got dumped. I can't believe it." She wanted to smack him.

"Bailey, please let me explain."

"No, Mark, I don't think so. You can turn your sorry behind around and go back to whatever rock on the side of a mountain you crawled out from under. I can't believe I actually considered a life with you. There's something wrong with me. But let me make myself perfectly clear. I never want to see you or hear from you again. Shove it up your ass, Mark. Now get out of my store."

"You heard the lady." Jack took a step around her, closing the space between him and Mark.

Mark turned on his heel and marched out of the store.

She dropped her head between her knees.

"That was pretty impressive." Jack put a hand on her back and helped her stand.

"I'm an idiot. Don't get involved with me, Jack."

"Too late." And he kissed her.

"Thank you, Mr. West." Bailey handed the paperwork across the desk.

Mr. West tapped the pages, then bound them with a clip. "And you're certain about this? You can't change your mind after we execute the request."

"I've never been more certain of anything." She stood and reached out her hand. "I appreciate you helping me with this and expediting my request."

He slid his warm, larger hand into hers. Mr. West had been a longtime friend of her father's. Bailey could trust him to do as she asked.

"The office will let you know when the papers are finalized."

"Thank you." She showed herself back to the lobby and out into the hot sunshine. August was on the horizon. Bailey wondered if the heat would hold all the way through to Labor Day.

She had nowhere to go now that she didn't own Tea and Tales. She'd have to touch base with her clients soon and tell them she was no longer relocating and schedule online appointments because she wasn't sure where she'd land. She was taking time to decide what came next.

She slipped behind the steering wheel and let the car take her where it wanted.

Her insides floated. She had made the right decision. The bookstore would go to Luther immediately. Because he was a minor, Jack was named as executor of the trust to manage in the best way he saw fit for Luther. Now he could sell the building and stop worrying about his money problems. Jack could focus on being a father. He deserved to be one. He was good at it even if he didn't think so yet.

She had helped Jack make his wishes come true. "Sorry, Beth," she said inside the car. "I loved you, but you were wrong on this one."

Everything must come to an end, even the good stuff. Jack deserved a second chance. It was his time to become like sea glass—broken but new and still beautiful. And he was.

Mr. West would take care of delivering the news and the contract. Bailey feared Jack would argue with her. He had resigned himself to the fact that Beth didn't love him. He might think what Bailey had done was out of pity.

It wasn't.

She turned right at the stop sign. She didn't want to own the store. She only wanted to be able to go there and find books, see some of the regular customers. Her memories with Beth were enough to hold her over. Beth was in the creases of her life. Bailey didn't need a physical building to feel close to her.

Bailey passed her father's old house. A young family lived there now, making memories. She missed her dad, but she was glad someone else owned that house. After the way her father had left it, she didn't want to have those sad memories replace the good ones, like Maren reading to her at night.

She avoided Jack's street. She wanted to be with him in the worst way, but she needed some time to process all that she had been through. She wanted her mind to be clear when she was finally with him.

No more thoughts about Mark. He had left the same day he had arrived. She was glad to see him go, but her pride was still bruised. She had to sit with that until the feeling was ready to leave. She couldn't rush it. She was embarrassed by being fooled by him again. She couldn't start an honest relationship with Jack while her grief— because what she felt *was* grief—still hung over her head.

She wanted to mourn Beth some before she began anything more with Jack. She would always miss Beth, that would never go away, but she hadn't spent much time with those feelings either.

Bailey simply needed time. She hoped Jack would understand when he got word from Mr. West.

She parked near the bakery. Something sweet would be nice. She had earned it. She pushed inside. The cool air refreshed her.

"Ciao, Bailey." Mr. D waved her over to the pastry counter.

"Ciao, Mr. D. What's good today?"

"Ah. Everything is good." He waved his meaty hand in the air. "How about an éclair?" He wrapped a chocolate éclair in wax paper.

"Mr. D, you are the best baker around. You can't retire."

He laughed. "Retire? What's that? What would I do anyway? Sit around and read books like Sophia?"

"Sophia does like to read. Wait? What day is it?"

Mr. D narrowed his eyes. "Tuesday."

"It's book club day. Mr. D, can you pack up three more of these? I have to get down the street."

She had forgotten that the Lilacs met today, and she had promised Natalie that she would stop by to see them. She wanted to tell the ladies she would be gone for a few weeks, maybe a month. She hadn't decided.

She hurried to the bookstore. The Lilacs had already begun their meeting. They all sat by the window, holding *Little Women* in their hands. Bailey pushed into the store.

"I'm sorry I'm late."

"Finally," Cara said.

"We weren't sure you would come." Natalie gave her a sideways glance.

"Bringing Gio's pastries doesn't forgive being late."

Sophia smiled wide. Bailey was certain Sophia only teased her.

"What are we talking about?" She looked around for a place to sit.

"Take Beth's seat." Natalie patted the stool beside her. "She would want it that way."

Jack called Bailey again, but she hadn't picked up the phone. He had to see her. He had to ask her if she had lost her mind. She had given him the greatest gift of his life. He needed to understand why she had allowed Mr. West to deliver the message, though. She deserved a proper thank-you.

If she wouldn't pick up the phone, he would go looking for her. "Hey, Luther."

"Yes?" Luther looked up from the fantasy book he read. Bailey had never come back to read with him, but at least Jack understood why. She had trusted him with something personal. Why hadn't she trusted him enough to tell him herself she was giving the store to Luther?

"Do you want to take a ride with me? I want to find Bailey."

"Are we going to the beach?"

"How about later? I promise." Because now he would have the time and the money to take care of them both which will leave time for the fun stuff too.

"Okay. Can we get ice cream?"

"Let's find Bailey first and see if she wants some too."

"Yes." Luther made a fist and flexed.

He drove by the bookstore. He wasn't sure if he'd find her there, but she might want to see it again before he took ownership.

He parked across the street. The Lilacs sat in the window having their meeting. Someone said something he couldn't hear, but they all laughed. His grandmother was missing all the fun. She loved her book club as much as anything. Maybe more than him.

He didn't—couldn't—believe that Grammie didn't love him. She had. The store had been around forever right along with that messy cherry tree that Bailey loved so much.

Grammie had wanted the store and its history to stay in the family. He glanced at Luther in the back seat. Luther stared out the window.

Luther was his legacy now. What did he want his son to think about him when Jack was gone? Did he have any traditions to share with him? He had better start coming up with some.

Sterling had never shared any family traditions with him other than work hard and make a lot of money. Grammie had been the one to make holidays nice for him. She had shared stories about her childhood and all the hours she had spent in that store at her father's knee.

He wished he could ask his grandmother more questions. Why hadn't he asked about how his grandparents had met. Did she ever want to go to college? Did she go to her high school prom? He had wasted so much time on things that weren't important in the end. He'd give anything to spend another five minutes with Grammie.

"Jack, are we going into the store?"

He turned in his seat. "How would you feel about calling me Dad?"

Luther wrinkled his nose.

"I'll take that as a no." Jack turned back and opened the door. "Let's go inside. Maybe one of the ladies has seen Bailey."

Jack asked the ladies about Bailey as soon as they crossed the threshold.

"She left about thirty minutes ago," Cara said.

"Did she say where she was going?"

Natalie flipped through a fashion magazine. Her gaze remained on the page. "She only said she was going back to Maren's to pack."

"Pack?" He didn't like the sound of that. She hadn't mentioned she was leaving town. She had also forgotten to tell him that she was handing the store over to Luther as a way to give him the store.

"She's leaving." Natalie finally met his gaze.

"Leaving permanently?" He couldn't let her do that.

"I think that's what she said." Natalie glanced at Cara and Sophia. They both agreed.

"Thanks, ladies. I have to go. Come on, Luther. We have to stop Bailey."

Chapter Thirty-Two

"You're going to let us know when you get there." Maren handed Bailey a box.

"Yes, for the hundredth time. It should take me about five hours to get to the lake resort." Bailey loved that her sisters worried about her.

"You're definitely coming back," Kassidy said.

"I'll be back by Labor Day, and we can have ourselves a big barbeque with lots of s'mores."

"I wish you weren't going." Kassidy pulled her into a big hug.

"I'll be back before you know it. You won't even miss me."

"We will." Maren pulled them both into a hug.

"What are you going to tell Jack?" Kassidy put another bag into her trunk.

"I'm going to call him from the road. Mr. West should've told him by now. I hate to see the store go, but it's the right thing to do."

"You're brave," Maren said.

"You're the bravest of the three of us," Kassidy said.

Maren nodded.

"You are both brave. Look what you've accomplished against all odds." Bailey took each of their hands.

A car shrieked around the corner and slammed to a stop in the middle of the road. Jack jumped out of his old beater.

"Bailey, you can't leave."

"Looks like you have some explaining to do." Maren kissed her cheek. "We'll be inside until you're done."

Kassidy and Maren left her alone. She closed the trunk. Jack jogged over to her.

"What are you doing here?" She soaked him in. He was gorgeous with his blue eyes and the crinkles around them. She would memorize every line and inch of him to hold close to her heart while she figured herself out.

"I had to find you. Why did you give the store to Luther?" His chest heaved with short breaths.

"You know why." She shoved her hands into the pockets of her shorts.

"That was the most selfless thing anyone has ever done for me."

"You deserve it. I don't want it anyway."

"Can I ask you where you're going?"

"On a trip."

"For how long?"

"A month or so."

"Were you going to tell me?"

"After I got on the road."

"Why not before?"

"Because you might try to stop me, and I need some time to deal with my emotions."

"Are you sorry you sent that guy away?"

"Absolutely not. He's not for me. But I was such a fool. How can I jump into another relationship with the sting of the old one still on my skin?"

"Because you love me." He took a step closer.

"Is love enough? Shouldn't I be the best version of myself for you?"

"First of all, you are the best person for me, just as you are. I don't want you any other way. Second, I sure hope love is enough, because that's about all I have to offer you right now."

"You're going to be fine now."

"I'm not going to sell the store. I'll take care of it for Luther. I'll do my best to keep it open if you'll help me try. He deserves a chance to know about his family's history. I want to research as much as I can about the store and my family. I don't know enough to share it with him."

"What are you saying?"

"I love that store and my grandmother. I love this tiny little town with its quirky residents and brine smell of the sea. I can't get rid of Tea and Tales. I don't want someone else erasing what my family has created. I have some ideas on how to expand it and bring in additional income. Maybe this is my new career path. Who knows?" He laughed.

"That's great news."

"I don't want to disappoint you either. Or Luther. I want to be the kind of man I always wished my father was. For once, I choose for love."

She leaped into his arms.

He held her close. "I do love you, Jack Billinger. I truly do."

He placed a soft kiss on her lips. "Should we tell Luther he owns a bookstore and that we're officially together?"

"Yes, please."

"Luther, pal, come out here." Jack waved Luther out of the car.

Luther ran to them.

Jack squatted down, eye level with Luther. "My man, everything is going to work out here with us. Bailey and I have some exciting things to share. How about over pizza?" Jack looked at her.

"I'd like that," she said.

"Are you going somewhere?" Luther asked. "I saw your suitcase."

"I'm not going anywhere for a while. Everything I need is right here." She glanced at Jack and then at Maren's house. She finally had everything she ever wanted.

"I'm glad to hear you're sticking around. But if you still need to take your trip, I understand. I never want to stand in the way of what you want. All I want to do is make you happy."

"You already do. I just want to be what you need."

"You are everything I need. Without you nothing makes sense." Jack kissed her again.

"Yuck." Luther scrunched up his face and shivered.

She and Jack laughed.

She stuck her hands in her pockets again. Her fingers curled around something hard.

She pulled out the last piece of white sea glass she had found the other day. They were all like this sea glass. They all, including Luther, had started out with broken pieces that had tumbled around for a while, for her and Jack much, much longer, but with the right amount of love and determination, they were all more exquisite than when they had started.

"Luther, this is for you." She handed Luther the sea glass.

"Wow. This is a big one." Luther looked up at Jack. Admiration spread across Luther's face as he held Jack's gaze.

"Can I keep it, Dad?"

Tears filled Jack's eyes. "You bet, pal." He turned to her. "Thank you. You gave me everything I've ever wanted. Even some stuff I didn't know I wanted."

She took his hand. "Thank you for showing me I can have roots and wings. I love you."

"And I love you, every wild and whimsical part of you."

Acknowledgments

~

As always, I have some important people to thank for the creating of this book. I can never do this alone.

When I met Lisa Olech at a readers' conference several years ago, I had no idea what a great friend and invaluable critique partner she would become. I was 40K words into this book and decided I hated Jack's goals. Not a great place to figure that out. I screamed for help and she came running. Jack ended up with new goals.

As always the incomparable Robin Rottner, my Content Editor, asks all the right questions so I can make this the best book possible.

My Executive Administrator, Joanne Gelderblom, weaves her magic on a daily basis and finds ways to give me time to write. I don't know what I would do without her.

My amazing son and historian, Joshua Wilk, answered lots of questions for me about the Civil War because of the references to *Little Women* in this book. Unfortunately, once I changed Jack's goals, the history lesson went too.

Last, but never least, I must thank all of you, reading

this book. Those two words are never enough. You bring my characters to life by believing in my story. Thank you for allowing me to give you an escape you must certainly deserve.

Read On!

xo

Stacey

Also by Stacey Wilk

The Brotherhood Protectors World

Winter's Last Chance

The Last Betrayal

Her Last Word

The Last Days of Christmas

Seduced by Denial

Chill in the Air

Fighting for Tessa

Nash's Promise

Cruz's Watch

Harlan Unleashed

Big Sky Country Series

Time Won't Erase

Stay Awhile

Love Never Ends

Dare to Tell (coming 2025)

About the Author

From an early age, best-selling and award-winning author, Stacey Wilk, told tales as a way to escape. At six she wrote short stories in composition notebooks, at twelve she wrote a novel on a typewriter, in high school biology she wrote rock star romances in her binder instead of paying attention.

But it wasn't until many years later, inspired by her children and a looming birthday, that she finally took her story-telling seriously. And published her first novel in 2013. Since then, she's gone on to publish thirty-one more so women everywhere can indulge in books that hook them heart and soul.

She isn't done telling stories. Not by a long shot. If you want to read her emotional and honest books about family, romance, and second chances, visit her at www.staceywilk.com

To see what she writes next, follow her Facebook

group for her amazing readers – Stacey's Novel Family
https://bit.ly/2FK8Lae

Or join her newsletter - https://bit.ly/2AoJEFk